JAKE'S LAW

A novel by J.E. Gurley

Dedication

I wish to offer my greatest thanks to my dear wife, Kim, for putting up with me and to my mother, who encouraged me to write. I also with to thank my gun enthusiast friends for allowing me to pick their brains (Brains!). Special thanks to my fellow zombie apocalypse writers, who continue to push the boundaries of the genre.

J.E. Gurley

Jake's Laws

1. Aim high; shoot straight
2. Long noses often get lopped off
3. A fool and his life are soon parted
4. Don't bring home more problems than you left with
5. In a lawless land, the biggest gun makes the law
6. Bad people deserve bad ends
7. Trust yourself first; others seldom
8. Use the tools you've got
9. Always have an exit strategy
10. Serve revenge in big doses
11. Be willing to lose it all
12. Stay focused
13. First things first

1

April, 15, 2015   Florence State Prison, Florence, AZ –
The cloying stench of death and the reek of the unwashed dying permeated the air. It clung to his clothing and seeped through the bandana covering his mouth and nose in a failed attempt to stifle the foul odor. A century of death and decay wept from the limestone walls like a miasma, joining this new source of foulness. Levi Coombs fought down the nausea gripping his stomach and grabbed the legs of the body, while Howard 'Ax' Axleman wrestled with the corpse's arms. Together, they flung the corpse onto the cart as they would a bag of manure. The body meant little to either of them. He was a convict like them, and cons meant nothing to anybody, people who society had disaffiliated, dismissed, and discarded. After three years behind bars, Levi had lost all respect for his fellow man and his fellow inmates. He had seen the worst society had to offer, all crammed onto a few acres tucked away out of sight behind high walls and razor wire, guarded by men with guns.

"Whew! He's ripe," Ax commented, wiping his hands on his pants and wrinkling his nose beneath his handkerchief mask.

"He didn't smell much better alive," Levi said. "Bastard's farts stank up the entire cell block."

Ax chuckled. "Yeah, Andrews was a piece of shit, all right. Still, it's a nasty way to go." He paused before glancing up at Levi. His brown eyes peering over his handkerchief looked troubled. "He might be the lucky one."

Levi glanced down at the corpse. The raw, ragged wound in Andrews' neck where a Staggerer had ripped out a fist-sized chunk of flesh might have killed him, but he was a dead man anyway. Like most of the population, Andrews had the Staggers, coughing up his lungs and crying like a child for his dead momma. The neat round bullet hole in his head had been added shortly after death by one of the few remaining guards to prevent Andrews from turning zombie like the others.

"None of us are getting out of here alive," Levi said. "The guards had rather see us dead than outside roaming free."

As they rolled the cart down the corridor, the squeaky wheels created ghostly echoes reflecting from the walls in the nearly deserted cell block, sounding like the moans of the dead. A few residents peered warily through their unlocked cell doors but elected to remain inside, choosing the relative safety of their cells over the freedom of movement. Just outside the cell block door, they dumped Andrews' body unceremoniously onto the growing pile of corpses ripening in the sun, disturbing the flies crawling over the bloated flesh. The flies rose from the corpses in a dark cloud, buzzing obscenely.

Andrews was the last body in Unit 8, at least so far. Death had become so prevalent, so expected, that no one in the unit held out much hope for their chances of survival. Most of them simply waited for their inevitable death. Levi wasn't that complacent. He wasn't going to join the pile of cremated corpses.

A guard stood outside holding a red plastic can of gasoline in one hand and a 9 mm Colt Carbine in the other. He eyed the corpses and the two men with equal disdain.

"Stand back," he yelled, waving the barrel of the Carbine at the two men.

Levi raised his hands as a gesture of submission and stepped back. Ax did the same. Both knew better than to argue with the guards. No one questioned whether a corpse was a Staggerer or a con who had failed to obey a guard's orders quickly enough. The guard emptied the two-gallon container over the pile of corpses, backed away several yards, and pulled a road flare from his back pocket. From past experience, Levi knew what was coming and retreated to the open door of the Unit 8 cell block. He glanced at the death house next door where legal executions had once taken place. Now, anywhere would suffice. Any execution carried out by a guard was legal. No one questioned their reasoning. No one cared.

The guard struck the flare on the concrete sidewalk and tossed it onto the stack of corpses. With a sudden *whoosh*, the bodies became a blazing funeral pyre, to be cremated without fanfare or ceremony, simply trash to be disposed of on the rubbish heap. The guard, his duty done, turned and left, walking past several blackened stains on the concrete from previous pyres. He paid no more attention to Levi or to Ax. His fellow guard in the tower at the corner of the wall had them in his sights. To the guards, the two cons were just pieces of meat awaiting disposal.

Levi was used to such callous treatment. When he had arrived at the Florence State Prison in 2012 as a three-time loser, he had been shoved into a cage and quickly forgotten. Living among thieves, murderers, rapists, gang bangers, and drug dealers, he had become as hard and as unyielding as the concrete surrounding him and as sharp as the razor wire running atop the walls. He had fought with guards and with fellow inmates, but mostly he had fought with himself. One thing only had saved him from descending into the dark pit of oblivion – the wild mustangs.

Training and caring for the wild mustangs the Bureau of Land Management brought to the prison had kept him sane. Breaking and riding the feral horses, even in the small dirt enclosure allotted to them, had given him his only taste of freedom, his only contact with a living creature pure and unsullied by man's dark desires or his need to screw over one another. Now, the mustangs were gone, released when the Staggers hit the state. The authorities had seen to the freedom of the animals but kept the cons inside to die.

Levi didn't know what the Staggers were, nor did he care. Rumors flew in a prison like toilet paper in a riot. Everyone had his tale to tell. All he knew was that people became sick, died, and came back to life. At first, they stumbled around like drunks, thus the name Staggers, but as time passed, they became fast, deadly killers consuming human flesh. The infirmary was full of the dead and the dying and only one overworked doctor remained on duty. Sick cons remained where they were, and the harried doctor came cell-to-cell checking on them when he could.

The first casualty Levi had witnessed in Unit 8 was Big Moose Callahan in for rape and murder. He fell ill and died within six days, hacking up his lungs like a TB patient. Before they could remove the body, Moose came back to life, attacked a guard, and ate his face. After that, all hell broke loose. The sick were separated from the healthy. Every cough sent men scurrying in the other direction.

Of the almost 4,000 convicts in the Florence State Prison, fewer than three hundred remained. The cons near the end of their sentences, or those deemed safe for early release, had been freed a few months earlier, leaving only the hardcore criminals. Since then, Levi had been attacked twice. He bore a livid scar on this right side where a shiv made from a toothbrush had almost punctured a kidney. The doctor had stopped the bleeding, stitched the wound, and returned him to lockup. Now, he carried a weapon of his own, a sharpened piece of copper tubing ripped from one of the bathroom sinks. Only one person had threatened him since, and his body had been burned with the Stagger victims.

A pall of black smoke, reeking of scorched flesh and gasoline, billowed around his face. He brushed back his long red hair and coughed. "We've got to get out of here," he told Ax.

Ax rolled his eyes. "Sure. Why don't you just ask a bull for the key?" he said, hitching his thumb at the retreating guard.

Ax's sarcasm annoyed Levi, but he let it slide. "I have a better idea," he said, his blue eyes twinkling.

Ax stared at him. "What?"

Levi shook his head. The best secret was the one only one person knew. "I'll show you tonight in the cafeteria."

He paced his small cell the remainder of the afternoon. The door wasn't locked. He could have walked the length of the entire cell block if he wished, or wandered onto the yard. The remaining cons could now come and go as they pleased within the confines of the prison, but few chose that option. The guards were trigger happy, and one stumble could turn a fall into death sentence. One cough could invite a bullet to the head. Having a barred metal door to shut if someone turned zombie was another reason most remained indoors.

That evening, in the much shorter than usual chow line, Levi took his place behind a con named McHugh, a great hulk of a man with a nasty disposition and a reputation for hurting people for pleasure. He didn't like McHugh, and McHugh didn't like anyone. He was taking a chance getting so near the quick-tempered con, but tonight the risk was worth it. As they shuffled down the food line, McHugh loaded his tray with double helpings of everything, growling his displeasure at the hapless servers who cowered from him. Levi placed nothing on his tray. His stomach still reeled from the stench of the dead. He remained close behind McHugh, following him down the serving line. As they neared a table, Levi raised his empty tray, slammed the corner of it into the back of McHugh's head with all his might, and then shoved the stunned man forward into the space between tables. McHugh, dazed by the unexpected blow, dropped his heaping tray of food and stumbled around groaning, banging into tables and reaching out blindly to maintain his balance.

"Staggerer!" Levi shouted at the top of his lungs and pointed at McHugh.

Other frightened voices immediately took up the yell. Cons scattered like frightened children as the guards closed in, shoving their way through the throng like bulldozers, swinging wooden truncheons at random heads too slow to move out of their way. Levi grabbed a confused Ax by the arm and yanked him along; joining one group huddled near the kitchen door. McHugh recovered enough sense to realize what had happened. He searched the room for his attacker. As his gaze fell on Levi, he raised his hand, pointed, and growled in rage. As he did, his head exploded, disintegrating from a flurry of bullets from frightened guards standing on walkways above the mess hall floor. Brains and blood sprayed the floor, the tables, plates of abandoned food, and the nearby cons. Men panicked. A melee ensued, as men scurried away from the gore, afraid the disease was spread by blood.

Mouthing a silent thanks to McHugh for his unintended aid, Levi and Ax eased through the kitchen door unnoticed. The cooks and cook's helpers were staring at the turmoil on the floor and paid little attention to them, as they slipped into one of the trash bins.

They waited for hours in the filthy bin, buried beneath scraps of food, potato peelings, and empty cans. The smell was nauseating, but not as bad as the burning bodies. Eventually, as Levi knew they would, the workers rolled the full trash bins to the incinerator room where trash was ground into small bits before being burned. As he hoped, with the shortage of guards, they were allowing the trash to build up before separating the recyclables from the burnable trash, if they still bothered with such petty details in a world no longer concerned with environmental issues. After the workers hauling the trash and the single guard accompanying them left, he and Ax slipped out of the bins.

Covered in food scraps, Ax looked around the room, his hands on his hips. "What now?" he asked.

Levi brushed a dried crust of mashed potatoes from his shirt and pointed up at the smokestack rising from the incinerator dominating the center of the room. A conveyor belt ran across the room, ending in the massive jaws of the grinder, last step before the incinerator. When active, the incinerator burned trash at temperatures of over 1000 degrees Fahrenheit. A series of recovery systems trapped and scrubbed harmful flue gases of their toxic chemicals. The system rarely worked as efficiently as the EPA required, but it was easier to pay the fines than to repair the unit. One benefit of the system was that the waste heat provided hot water for the showers. Now, it was silent.

"We climb out there," he said.

"Are you crazy?" Ax replied. "We'll fry."

Levi smiled. "Relax. The incinerator is off. We can stand a little heat. There's a maintenance ladder inside. Once we're outside, another ladder will take us back down to the roof. From there, it's a hop, skip, and a jump over the wall."

Ax eyed the incinerator with trepidation. "What if they decide to start it up?"

He chuckled. "Then, my friend, we die a horrible death."

After using a metal rod to pry open the small maintenance door used to remove ash from the incinerator, and wriggling his way through the tiny opening, Levi stood inside the narrow chimney and stared at the small circle of moonlight above him. It represented freedom. Ax, groaning and bitching, forced his bulk through the small opening and stood inside the smokestack.

"Christ Almighty, it's hot in here," he said, wiping sweat from his brow with his hand.

"And you say you're from Arizona," Levi chided.

The heat from the idle burners was stifling, not hot enough to kill, but enough to discourage them from spending any more time inside than necessary. He didn't see the need to inform Ax that he had tripped a sensor when he had opened the incinerator door. It was unlikely any guards were monitoring the trash room, but if so, they would likely be shot dead before they made it to the wall. Once outside the walls and a decent distance away, they would be safe. Too many cons had died during the plague for the guards to expend time and energy chasing down and re-capturing escapees.

He climbed up the narrow ladder first with Ax following closely behind him. The rungs were hot, but his hands had become tough from roping and breaking wild mustangs. The heat didn't bother him. It was barely as hot as Yuma on a midsummer's day. He closed his eyes as he climbed and imagined the feel of cool free air on his face. However, Ax had been an accountant before accidently killing his client during an argument over dubious money movements. His hands were soft as a baby's ass.

Ax seemed a strange companion for a prison break. He had no skills. He was lousy in a fight. Levi had taken pity on him one day when two cons started shoving him around. He had given Howard the nickname 'Ax' to make him at least sound tougher than he was. He wasn't a friend. Levi had no friends. The only thing Ax could offer Levi was the ability to watch his back after they escaped. He couldn't stay awake twenty-four hours a day and he didn't want to wake up with a Staggerer munching on his leg. There was no one else in the prison he could trust not to slit his throat in his sleep.

Ax's constant stream of complaints as they climbed grated on Levi's nerves. "Shut the hell up," he finally shouted down to his reluctant companion, "and climb."

At the top of the smokestack, he peered over the edge. Only two of the guard towers were manned full time, both at opposite ends of the yard, the reason he had chosen this particular spot to make his escape. The tower nearest them was manned only occasionally. He couldn't see anyone in it, but no lights didn't mean no guard. The searchlights from the other two towers swept the walls at roughly five minute intervals, just long enough to climb the wall and get over the top. If the dark tower was manned, or if they took too long to scale the wall, they would be shot. It was a risk he was willing to take. Remaining inside was quickly becoming a death sentence.

They descended the smokestack to the roof, lay flat while the searchlights passed over them, and then shimmied down a drainpipe to the ground. Moving in the shadows as much as possible, they made their way to a small metal tool shed near the east wall. The shed was locked, but that didn't matter to Levi. He had made other arrangements.

"How are we going to get over the wall?" Ax asked. His gaze followed the twin searchlight beams as they swept along the walls and the courtyard.

Levi had meticulously planned his escape. To answer his companion's question, he produced a length of old fire hose from beneath a pile of depleted fire extinguishers awaiting refills. A two-barb hook he had fashioned from copper pipe had been shoved down the mouth of the nozzle to make a crude grappling hook.

"With this. I made sure I was on the fire extinguisher detail. We hook the wire on the wall and climb up."

"We'll be cut to shreds," Ax moaned. "Besides, the wire's electrified."

Levi grinned and pulled a roll of copper wire from his pants pocket. Tied in a loop at one end serving as weight were several half-inch steel nuts he had been surreptitiously removing from the garage for weeks. He threw back a dusty tarp to reveal a rolled up and discarded bunk mattress. He had spent three weeks stealing small snips of copper wire and secreting the other items near the shed. All he had needed to set his plan in motion was help from the hapless McHugh.

"We short out the fence and lay the mattress over the wire."

Ax frowned. "Why didn't you tell me about all this?"

"Because you've got a big mouth. Now, come on."

When the searchlights had reached the far end of the yard, the two rushed across the open space and hugged the shadow of the wall. Levi attached one end of the copper wire to a metal drainpipe and flung the heavy, weighted end over the razor wire, releasing his grip before it touched the wire. Sparks flew as the wire shorted. The searchlights went dark as the fuses blew. Quickly, he stepped away from the wall and twirled the fire hose to gain momentum. Then he tossed it up and over the coiled razor wire. On his first attempt, it fell short. The barb caught on the lip of the wall. It took him several heart-stopping moments to free the hose and try again. He sighed with relief as it snagged the wire on his second toss. He handed one end of the hose to Ax.

"Now, pull."

The wire stretched taut but remained in place, secured by the steel posts embedded in the concrete. Hoisting the mattress over his shoulder, secured by a piece of twine, Levi began climbing the hose hand over hand, feet braced against the wall. He reached the top, slung the mattress over the wire, and signaled for Ax to follow him. The out-of-shape accountant struggled up the hose, eating away at their precious time. The searchlights flared as an emergency auxiliary circuit was thrown. They had very little time remaining. Levi considered leaving his companion behind, but the frightened Ax redoubled his efforts. With both of them on the top of the wall, protected from the sharp wire by the mattress, Levi pulled up the hose, dropped it over the outside wall, and slid down the other side.

The hard earth beneath his shoes renewed his strength. Years in the prison had dulled his senses. Now they were fully awake, revitalized. He took a deep breath. The air, free of the stench of other prisoners and death, filled his lungs with joy. He would not go back to prison.

Ax's descent was ungainly, but he managed to reach the ground without falling to his death. Heading southeast, they passed the water tower he had gazed upon so many times. It had stood like a giant taunting his confinement. They soon reached the Florence Canal, the first of three they would have to ford to reach safety. The water was cold but only reached to his knees. As they waded across it, the first sirens began wailing behind them signaling their escape. They had no time to stop and rest.

They encountered the first zombies stumbling along the railroad tracks. The creatures were gaunt and slow moving. Until he saw them, Levi had no true idea of how bad the situation outside the prison walls was. The creatures were starving because human prey had become scarce. That meant either few living people remained in the area, or they were remaining indoors. That was bad for the survivors, but good for them. With few people watching, they could make good their escape. The zombies spotted the two humans and gave half-hearted chase, but their emaciated condition slowed them down. Levi easily outran them, but Ax struggled to keep up. Levi didn't bother looking back. Ax either kept up or he died.

At the Central Arizona Project, the last and the largest of the three canals they would have to cross, Ax knelt on the ground catching his breath while Levi studied the current. The CAP was deeper than the other canals, and the water, fed by pumps, ran swiftly. The ribbon of concrete meandered from the Colorado River to points throughout the state, delivering water to farms, cities, and reservoirs. There was no way across except for the bridges at the roads, and they would be watched. They would have to swim. He took a deep breath and dove into the frigid water without hesitation. He didn't know if his companion could swim, but such thoughts didn't enter his mind. He was free, and he intended to remain so at any cost.

An hour later, wet, cold, and exhausted, they reached a mobile home on the outskirts of Florence. It appeared abandoned, but the pair approached carefully. Now was not the time to receive a load of buckshot in the face from an overly cautious homeowner. The door wasn't locked. Inside, the trailer was empty of people with signs of being hastily abandoned. Stale, rotting food remained on the table. Drawers had been pulled out of counters and their contents dumped on the floor. Levi stripped off his wet prison uniform, toweled dry, and in the pile of discarded clothing on the bedroom floor found a pair of pants and a shirt that fit. There was no food in the cabinets, but he discovered a six-pack of hot beer beneath the sink. He popped a top and guzzled it down, his first taste of beer in three long years. It tasted like manna from heaven.

Ax walked into the small kitchen from the bedroom looking ridiculous in a too small ASU jersey and a pair of bright red exercise shorts. His pale legs almost glowed in the darkness of the trailer. "What's next?" he asked.

Levi collapsed into a chair and finished his beer. "We wait until things die down, and then make our way to Tucson."

"Why Tucson? I'm from Phoenix."

Levi shook his head. For an accountant, Ax could be incredibly stupid. "And I'm from Yuma, and those will be the first places they look for us." He picked up a straw Stetson sitting on the coffee table and tried it on. It fit. Soon, they would need food and transportation, but he knew the police would give up the chase quickly. They had bigger problems to deal with than a pair of escaped convicts. Once the commotion died down, they would find refuge in Tucson. A breakdown in society was an opportunity for men like him. With a few like-minded individuals, they could survive the apocalypse nicely, taking what they wanted, living like kings. He lay back in his chair, crossed his legs, closed his eyes, and dreamt of his future in the new world.

2

June 7, 2016   Split Rock Canyon, Galiuro Mountains near San
Manuel, AZ –

Jake Blakely laced up his boots while the coffee brewed. The
aroma of freshly ground French Roast filled the kitchen and drifted
down the hallway, helping to clear his head almost as much as the
coffee itself would. He didn't often overindulge in alcohol – just a
couple of beers or a glass of whiskey every now and then – but
yesterday had been a special occasion, an anniversary of sorts. It
had been exactly one year since the world, his world, had ended; a
reason to celebrate or to commiserate, depending on one's point of
view. Others might argue the exact date, but for him, June 6, 2015
was the one he had red-lettered on his mental calendar. June 6,
1944 was D-Day, the invasion of Europe. June 6, 2015, exactly
seventy-one years later, was his personal E-Day, the end of his
world when almost everyone died. In comparison, a slight
hangover headache didn't seem much to complain about.

Boots laced, but the coffee not quite finished brewing, he
walked to the window and gazed out over his domain. Split Rock
Canyon was a narrow defile thrusting six-hundred yards into the
rugged Galiuro Mountains north of Tucson, Arizona. His home,
built of native stone and Ponderosa pine logs, rested on a ledge
fifty feet above the canyon floor, accessible only by a set of fifty-
five hand-hewn steps and a twelve-foot-long plank bridge
spanning a narrow cleft in the cliff face. His view of the canyon
was spectacular, one of the reasons he had chosen such a remote
site for his home

A soft sigh escaped his lips, as he noticed two figures beyond
the gate lumbering up the dirt trail. His day wasn't starting out
well. Even fifteen miles from San Manuel, zombies still managed
to find him, roaming along the river from the local farms and
ranches. He believed the creatures could smell living flesh, sought
it out as a bat seeks cactus blossom pollen. He seemed to be the
only living flesh in the area. Moving to the living room, he picked

up his Browning X-Bolt rifle always kept handy beside the sofa, and stepped out onto the balcony.

He sighted his first target through the scope. The creature wore ragged jeans and t-shirt but had no shoes. Its bare feet were lacerated and bleeding. Its eyes, retaining none of the qualities of a living human, scanned the fence hungrily, like an animal. Carefully centering the crosshairs on the zombie's forehead, he took a deep breath and slowly released it as he squeezed the trigger. *Jake's Law #1 – Aim high; shoot straight.* The zombie collapsed before the echo of the shot reverberated from the canyon walls. The heavy .308 Winchester round took out the back of the creature's head, spraying a fan of blood across the sand. He had learned from experience that head shots worked best. You could kill a zombie if you inflicted sufficient damage to vital organs, but a single round to the brain worked just fine and saved ammunition.

The second creature stared at its fallen companion with disinterest for just a moment, as if judging it as a possible source of food, and then returned its attention to the gate. As Jake sighted it in his scope, he was shocked to recognize the creature as one of the area ranchers, an old man named Caldwell. He had met Caldwell once or twice at the grocery store in Catalina when Caldwell had struck up a conversation. He had seemed a nice guy, but whatever the creature now was, it was no longer Caldwell. It joined the first zombie a few heartbeats later with Jake's second well-placed shot. Shortly, he would transport the bodies to a nearby gully and incinerate them, but not before breakfast and an aspirin for his mounting headache. He hated to face zombies, alive or dead, before his first cup of morning coffee. At the noise of the percolator gurgling, he set aside his rifle and strode across the room to the kitchen.

For twelve years, Jake had been a Pima County Deputy Sheriff, dealing mostly with search and rescue situations. On the side, he had operated an online website for hunters and survivalists – preppers. He had also sold and repaired guns at local guns shows and often acted as a guide for area hunters. It never made him rich, but it kept him in beans and beer and off the grid. Now, there was no law but his law, Jake's Law. Gun shows were a thing of the past, and no one hunted for sport anymore. Those who had survived the apocalypse needed no advice on surviving, and those who hadn't were beyond caring. Now, he killed zombies and tried to survive.

E-Day had come for Jake on June 6, 2015, at four p.m. Washington time when the President of the United States declared Martial Law and dispatched troops to control the growing civil unrest racking the country. It had been the last straw to an already distrustful populace. Armed militias fought the troops, local police fought the National Guard, and private citizens fought with one another. Cities burned and chaos ruled the land. No longer safe in the streets, people huddled in their homes and died of starvation. Now, one year later, only the undead walked the decaying streets of America.

After a breakfast of bacon, grits, and scrambled eggs, he washed the dishes and puttered around the house for a while in a futile attempt to postpone his grisly chore. Finally, he could put it off no longer. The longer the bodies lay in the sun, the riper they would become. He washed his face in the sink, combed his too-long brown hair, and took his morning dose of Actos. Lean and muscular, his Type 2 diabetes had taken him completely by surprise at the age of twenty-three. His body's cells no longer properly utilized the insulin his pancreas produced. Left untreated, attacks of hypoglycemia left him weak and dizzy. The Actos, or *Pioglitazone*, a *Thiazolidnedione* drug, kept his diabetes under control but sometimes caused edema. Thus, he often had to take Torsemide, a diuretic, to reduce swelling. It was a vicious cycle.

His disease had cost him his Army career. As a weapons specialist for a recon squad in the 1st Reconnaissance Battalion in Afghanistan, he had thought being tired and achy had just been part of the job, the cost of maintaining his country's freedom, but one particularly severe dizzy spell had led to his diagnosis and subsequent discharge. It hadn't been bad enough to prevent him from becoming a Pima County Deputy. It had taken the end of the world to end that career. Now, at thirty-two, he was just another survivor.

His small ranch was more than his bastion of freedom from the grid. It was his fortress. It was his little slice of heaven, a *prepper's* dream. Those who had called him paranoid were now either dead or dying. However, he took no comfort from their misery. To him, it had simply been a matter of being prepared for any emergency. A plague of zombies had been very low on his list of catastrophes. Luckily for him, like thirty percent of the population, he was immune to the virus, but he wasn't immune to zombies.

As he strode to the door, he strapped on his .45 and picked up his shotgun. His fingers lightly caressed the metal five-pointed star lying on the table, his great-grandfather's Arizona Ranger badge. Its surface wore the patina of time, but bore a slightly shinier spot where a bullet had grazed it in 1886. He picked up the badge and clipped it to his shirt. He was no longer a deputy. There was no longer any law. He wore the badge as a reminder of *Jake's Law #5 – In a lawless land the biggest gun makes the law.*

Grabbing a can of kerosene, he trudged down the path to the shed where he stored his ATV. After hooking up the small trailer to the Polaris Ranger, he drove down to the metal gate in the ten-foot-high stone wall which he had laboriously constructed across the canyon by hand. Working alone, it had been a gargantuan effort, but in hindsight, the fence had probably saved his life. He had since topped it with coils of razor wire. The canyon walls were too steep to easily climb and the terrain too rugged for casual hikers or unwanted visitors. He pressed the button on the remote and waited for the gate to roll open.

He disliked getting near zombies, dead or alive. Immune or not, he still hated taking unnecessary risks. His attention was so focused on the two corpses in front of him, so dreading his task that he failed to see a third zombie hidden within the early morning shadows of the wall. He stopped the ATV and had taken only two steps from it, when the zombie, an emaciated scarecrow, lurched toward him, the low growl erupting from its throat his only warning.

Jack's Law #12 – Stay Focused. His wandering mind had almost cost him his life. He swung the barrel of the shotgun and fired from the hip as he fell backwards, taking no time to properly aim. From less than six feet away, the .36-inch diameter triple-ought buckshot pellets tore through the zombie's torso like a scythe, ripping open his abdomen and sending him spinning to the ground. Severely damaged, it continued to reach for him with one outstretched hand, dragging its body behind it as it crawled toward him. Jake cursed himself for his stupidity and fired another round into the creature's head. Brains and skull fragments splattered the ground, as the head disintegrated from the barrage of steel pellets.

He picked himself up, dusted off, and set about his distasteful task. The mask he wore over his mouth and nose helped reduce the stench, but even live zombies stank of rotting flesh as outer layers of flesh decayed and sloughed away. Dead ones smelled worse. Using latex gloves, he rolled the three corpses in plastic sheets and loaded them onto the trailer. On the dirt where the zombies lay, tiny black worms no larger than snips of sewing thread wriggled in pools of rapidly congealing blood, the Stagger's culprit, the adult parasite. Jake suppressed a shudder of revulsion and splashed kerosene over the ground. He ignited it with a match and watched the tiny parasites shrivel and burn.

Satisfied he had killed them all, he drove two miles to a gully, and dumped the corpses over the edge. They rolled down the embankment to join the dozen or so skeletal remains of previous visitors. He poured a liberal amount of kerosene over them, lit a rolled up piece of newspaper, and dropped it into the gully. The flames spread quickly, engulfing the zombie corpses. He preferred to incinerate the corpses rather than risk scavengers eating them. He knew that heat killed the parasitic worms, but he didn't know if it destroyed the encapsulated sporazoa through which the disease spread.

He backed away from the acrid cloud of thick, black smoke, but lingered for a while to assure total cremation. While he waited, he climbed atop a ridge and scanned the horizon toward San Manuel through his binoculars. The small city once had a population of 3500, evenly split between Hispanic and whites, but had been hemorrhaging people since the closing of the copper mine in 2003. He had shopped there, picked up his mail at the local post office, ate at the Subway and the *Las Casas* Restaurant, and drank a few beers at Michael's Bar, but he had never considered himself a part of the town.

A loner by nature, the people of San Manuel were as foreign to him as the population of Mexico or India. He understood their language and their customs, but not their need to congregate in large numbers or their zeal of a lifetime's pursuit of the almighty dollar simply to die at an early age, exhausted by life and slightly less poor than before. His solitary life didn't appeal to many.

Perhaps he was lacking an empathy gene or suffered from a lack of whatever chemical drove people to seek human companionship. Whatever its cause, it had made him fit to survive in the new world rising from the ashes of the old.

A pall of smoke rose over the town, as it had for the past two days. Some large building was burning, or maybe it was an out-of-control grass fire. With no firefighters remaining, a grass fire could rage for weeks. He had watched one burn the north slopes of the San Galiuros a few months earlier, covering almost three hundred acres. He was safe enough in his remote canyon, but the smoke had made breathing difficult. From the amount of smoke visible, perhaps the entire town was in flames. Briefly, he considered the possibility that the army had arrived and was burning bodies as he was doing, but the chances were remote. Last, he had heard, the U. S Army had disintegrated into a dozen regional armies trying to eradicate the zombie threat and restore order in confined areas, like Phoenix, Portland, Miami, Dallas, and Atlanta. His curiosity begged him to investigate, but his common sense told him to wait. Whatever the cause, he could do nothing about it. *Jake's Law #2 – Long noses often get lopped off.*

By the time he returned to his ranch, the sun had topped seven-thousand-foot Basset Peak a dozen miles to the southeast. He thought he saw a brief glint of metal from the B-24 bomber that had crashed there in 1943, killing the entire crew, but it was probably just his imagination. Soon, the cool shadows would evaporate in the mounting heat, introducing the start of another smoldering day to his canyon.

He took his second cup of coffee of the morning on the balcony, dragging his favorite leather chair outside to sit in the sun. He pushed an errant lock of hair back under his University of Arizona baseball cap. Soon, he would have to use the clippers to chop it to a more manageable length. He shaved every other day more to retain the habit than a dislike of beards. Personal hygiene and grooming were often the first habits to disappear in a crisis situation. He refused to give in to such a slacker mentality. He had carefully prepared for an emergency, and he wasn't going to let the small things ruin his plans.

His ranch reflected his careful planning. A shallow wash ran the length of the block fault uplift canyon from Split Rock Falls at the head of the canyon to the desert beyond. During the summer monsoon season and the winter rains, the wash ran brown with muddy water. He had built a dam across the head of the wash from native stone, creating a small retention pond for irrigation. Now, the pond and the wash were bone dry, but his one-hundred-fifteen-feet-deep drilled well tapped a small aquifer and supplied more water than he needed in the dry seasons for his garden. His crops – mostly beans, peas, okra, carrots, tomatoes, lettuce, peppers, and corn – thrived in the irrigated soil. Canned goods were growing scarcer and becoming more difficult to procure by scavenging. It was easier and healthier to grow fresh vegetables.

His small ranch also housed four pigs, a chicken coop with fifteen hens and two roosters, and two goats, supplying him with meat, milk, and eggs. He hunted as often as possible to supplement his meat, but game was becoming scarce on the lower elevations. A large ironwood tree and a few sycamores provided some shade for the animals to escape the worst of the day's heat. He had planted two lemon trees, an orange tree, and an avocado tree a year earlier. If he survived long enough, he would have fresh fruit to supplement his diet. A small smokehouse beside the original ranch house was filled with hanging slabs of bacon, ham, venison, and pork sausages.

The one thing he had not prepared for was the loneliness. He had considered himself a hermit, seeking out companionship only on rare occasions and only on his terms, but at least he had been able to walk among people without the need to interact with them. Now, the lack of companionship was taking its toll on him. On his infrequent trips to scavenge for supplies or to raid a pharmacy for his medication, he saw many zombies but few living souls. Survivors had, like him, learned to hide. He often wondered if eyes watched him from behind curtained windows as eager for fellowship as he was. Only the fear of being greeted by a bullet prevented him from knocking on random doors. He found himself watching old movies on his DVD just to hear the sound of human voices. Lately, he had developed an unhealthy lust for Ingrid Bergman. He had once watched *For Whom the Bell Tolls* three times in a row just to gaze into her mesmerizing blue eyes.

A sudden sound tore his mind from his daydream. He glanced down the canyon in alarm, but it was only the two roosters fighting for territory, not coyotes. Predators like coyotes and mountain lions were becoming more numerous and bolder and had made several attempts at his animals. The chickens quickly settled back down. It amazed him how much like chickens humans were. They staked out claims to small parcels of land and fought all comers for a few kernels of corn. That same lack of cooperation had doomed mankind. Now, the zombies ate humans like humans ate chickens. He wondered if they considered humans to be finger licking good.

The temperature soared as the day wore on. By noon, his thermometer read 101. It was almost monsoon season, but he thought it would be weeks before the monsoons came, bringing with them a few clouds, a brief respite from the heat, and life-giving rain. He retreated to the relative coolness inside. He hadn't installed air conditioning. That would have been too large a load for the solar panels, but he had fans. They moved sufficient air to keep the inside of the house comfortable. Part of the rear wall of the house was built into the solid cliff face, providing a heat sink that retained the heat of the day in the winter and the cool of the night in the summer.

His roof-mounted solar panels provided electricity for a refrigerator to store food, but he kept his refrigerated supplies to a minimum in the event of several consecutive cloudy days. Mostly he used it for beer. A large pile of oak firewood chopped and split from trees higher up the slope was stacked beside the house. The wood fueled his fireplace, offering heat in the winter and doubling as a means of cooking if he ran out of propane for the stove.

He pitied the survivors living on scraps and huddling in their homes afraid to venture out for supplies, but not enough to search them out and invite them to share his domain. He had prepared and they hadn't. It wasn't quite survival of the fittest, but it came damn close. Those in the large cities had fared worst. When supplies had stopped entering from outside, riots had broken out, then full-scale turf wars over limited resources. He had heard tales of cannibalism, but he didn't know if they were true. However, determined people often did whatever was necessary to survive.

By late afternoon, he had grown restless. The continued cloud of smoke over San Manuel disturbed him. He knew a few people still lived there, though he didn't know how they managed to survive in a town filled with thousands of zombies. *Probably less than that*, he corrected himself. Many people had fled the city for imagined safety in the FEMA shelters set up in Phoenix and Tucson. Others had been killed by zombies, mostly infected loved ones they had refused to restrain, and a few had chosen suicide when they had become infected. By his estimate, less than a few hundred zombies remained in the area, enough to pose a considerable problem, since the only road out of the area led right through town. *Too many to shoot.*

When he went among the zombies, he carried his R-15 450 Bushmaster. Its light weight made it portable. He had replaced the weapon's original clip with an aftermarket thirty-round clip. The semi-automatic used the same .45 caliber 260-grain ammunition as his Remington Model 1911 R1 pistol, reducing the different types of ammo he needed to keep on hand. He had other weapons, like the Versa Max 12-gauge shotgun, but those two sufficed in most instances. He also carried a crossbow for silent killing. He had learned that noise attracted zombies. The Parker Concorde bow fired twenty-inch bolts like a rifle, complete with 3X scope and pistol grip. It cocked automatically at the push of a button, using a CO2 cartridge. It was a formidable weapon, saving the R-15 for difficult situations.

In his recon unit in Afghanistan, he had been the SDM, the Squad Designated Marksman, and had carried a modified M16. Such a weapon was illegal in the US, but he doubted anyone cared now. 45 caliber ammunition was easier to find than the 5.56 mm the M16 used, so he preferred the R-15.

The drive into town was a rough one, even for his four-wheel drive jeep. His dirt trail had suffered during the spring rains. He had tried to repair the worst spots, but without heavier equipment than a rake and a shovel, it was only patchwork. Soon, he would have to find a small bobcat bulldozer for more permanent repairs or risk being stranded and on foot. San Pedro River Road proved little better. It was gravel and wider, but the washes were almost impassable and the innumerable washboard ruts jarred his spine. Grass and weeds thrust upward through the packed gravel. In some places, it was difficult to tell road from desert. Already, the land was busily reclaiming what man had wrestled from it.

A few miles from San Manuel, the gravel road became pavement. He stopped the jeep and killed the engine, listening before he entered the town. The sharp report of a gunshot was followed by two more, then silence. Someone was alive and in trouble. He hesitated. He didn't like getting involved in other people's problems, but he was curious about the smoke. He unsnapped his holster and laid the R-15 across the seat beside him just in case, and continued down the road.

The town of San Manuel was mostly located off the main road. He usually avoided the densely packed neighborhoods and its inherent local zombie population. However, this time his curiosity compelled him to enter the town. A cloud of smoke rose from the combined junior high and high schools. A large part of the main was already gone. Fingers of steel rebar and thick support columns protruded through piles of smoldering brick and rubble. Another section was mostly intact but in flames. Smoke billowed from the windows and curled over the eaves. A man stood near the school entrance shooting zombies as they emerged from the flames. Some of the creatures' clothing was on fire, their flesh seared and blackened from the inferno, but they charged him, heedless of the flames consuming them. Jake silently saluted the man's ingenuity in herding the zombies into the school to dispose of them en masse. He watched him take down several of the creatures in this manner, but as a wall collapsed, more than a dozen creatures rushed from the ruins. The shooter turned to run toward a nearby Toyota pickup, but he was overweight and ran too slowly. Jake saw that he would never make it before he was overtaken.

He was torn. He could either watch the man die or help him. The ex-deputy in him pushed him to help, but the survivalist cautioned against risking his life for a total stranger. Deciding he had watched too many people die, he picked up his R-15 in one hand and drove closer. The man didn't hear or notice the jeep until Jake began firing the Bushmaster into the mass of zombies. Then, startled, the stranger cowered behind his pickup. Jake finished off the zombies and parked a few yards away, waiting. The stranger watched Jake for a couple of minutes before emerging from behind his vehicle, his rifle cradled in his arms, handy but not threatening. Jake exited the jeep. He left his rifle on the seat, but he had his pistol on his hip, so he felt safe.

"Nice job," he said, nodding his head toward the burning school.

The man, shorter than Jake by three inches, slightly balding, and severely overweight, smiled. He pushed his glasses up the bridge of his nose, and said, "I lured about fifty inside a couple of days ago and set it afire. I thought the fire would kill them all, but it died out. I tried again last night, but a few managed to escape. I was cleaning up."

"I saw the smoke and was curious."

The man stared at the smoke rising into the sky for a moment. "Thanks for saving my ass, Deputy. I can usually hit what I aim at, but I can't shoot fast enough to take on a group like that."

"You need something bigger, and I'm not a deputy anymore."

The man stared at the badge more closely. "A Ranger?"

"No. This belonged to my great-grandfather. I wear it as a reminder."

"A reminder of what?"

Jake tapped his pistol. "That this makes the laws now."

The man shrugged. "If you say so." He kicked at the dirt with the toe of his boot. "I can cook up some stew if you're hungry. I live in Oracle."

"Why come out here to kill zombies? Aren't there any of the bastards in Oracle?"

The man frowned. "Too damned many." He glanced at the building. "I taught high school science here. Some of those zombies were my students. I needed to … tidy up."

Jake noticed movement in the distance – more zombies drawn by the noise. "We had better get out of here before reinforcements arrive."

"You don't look like you're afraid of a few zombies. You've got the firepower. Let's wipe them out." A look of grim determination swept over the man's face. Jake recognized the look of a zealot. Zealots had no instinct for survival.

He shook his head. "It's not my war."

"Not your war? That's a curious attitude. Whose war is it, do you think?"

"We lost the war. Clean up isn't my thing. I kill zombies when they get in my way. I'm not angry with them the way you seem to be."

The man nodded. "Yeah, I guess you're right. I'm at war with them. I hate them with the same degree of passion I had about teaching." He glanced at the burning school. "Maybe I'm simply teaching them a lesson."

"Do you think they learn?"

"About as well as some of my students did," he snorted. "Now, about that stew. My name's Reed by the way, Alton Reed."

The sound of a human voice sounded strange to Jake after so long alone, but he found it sweet in his ears. A few minutes of conversation and a shared meal wasn't a commitment to humanity. "Sounds good. My name's Jake Blakely."

"Great! Follow me, Jake."

He followed Reed's pickup out of San Manuel past the abandoned smelter. Jake had watched the demolition of the twin, five-hundred-foot smokestacks that had once stood there in January of 2007, while sitting in his jeep nursing a six-pack of beer. It had been the most excitement the town had experienced in years. As he drove by the abandoned local Pinal County branch sheriff's office, memories of his days as a deputy in nearby Pima County rushed over him. Not all of them had been good, but he especially missed the search and rescue missions. Hikers were always getting lost, injured, or trapped on a cliff. It was certainly better than writing tickets and getting involved in domestic disputes.

They continued through the winding canyons surrounding San Manuel to Oracle. Just past American Avenue, the main street for downtown Oracle, Reed crossed Tucson Wash and turned onto Goodman Ranch Road. They drove about three miles out into the desert before reaching a parked RV, a Country Coach Magna, nestled in a little depression between copses of saguaros and mesquite. Reed pulled up beside the RV, stopped, and hopped out.

"Here's home," he announced, waving his arm at the vehicle.

A small gas-powered generator sat humming beside the RV, supplying electricity. Inside, the forty-two-foot RV was cramped with stacked boxes of canned goods and bottled water. A hacksaw and short lengths of steel pipe littered the floor. Reed dropped his rifle on the couch beside a 20-gauge Marlin shotgun. Jake took a seat at the table while Reed opened a can of beef stew, poured it in a pot, and set it on the stove. He added a few herbs and a splash of hot sauce. After a few minutes, the delicious aroma of hot stew filled the trailer. His host ladled out two bowls of stew and produced two bottles of cold beer.

"Do the zombies bother you out here?" he asked, as he lifted a spoonful of stew to his mouth.

"Not much. If it's just one or two, I kill them with a Kaiser blade to be quiet." Reed grimaced. "I used to live in a comfortable house in Oracle, but it got too crowded with rowdy undead neighbors. I found this RV, and now I simply pick up and move if things get too dangerous."

Curious, he asked, "Why do you remain here?"

Reed wrinkled his brow and frowned. "It's my home. I grew up in Oracle. I left once, but I came back. I've got no place else to go." He shoveled a spoonful of stew into his mouth and took a sip of beer. "I've seen your jeep around a few times but stayed hidden. I didn't know if you were friend or foe. There are a lot of bad characters running around. I've seen some dead bodies with bullet holes in them. They weren't zombies."

Jake nodded. He had encountered murder victims as well. Not everyone believed in the sanctity of life. "Bad times," he said.

"Bad times indeed," Reed agreed. He stopped eating, folded his arms on the table, spoon in hand, and stared at Jake. "Why did you help me?"

Jake shrugged his shoulders. He had been asking himself the same question. It was a first for him. "I don't know."

Reed leveled his spoon and pointed at Jake, as if he were calling upon a student to answer a question. "I think it's because you craved a human voice. I know I do. I'm used to thirty kids screaming and yelling all day. The silence is killing me."

"Not as fast as the zombies will."

Reed nodded his head. "True. True. I knew shooting zombies would bring more, but I was angry. I took a chance." He stared at Jake. "Will we be two ships that pass in the night?"

Jake took a sip of his beer, a Dos Equis, and then returned Reed's steady gaze. "You looking for a play date?"

Reed laughed, slapped the table with the palm of his hand, and laughed again. "Good one. No, I just thought we might cooperate a little. You know, scavenging. Two sets of eyes, two guns… You know I can shoot."

"Maybe, but I'm not ready to adopt you yet."

"Good enough. We'll feel each other out a bit first. There's a CVS pharmacy in Oro Valley that I don't think has been completely stripped. Oh, the real drugs, the Oxycontin, Vicodin, etcetera are probably gone, and the Valium. Hell, I take a Valium every now and then. Who wouldn't in this mess, but I've got asthma. I need *Millipred* and more inhalers. The pollen count is rising, and I don't need another asthma attack. The last one almost did me in."

Jake didn't know if he trusted a man who took narcotics, even something as common as Valium, but he understood Reed's medical problems. He needed more Actos and supplies for his first aid kit. "Okay, but we take two vehicles."

Reed smiled. "Let's eat first."

The stew hit the spot. It had been cooked and canned by Armour and Company, but Reed's addition of dried herbs enhanced the flavor. The beer hit the spot as well. The irony of the two of them together didn't amuse him. Reed, a high school science teacher and a decent shot seemed capable of surviving the zombie apocalypse, yet required modern medicines to function, while he, a survivalist and an avid hunter, also needed medication to survive. That two people blessed with immunity to the Staggers might die as their drug supply dwindled had to be a cosmic joke.

After the meal, Reed tidied up quickly, as he seemed in a hurry to leave. Jake visually inspected Reed's trailer while Reed washed the dishes. Boxes of ammunition and a pair of binoculars lay beside the two guns on the sofa. A trashcan overflowing with empty cans, water bottles, and short pieces of metal pipe was pushed up against the sink. Together with the pieces of pipe on the floor, it looked as if Reed was doing a little plumbing. The cases of food and water were neatly stacked, but the bed down the short hallway was unmade. Clothes were strewn on the floor.

"There! Finished," Reed announced as he dried his hands on a dish towel.

As they drove south, they passed many vehicles abandoned when their drivers succumbed to the disease. Most of the zombies had ambled into the nearest towns or wandered into the desert to die of starvation. They were forced to drive around a jack-knifed semi blocking most of both lanes near Biosphere 2. The rear door had been forced open and the contents scattered. Instead of the hoped for food someone had expected, the truck's cargo had been cell phones and electronic devices. Discarded boxes of them lay scattered in the ditch.

At one point, Reed swerved his Toyota onto the shoulder at forty miles per hour to take out a female zombie clad only in panties and slippers. The woman turned at the sound of the truck but showed no awareness of her immediate danger. As the truck's right front fender crushed her chest, she spiraled into the air, and landed in a broken heap in the ditch. Jake shook his head in dismay. Reed's personal vendetta against zombies could get him killed. A simple flat tire could strand him out in the open miles from shelter. He understood the former teacher's hatred for the creatures, but he refrained from foolish actions. *Jack's Law #3 – A fool and his life are soon parted.*

Catalina was a small town flowing along both sides of the highway. One strip mall where Jake had sometimes eaten breakfast was now only blackened ruins in a sea of cracked asphalt and rusting automobiles. Many other buildings had suffered similar fates, as unattended stoves and ovens had ignited gas leaks or other flammable material. Some fires had been deliberately set by vandals or looters. Zombies roamed the parking lot of the *Basha's* grocery store where he had once shopped and attempted to pursue the two vehicles, but moved too slowly to present a problem. As one of the creatures rushed down the hill on which the grocery store was situated, it stumbled and rolled head-over-heels to the bottom. It picked itself up, looked around as if searching for whoever had tripped it, and continued toward the highway. Freshly turned zombies or zombies who had just fed, Runners, could move swiftly, but the longer they existed without feeding, the slower and weaker they became, Shamblers. He didn't know how long they could survive without eating, but so far, he had encountered no zombies dead from natural causes.

In Oro Valley, beyond the pass between the Tortalita and the Catalina mountains, the devastation was less severe, but vehicles filled the parking lots of the Oro Valley Marketplace Mall, including military trucks and police squad cars. Jake frowned at the empty squad cars. He might have known some of the officers that had driven them, not friends but at least acquaintances. The remains of a FEMA medical tent city in the open area between parking lots lay scattered by the wind. The shattered chain link fence that had protected it and the weathered skeletons dotting the asphalt around the tent reminded him of the confusion and misery of those final days when he had still been a cop. He had helped ferry the sick to the FEMA facility after the Oro Valley Hospital had become overwhelmed with patients. Some had gone willingly. Others had gone in handcuffs. None had survived. They had simply died away from home and loved ones. His participation in such acts of forced incarceration had been one of the turning points in his decision to quit the force. His dwindling faith in the government's ability to solve the problem wasn't as strong as his faith in himself.

Zombies roamed the empty stores and parking lots in search of food. Many turned their heads in his direction at the sound of the jeep and the truck, but even with their limited mental capacity, they knew the vehicle was too far away to chase after them.

Further south, across from a large shopping center, several corpses littered the CVS parking lot. Jake didn't bother to check if they had been zombies or victims of zombies. The unmoving dead no longer mattered. As Reed had said, the store had been looted of most food items, narcotics, medical supplies, and oddly enough, cosmetics. The odor of rotten food spilled from open cooler doors. The stringent smell of vinegar rose from a broken case of soured apple juice. As he walked deeper into the store, glass from broken bottles of wine and liquor crunched beneath the sole of his boots. The corpse of a young man lay on the floor between aisles. He had been dead many weeks. His decaying body had almost mummified in the dry heat. From his withered arm protruded a hypodermic syringe.

"Poor bastard couldn't even wait to get home before shooting up," Reed observed.

"Small loss," Jake replied, stepping over the body, instantly dismissing it. He had witnessed many similar scenes as a deputy. To him, drugs were a pipeline to death, and dead junkies didn't bother him. He had become apathetic to people willing to commit slow suicide. It was their families he felt sorry for, not the junkies.

In the pharmacy section, the shelves been thoroughly ransacked, especially of aspirin, cough syrup, and disinfectants. Some bottles had been deliberately broken in anger, spilling their contents across the floor. Tablets were crushed to a fine powder by the tread of many feet. Reed searched through a pile of rubble and grabbed three boxes of inhalers that looters had missed and stuffed them into a bag he carried. Jake located a large bottle of Torsemide, but only two bottles of Actos, enough for sixty days.

"I can't find the Millipred," Reed mumbled, as he tossed aside boxes in his search.

Jake scraped up a large handful of aspirin that had spilled from a broken bottle and shoved them into his pocket. "Try the customer Will Call," he suggested, as he picked up a box of bandages and antiseptic ointment.

Heeding his advice, Reed checked the packages that had been waiting for customers who would never pick them up. "Yes!" he cried in triumph, holding aloft two vials of Millipred. He read from the package label. "Thank you Mr. Dexter Ellis for your generous donation to the Alton Reed Medical Fund."

At the sound of broken glass crunching, Jake motioned Reed to silence. Laying his supplies on the counter, he edged toward the noise. He had taken only two steps toward the customer counter, when a zombie thrust its head through the glass, smashing it. Broken shards stuck in the creature's head, as well as Jake's arm. He leaped backwards to avoid the zombie's clutching hands. He plucked the glass from his arm and wiped the blood on his pants. Reed dropped his load of supplies and pointed his rifle at the creature. Fearing the noise would attract more zombies, Jake cautioned him with a wave of his hand to wait.

This zombie was no Shambler. It was a Runner, fresh from a kill, eager for more flesh. Barely dried blood coated its mouth and upper torso. It tilted its head to one side and sniffed the air, keening at the smell of Jake's blood. He had left his knife in the jeep. Keeping his body away from the zombie's flailing arms, he picked up a long sliver of broken glass, and wrapped one end in a white pharmacist's smock hanging on a hook. Leaping forward quickly, he jabbed the glass into the back of the creature's neck between the third and fourth vertebrae and twisted until the shard snapped in his hands. The zombie groaned and died, the glass severing its spinal column.

"That was close," Reed said.

Jake took a deep breath and nodded. "Too damn close. It's time to leave." He tossed the bloody smock on the floor and took a closer look at the zombie, a middle-aged male whose clothing was surprisingly clean except for the fresh blood stains. He had turned only recently and fed even more recently. "There's bound to be more around."

Reed pointed to Jake's arm. "You had better see to that."

Jake glanced at the wound. Already, the blood flow was slowing. He dismissed Reed's concern with, "I'll be fine," but he did apply some of the antiseptic ointment to prevent infection. With no doctors, prevention was tantamount to survival.

On the way out, he picked up a collapsible water hose to add to his irrigation system. Reed grinned but said nothing. Satisfied with his haul, Reed was ready to return to his RV, but Jake decided to look around. It had been many weeks since he had last ventured so far from home, and he wanted to discover what was happening in the dead city, and to see if the military had managed to secure the area.

"I'll be along later," he told Reed." Maybe I'll see you in a day or two." Having someone to talk with had been more pleasant than he had expected. Having met someone, he was reluctant to sever the relationship, but even more reluctant to commit himself.

Reed replied, "If I have to move, I'll be in Oracle Park."

After they had parted company, Jake continued south on Oracle Road. A barricade had been hastily thrown across the road at one intersection in an attempt to block incoming traffic in the mistaken belief that the Staggers was restricted to transmission by contact, rather than airborne through mosquitoes, flies, and other insects. Lines of abandoned vehicles filled all lanes. Several disintegrating corpses lying in and around the vehicles spoke of the determination with which the erecters of the barricade had fought to keep out strangers. In the end, their efforts had been futile. The city had died.

He detoured along several smaller side roads to bypass the barricade, detecting signs of life in a few houses – fresh wash hanging on clotheslines, cars not covered by pollen or fallen leaves, indicating they had been driven recently, and subtle movement behind curtains as he passed. It could have been zombies, but the movements were so furtive that he believed frightened survivors lived there.

He saw many zombies, hundreds, in fact. He ran a few down with his jeep when they stepped in front of him, but he didn't go out of his way to kill those wise enough to remain off the road. Most of the houses had been ransacked or looted. Broken windows, smashed doors, and scattered debris were the calling cards of human scavengers; human skeletons, the leftovers of zombie attacks. Here and there, he saw signs that some people had banded together at schools, churches, or businesses to combat zombies or looters – chain link fences and walls constructed from metal freight containers or overturned vehicles; the bodies of looters hanging from trees and streetlights; piles of cremated zombies in empty lots or washes – but nowhere did he see groups of living people. They had either fled or had fallen victim to marauders both human and inhuman.

Parking atop a ridge south of Canada del Oro Wash, he had a sweeping vista of Tucson with the backdrop of the Santa Rita Mountains towering to the south. The city certainly appeared dead. The streets were deserted of traffic. No smoke rose from chimneys. No sounds stirred the still air. Entire neighborhoods had been razed during riots or brush fires. Perhaps the clearest indications that the city was lost were the flocks of buzzards circling overhead and the packs of wild dogs and coyotes roaming the streets. All three groups of scavengers competed for the same food source, dead bodies. Murders of crows patrolled the parking lots and buildings, their ebony wings glistening in the sun. It was a city of the dead and the dying. Scavengers, winged, four-legged, and two-legged, ruled the city.

He had seen enough. The sight of the dead city depressed and sickened him. Further explorations would prove nothing. If anyone remained alive in Tucson, they were hiding and would soon become victims, or they were predators living off the bloated corpse of the city and the few remaining survivors that crawled through its innards like maggots. He turned away and started home.

3

June 7, 2016 Oro valley, AZ –

Jake was intent on reaching home, so intent that he almost failed to see the woman racing across the road, pursued by three fast zombies, Runners. He slammed on the brakes, sliding to a halt to miss her. One of the creatures focused its attention on him rather than the girl. Jake grabbed his crossbow and leaped from the jeep. His arrow struck the creature in the right side of its temple and passed completely through the skull in a fine spray of blood. The zombie took two faltering steps, teetered, and collapsed beside the road, rolling into a ditch. Before it hit the ground, Jake was in pursuit of the other two creatures.

The woman was fast, but she was clearly tiring. She stumbled, righted herself, and then stumbled again, this time falling and rolling across the ground. She picked herself up and saw that her pursuers were gaining. Changing directions, she raced toward a nearby building, limping slightly.

Jake stopped long enough to eliminate a second zombie with a bolt through its head, but the other Runner was too far away. He raced to catch up. The woman scrambled up on the flat roof of the building using a Palo Verde tree as a convenient ladder. *At least she has more sense than to get herself cornered inside a building*, he thought. When he got within range, he took steady aim and dropped the last Runner, who was intent on getting at the woman, clawing at the tree in rage. The woman noticed Jake but made no effort to vacate the roof.

"Come down. We have to go before more show up."

She still didn't budge. He was on the verge of leaving her, when she began to climb back down. As she did, a branch snapped, and she plunged ten feet to the ground. Jake watched her fall in slow motion, knowing he could never reach her in time. She landed with a sickening thud on her right side and lay there groaning. He rushed to help.

She was young, perhaps twenty-two or twenty-three, slim and athletic, but looked as though she had missed a meal or two lately. She looked up at him and grimaced, as she tried to sit up.

"I think I sprained my shoulder," she said.

"Lucky you didn't break your fool neck," he replied a little harsher than he had intended, but continued, "What were you doing out here unarmed and baiting zombies?"

"I don't like guns," she said.

"Then keep dying a horrible death real high on your list of things to do, 'cause that's what's going to happen to you." He raised his crossbow into the air. Her eyes followed it. "Either you kill them, or they'll kill you. Being a pacifist nowadays is a death wish. You can't always depend on someone who doesn't share your disdain for self-defense to help."

"You're a cop. Isn't that what you do, save people?"

He didn't feel like repeating his great-grandfather story about the badge. "I'm not a cop, and I normally don't save people. Today was your lucky day. Now, why were you running?"

"My friends and I were holed up in a house a couple of miles away. Ben got careless on a food run and zombies followed him back. We didn't know they were there until they broke the door down. One grabbed Liz." She paused and closed her eyes. After a few seconds, she continued, "Ben tried to save her. They both died, horribly," she added, looking up at him with a sneer. "I ran."

She was angry with herself for deserting her friends. He decided to wise her up. "Smart move. They're dead. You're not."

Some of the anger drained from her face. "I would be if not for you. By the way, my name is Jessica."

Her sudden shift from disdain to praise caught him off guard and embarrassed him. He helped her to her feet using her good left arm. "You had better come with me, Jessica. I'll see what I can do about that shoulder. Can you walk?"

She took a few uncertain steps. "I can manage, but my shoulder is numb."

He noticed her right arm dangling loosely at her side. "You've dislocated your shoulder. Here."

He handed her his crossbow, and then grabbed her right arm. Before she could protest, he pulled it outwards and up. She yelped in pain, as the bones slipped back into place.

"That hurt like hell," she snapped, drawing back from him.

In the Army, he had become a Jack-of-all-trades. A little medical knowledge went a long way fifty clicks from the nearest medic. He knew how much pain he had caused her. "It will heal," he replied. He took his crossbow from her. "Let's go."

She followed, limping badly. She had run a couple of miles wearing shorts and sandals with hungry zombies in hot pursuit. Her legs were covered with numerous scratches and scrapes. Several prickly pear cactus spines protruded from her flesh. Her t-shirt was ripped in several places, exposing one of her small, naked breasts through the fabric. He tried not to stare at it, but the sight stirred something in him. He fought it down, as he wrapped his arm around her waist to help her walk. She didn't protest.

Back in the jeep, he offered her water and a protein bar he kept handy in case of an attack of hypoglycemia. She accepted both eagerly, downing the bar in three quick bites.

"Thanks," she said, still chewing. "What's your name?"

"Jake Blakely." He fished another bar from his bag and handed it to her. "You can't go back home," he said.

She shook her head. "No, Jake, I can't." She glanced around. "I know the area. I'll find some place safe."

"And starve?" he asked. She didn't reply. "Look, it's not safe here. I've got a place north of here that's secure, and I have plenty of food." He wrinkled his nose. "I've got hot water for a shower, too. I don't make any promises, but at least you'll have a meal, a shower, and a place to sleep tonight."

She looked at him undecided. He guessed at the reason for her caution.

"If I wanted to rape you or kill you, I could easily do it now, and I wouldn't have had to waste precious protein bars."

She smiled sheepishly at him. "You're right. I'm being foolish. I accept."

"Just as long as you know I'm not adopting you. When your wounds heal, you're gone."

"Fair enough. I don't want to be a bother."

"Too late for that," he replied, as he cranked the jeep, mentally kicking himself for ignoring *Jack's Law #4 – Don't bring home more problems than you left with. Especially a good looking problem,* he added.

* * * *

Later, after a shower, Jessica looked almost human again. Her short red hair hung in wet curls on her scalp. He had given her one of his t-shirts to replace her torn one. It was too big for her small frame, but at least it hid her breasts. While she was showering, he had considered his options. He had broken *Jack's Law #2* twice today already, and his nose was feeling rather tender. He had saved Reed, and now Jessica. He didn't know what had gotten into him, but now she was here, and he was responsible for her.

"Sit down," he said.

He broke out his medical kit and tended to her cuts and scrapes. They were numerous but less serious than they had first appeared. He had painfully plucked out the cactus spines with a pair of tweezers before her shower to prevent them from breaking off and becoming infected. A few of the deeper gashes still bled. She winced, as he applied antiseptic spray and covered the wounds with bandages. Her sprained ankle and dislocated shoulder would heal with sufficient rest. Afterwards, as he put away his first aid kit, she smiled at him.

"You have gentle hands, Jake."

Embarrassed, he ignored her comment. "I've got aspirin for pain, if your shoulder is bothering you?"

She moved her right arm experimentally and bit down on her lip. "A little stiff, but I'll hold off on any pain killers for now. I don't like drugs. I guess I won't be doing any yoga for a few days."

He looked at her in surprise. "Yoga? Are you a health nut?"

"If that's what you want to call it. I teach, uh, taught yoga and nutrition. I try to maintain a healthy body – no meats, grains, processed or fatty foods."

He laughed aloud. "Boy, did you choose the wrong time to be picky."

She stared at him for a moment, finally got his joke, and laughed with him. "Yeah, it hasn't been easy. I guess I'll have to alter my diet, but I think my healthy lifestyle is the reason I haven't gotten the Staggers."

"If that were true, I'd be dead. I can offer fresh vegetables, eggs, and cheese if you're not a strict vegan, but everything else is canned, smoked, or still walking around on four legs."

"Cheese?" she asked in disbelief.

"I have goats. I milk them and make cheese, mostly feta, but I have a good imitation of Italian caprino aging. Of course, I have a block of cheddar around somewhere if you prefer, but I salvaged it from a grocery store. I keep goats because cows require too much space to maintain even a few of them."

She nodded. "How do you know about making cheeses?"

He waved his hand at the bookcase against one wall. "Books. You can learn anything from books, although my first few efforts were unappetizing messes."

She looked at his modest but eclectic collection books. "Are all deputies survivalists?"

He smiled at her question. "Not all. Some of my colleagues called me a kook. I consider myself a prepper, ready for almost any eventuality."

"Even a zombie apocalypse?"

He shrugged his shoulders. "The principle's the same. Survival is survival."

"I suppose." She glanced around the room, noting the disarray. "Are you married?"

He laughed. Never a very neat person, he had clothes lying across the back of the sofa and dining room chairs, books piled on tables, and the furniture was coated in a fine film of dust. "Do you think a wife would let me keep the house this messy?"

"Have you been?"

He shook his head. "No. I came close once or twice, but it didn't stick, or maybe I didn't stick with it long enough for it to take. Either way, I live alone."

"Me, too, live alone I mean. I had a boyfriend, but he died."

Jake simply nodded. There was nothing he could say that would matter. A lot of people had died. Death had become as casual as sex had once been. Death didn't really matter until it came your turn. "No family?"

She shook her head. "No. My father left when I was ten. Mom died two years ago. At least she didn't see the shit hit the fan."

"Do you want to survive?" he asked.

She stared at him with her head tilted to one side. "What do you mean?"

"If you want to live, you've got to get over your distaste for guns. Running fast just won't cut it."

"Guns kill people."

He laughed at her twisted logic and watched her jaw tighten. "I've owned guns all my life, but the only people I've killed were shooting at me in Afghanistan. A gun is a tool, nothing more. I used them for hunting. Now, I use them to stay alive. If it's guns in general you don't like, learn to use a bow or a sword, but you can't always depend on someone else to save your ass."

"I've been doing all right," she said.

"Maybe you should ask your two dead friends how they feel about that."

She recoiled as if he had slapped her. His barb had struck deeply, just as he had intended. Trying to hang on to one's beliefs was one thing, but allowing them to kill you was foolish.

He continued, "There are people out there who would kill you for fun, and about half a million creatures that want to eat you. You have to learn to defend yourself, or you'll die. It's as simple as that. You can only hide so long. You'll have to go out among them some time. You need to be prepared."

"You seem to have a pretty good hiding place here," she shot at him.

"I spent years preparing it, but even I have to go out at times. I prepared for that too." He decided to soften his rhetoric. She had survived so far, so she had some skill at it. He was pushing her into an uncomfortable area. Some people had an unreasonable attitude toward guns, somehow seeing them as more dangerous than other weapons. It would take time for her to adjust to the new reality. "Look, you can stay here for a few days while you heal properly. I can teach you how to shoot a gun or a crossbow, if you want. If not," he shrugged, "I'll drop you off wherever you want to go, and you're on your own."

She turned her head to stare out the window. After a minute, she looked back at him. Her cheek was damp, but he didn't think it was from her shower. "I should be grateful. You saved my life. You took me in and tended to my wounds. I realize my dislocated shoulder would have doomed me. I'll ... I'll consider what you've said."

"Fair enough." He jerked his thumb toward the small kitchen. "I'll whip up a salad and a couple of cheese omelets."

She smiled. "That sounds delicious."

It was strange watching someone else eat. He hadn't paid attention to Reed eating, but he ate like a man, shoveling food into his mouth with a purpose. Food was energy. Taste was secondary. Jessica ate methodically and deliberately, examining each bite of food before placing it in her mouth; savoring it to allow her taste buds to relish the flavor before chewing and swallowing. He forced himself to slow down. Like Reed, he had a supply of dried and fresh herbs and used them to vary the taste of his meals – Mexican spices one day, Italian the next, and so on for a culinary trip around the globe – but he could eat anything placed in front of him. One day he might have to exist solely on the two hundred MREs he had in storage and wanted to enjoy as much variety as possible before then.

He found it impossible not to stare across the table at Jessica. She was so intent on her meal that she failed to notice his gaze. He had to admit that she was pretty in a plain sort of way, not magazine model beautiful, but certainly a cut above most women. He normally preferred women with a little more meat on their bones and larger breasts, but she was sexy in a Disney Princess sort of way. At first glance, she looked emaciated – high, thin cheekbones and a petite frame – but her lithe body was well-muscled. Her yoga exercises must have helped. He personally didn't see much use in twisting your body into outlandish pretzel shapes, but it had worked for her.

"Trying to decide if you like what you see?"

He jumped, caught red-handed examining her. "Just wondering if I should take up yoga."

She smiled. "It couldn't hurt. I also used to run five miles every morning. I tried to take care of my body."

"It's a nice body."

She stopped eating and stared at him. "I'm glad you noticed. I was beginning to think you might be gay. That would be just my luck."

That brought a chuckle to his lips. "No, not gay, just careful."

"Have you decided yet?"

"Decided what?"

"If you want to screw me."

Her casual manner took him by surprise. In spite of himself, he blushed. He had been brought up believing men were the beasts, always thinking about sex, but she was more comfortable with the idea of casual sex than he was. He fought to recover his aplomb.

"Do you think if you put out, I'll let you stay?"

She didn't flinch at his accusation. She took another bite of her omelet and said, "Something like that."

"As much as the idea appeals to me, and believe me it is appealing, I can't be bought by a roll in the sack. You go or stay strictly on the concept of mutual benefit. If you can't benefit me other than with sex, I don't need another person around to take care of. I don't want the responsibility."

She nodded. "Fair enough, but I don't want to go back out there alone. I'll probably die. You teach me how to shoot, and I'll teach you how to take care of your body." She waved her hand over the table. "What you're eating won't supply all your nutritional requirements. I saw the Actos in the jeep. If you have diabetes, you need to be especially careful of your diet. You need vitamins and supplements. You need less red meat; more white meat and seafood. You need someone to watch your back."

He jerked his head, stunned by her outpouring. "Jesus, you sound like a salesperson trying to sell me a used car."

"I'm trying to sell myself. Sex is just part of the package. You're good looking, and I'm no virgin. It has probably been a while for both of us. We can be, ah, mutually beneficial, as you say."

Her smile sliced right through his resolve. Her offer did have merits. She was certainly right about it having been a long time since he had sex. A quick mental vision of her naked in bed flashed through his mind, stirring his manhood. He shook his head to vanquish the alluring image. Sometimes, being a gentleman was difficult. Other times, it was downright impossible. Her offer also drove home the fact that he needed someone around. Except for his brief encounter with Reed, he had been alone since before E-Day a year earlier. The life of a hermit sounded great when no one was around. It was easy being a loner when you're alone. When faced with the possibility of companionship after a year of solitude, it lost some of its appeal. He thought of the scene in *Young Frankenstein* where the blind hermit Gene Hackman invited the monster into his hut, eager for the company, little realizing the danger. He felt a little like Hackman.

He swallowed hard, and then said, "First, we see if you can shoot." *There goes Jake's Law #4 – Don't bring home more problems than you left with.*

5

June 9, 2016   Oracle, AZ –

They rode into town ready for trouble, eager for it, in fact. Well-armed men didn't fear zombies or survivors. Fear was for loners and losers. Levi Coombs and his gang of marauders treated both groups the same, as obstacles to overcome. Oracle, Arizona was a small town north of Tucson, sparsely populated even before the apocalypse. There would be fewer zombies in Oracle than in Tucson, offering fewer risks to his raiding parties. Over the past year, he had gotten proficient at taking what he wanted. He expected little resistance in a town where the dead prowled the empty streets like packs of stray dogs, starving for flesh.

The roar of the big diesel U.S. Army truck they had liberated from an abandoned FEMA facility and the line of motorcycles trailing it rumbled down American Boulevard, attracting the attention of the mindless creatures. They turned and stared as the small convoy pulled into the parking lot of the ubiquitous Dollar General store every small town had.

Levi stepped down from the truck and surveyed the store. The glass front door was smashed, and broken glass littered the asphalt around the entrance. More ominous were the two skeletons beside the doorway picked almost clean by zombies and scavengers. He dropped his Marlboro cigarette to the ground and crushed it beneath the toe of his cowboy boots. He pushed back the dirty straw Stetson he wore and ran his fingers through his goatee as he surveyed the area. He then looked at the first two bikes, raised a finger and swirled it in the air, and pointed down the road.

"Go find us a place to live."

Ax nodded and gunned the engine of the Harley he rode, leaving a trail of rubber and smoke as he left the parking lot. The former accountant had undergone a major transformation since their escape from prison fourteen months earlier. His hair hung to his shoulders from beneath the biker's helmet. No longer frightened by every zombie they encountered, he had become Levi's second-in-command, almost as ruthless as the leader to which he was devoted. A second bike followed Ax down the road.

Levi stared at his remaining companions, a motley group of bikers, ex-cons like him, and street scum lucky enough to be immune to the Staggers. "Let's see what the locals missed."

He shouldered the M16 he had taken from a home they had raided a few weeks earlier and sauntered toward the store, stroking his goatee. He stopped when a Staggerer wearing a filthy, tattered pair of green mechanic's coveralls appeared from around the corner of the building. A tire gauge and a Phillips-head screwdriver protruded from the creature's breast pocket. The blood-smeared name tag above the pocket read 'Bobby'. A second zombie stumbled into view close behind the first, a naked man covered in cuts, lacerations, and cactus spines.

Levi winced at the second creature's grisly condition. "Mindless bastards," he said.

From experience, Levi knew to aim for the head. He placed his first shot in Bobby's forehead from ten paces. The back of the creature's head exploded, splattering the front of the metal building with a spray of dark blood and matted brains. The body hit the pavement, shuddering slightly. The screwdriver fell from the creature's pocket, landing beside the twitching fingers of the hand that had once wielded it. The second creature stepped over its companion and lunged at Levi. He sidestepped it easily and clubbed it across the back of the head with the butt of the rifle. The zombie collapsed on the pavement, adding more scrapes and cuts to its already tortured body, as it skidded in the gravel. Before it could rise, Levi lowered the barrel of the M16 and delivered a can't-miss shot from a distance of twelve inches. The head disintegrated, leaving a bloody pulp on the ground. Levi eyed the mass of wriggling worms that had changed the creature from a human into the walking dead and spat at them, knowing they would soon wither and die in the heat of the day.

Posting two men outside to take care of any stray Staggerers, he led the others into the darkened store's interior. The building had been thoroughly looted of food and canned goods, but they found flashlights and batteries, boots, clothing, tools – things that would eventually come in handy. Moving like a precision team, they quickly gathered and piled their loot by the door. Outside, sporadic shooting told him the area was getting hot with zombies.

"Time to leave," he announced. He wasn't afraid of a few zombies, but night was falling and darkness made it more difficult to see the creatures coming. There was no reason to take unnecessary chances. Houses were safer to loot. "Let's see if Ax and Spence found us some good digs."

As they were loading the truck, an elderly couple emerged from a house across the street. They held hands as they crossed the highway, looking both ways as if expecting traffic. Levi chuckled at the useless gesture. They both wore reasonably clean clothing and appeared well fed, a fact which immediately attracted Levi's attention. The man spoke first.

"I'm Charlie Drake. This is my wife Emma. Are you boys with the military?" He waved his hand toward the army truck.

One of the men behind him snorted. Levi smiled.

"We're what you might call independent contractors. How have you two managed to survive this long surrounded by zombies?"

"Oh, Emma is quite a canner," Charlie said. He patted her hand. "We have quite a supply of canned goods."

"Charlie," Emma warned quietly. "We don't know these people."

Charlie turned to her. "Hush, Emma. These boys are here to help us." To Levi, he said, "If you like, we'll feed you boys. Then you can take us to one of the shelters the military have set up."

Levi nodded to Slant and grinned. Slant smiled, dismounted the Harley he straddled, and walked over to the couple. "We'll take real good care of you," he said.

Before the man could react, Slant drew the pistol from the holster he kept slung over his shoulder and shot the man in the head. The woman, knowing what was coming, made no attempt to flee. She closed her eyes, bending over slightly as she still clutched her dead husband's hand in her own. Slant placed the barrel of his pistol to her forehead. She smiled at him as he pulled the trigger.

Levi stared down at the dead couple. "Old people shouldn't clutter up the planet. It's a new world." He nodded toward the house the couple had come from. "Check it out. Take anything useful. Now, let's clean this town out."

They spent the remainder of the day looting and stripping houses of anything of value. Most of it was junk, but he allowed his men to take what they wanted. For them, the process was as much for relaxation as it was for survival. To keep them, he had to keep them happy. Killing made them happy. Personally, he didn't care if the home's owners lived or died, but he didn't share. He needed what they had. As he saw it, he was doing them a favor by ending their miserable existence. Survival was difficult at best, impossible without food, weapons, or water, and he needed them all.

Ax had located a two-story house that served their purpose. It possessed a balcony from which they could keep watch, and a heavy wooden front door to keep out unwanted visitors. The house came with a well-stocked bar. His men started on the liquor first thing. Levi knew it would be useless to try to stop them, so he joined them, drinking just enough to keep a good buzz going, but not enough to lower his guard. He trusted Ax, but none of the others. Given the opportunity, they would kill him as handily as anyone else.

Ax had found a hoard of canned goods and walked around the house eating from a can of cold beef stew with a long wooden spoon. Food had become his escape, his comfort. He dug into the can as if it might be his last meal.

"Make sure one of these asswipes stays sober enough to stand guard," Levi told him.

Ax nodded with a spoon in his mouth.

"And try to leave some food for the rest of us," Levi growled.

Ax smiled and swiped his mouth with the back of his hand. "There's plenty."

"There won't be if you keep chowing down. You look like a full tick."

Ax patted his rotund belly. He had gained twenty pounds since their prison escape. "I'm stockpiling for rainy days."

Levi pointed to Ax's empty holster. "Keep your damn pistol handy. It's a dangerous world."

Ax turned around and returned to the kitchen, either to fetch his pistol or get more food. Levi wasn't sure which. He located the master bedroom at the end of the second-floor hallway. The furniture was large and ornate, too dark and baroque for Levi's tastes, but the king-sized bed was clean and looked comfortable. He stripped off his clothes and lay down naked. He hoped that somewhere in the town they would find a woman or two. It had been too long between women and the need for satisfaction drove him. He would use her, and then pass her on to his crew, as he had dozens of previous women. Women were a commodity, as scarce as weapons and as precious as booze and drugs. They were tools to keep his men in order, treats to be doled out or withheld at his whim. He had no room in his life for female companionship. Life was hard, and only a hard man could survive.

He glanced down at his erect penis and laughed. "And I'm a hard man," he said.

6

June 9, 2016   Split Rock Canyon –

Jake allowed Jessica a full day to rest her shoulder and ankle. They used the time to get better acquainted. They talked, but neither one offered many details of their pasts. The conversation ranged from horror stories about surviving the apocalypse to favorite movies. She shared his love of old classics, but not his love of war movies or westerns. Eager to see if she could handle a weapon, he coaxed her outside for target practice after a lunch of steamed fresh vegetables and grilled cheese sandwiches.

First, he familiarized her with the operation of both the rifle and the pistol, letting her learn the feel of them in her hand. Then he showed her how to shoot. After a couple of hours of practice, he realized that she would never be another Annie Oakley, but she could hit the center target four out of ten times with the rifle, and three times out of ten times with the pistol; not bad for a beginner. Although she was a leftie, he thought her aim might improve as her right shoulder healed. Despite her initial reluctance to handle either rifle or pistol, once she saw what she was capable of, she began to enjoy it. However, he wondered if she would be able to pull the trigger on a human or an inhuman adversary. Target practice was a game, a sport. Killing was a survival tactic.

He gave her a tour of the ranch. She was fascinated by the animals, especially the goats, which came up to her and allowed her pet them and to feed them by hand, something they wouldn't tolerate from him. He didn't know if she was genuinely intrigued by his set up, or if she was trying to ingratiate herself into his good graces. His natural distrust of his fellow man, or woman, had hazarded several earlier relationships. *Jake's Law #7 – Trust yourself first; others seldom.*

She leaned back against the fence and pointed to the three-hundred-gallon water tank on a ledge above the house. "What's that for?"

He forced his eyes away from her breasts, which though small jutted provocatively beneath his oversize shirt. "Water storage. I pump water from the well into the holding tank. It keeps the water pressure high enough without using the pump every time. That saves electricity and wear and tear on the pump."

"What about sewage?"

"I have an eco-friendly sewage tank that efficiently digests the waste. The runoff is clean enough to use to water the plants."

She pointed to the stone dam and smiled. "Is that your swimming pool?"

He swiped the sweat from his forehead with the palm of his hand, and then wiped his hand across the front of his shirt. "When it's full of water. Maybe when the monsoons get here."

"Solar panels on the roof, a well, water tank – you thought this out pretty well, didn't you?"

He shrugged and pointed to a small adobe brick building near a tall sycamore tree. "My grandfather owned this ranch. He lived in the old house over there. He built it in 1943. He planted the tree when he started the house. I use it for a work shed. I was a county deputy, but I ran an online survivalist and hunter website on the side. I also repaired guns."

One of the goats stretched its neck through the fence and brushed the back of her leg for attention. She turned and began petting its head. "You saved my life."

He didn't know what to say without sounding smug, so he said nothing. When she finished petting the goat, she turned and moved closer to him. She leaned forward and kissed him on the lips. Before he could respond, she backed away. It was a coy kiss, but one filled with promise.

"Thank you," she said.

As she walked away ahead of him, his eyes strayed to her hips. Was she sashaying for his benefit, or was that the way she normally walked? He hadn't paid close enough attention before, but he was now.

He had spent the last two nights sleeping on the couch, offering her his bed in a gentlemanly manner. He had hoped that she might slip into bed with him or invite him into hers, but she hadn't, and he didn't want to force the issue. Her casual offer of sex had weighed heavily on his mind, but somehow, he couldn't bring himself to make that last bit of commitment. He was a loner, yet he knew that once committed, he could never send her away. The world had changed, and to a degree, so had he.

As he watched her, he felt his resolve weakening with each step. The idea of sex with her excited him. It had been a long time between lovers, and it had looked as if it might be even longer. He wondered how the agility of her yoga movements translated to sex. It would be interesting to find out.

To his delight, when he reached the house, he found her already naked and waiting in his bed. He felt a surge of relief that she had made the first move. He wasted no time removing his own clothes, flinging them across the room. She reached for him eagerly, and his body responded. His mouth found hers, and then moved down her body, pausing briefly at her breasts. Her soft moans and quiet whispers urging him on only intensified his lust. When she flipped him over onto his back and straddled him, he didn't complain. He soon learned that he had been right about her yoga.

Afterwards, she snuggled against his side. He was angry at himself for giving in so easily, but satisfied enough to know not to mention it to her. Somewhere along the way, he had made his decision. He wanted her to remain with him. He needed her to stay. If she had manipulated him, it wouldn't be the first time a woman had used sex to get her way, nor the first time a man had given in for the sake of sex. She got a safe haven. He got companionship. He considered it an even trade.

As if reading his thoughts, she said, "You can still send me away if you want. I'll understand. I won't complain. I needed this as much as you did. It's been too long."

"We'll see how things go. If you get fed up with me, let me know."

He felt her head nod against his side. Then she fell asleep. Thinking that she probably needed the sleep, he eased out of bed so as not to wake her. He strode naked to the balcony. The sun was hot on his skin, but years of outdoor living had tanned and toughened it to a thick hide. *Not thick enough that a red-headed slip of a girl couldn't crawl beneath it*, he mused. He glanced back at her sleeping on the bed and experienced a *déjà vu* of other girlfriends lying there. They hadn't meant much to him, just temporary companionship. Breaking ties with them had been easier than it should have been, and once gone, he had quickly forgotten them. Why then did this girl affect him so strongly?

Because she might be one of the last women on Earth? He thought it must be more than that.

A thought, dark and morbid, came to him. He tried to dismiss it, but it lingered like the aftereffects of a bad dream. *Maybe I just want someone to bury my body and grieve over me when I die.*

* * * *

June 10, 2016   Split Rock Canyon –

Jessica got the chance to prove her value to him the next morning. A single zombie, its clothing torn and tattered, and with strips of dead flesh hanging from its arms, waited for them outside the wall. He could have shot it easily from the balcony, but he needed to find out if Jessica was capable of facing a zombie and dispatching it. The creature was already dying, barely shambling along. All skin and bones, the creature's backbone was almost visible through its stomach. It posed no serious threat unless she strayed too close. It was the perfect opportunity to test her mettle.

"You kill it," he said, as she stood beside him staring down at it.

She gazed at him in horror. "Me? I've never shot a zombie."

"It's time to learn. Use the rifle."

She looked at the creature and shook her head. "It's too far away."

"We'll get closer."

She shook her head more emphatically. "No."

"If you can't shoot a zombie, you're no good to me." He kept the tone of his voice even, but she understood the veiled threat – shoot it or leave.

She licked her lips and glanced nervously between the zombie and Jake. "What if I miss?"

"I'll be there."

She nodded, but didn't look as certain as she pretended. "Okay."

He handed her the Browning and picked up the Versa Max 12-gauge. She walked down the path slowly, glancing at him questioningly when he opened the gate and motioned her through. The zombie tottered toward them, its mouth moving as if trying to speak. The only sound that came from its throat was a muted mewling.

"Notice how thin and emaciated it is and how slowly it moves. I call them Shamblers. It will die soon unless it feeds. They're no real threat unless they outnumber you or catch you by surprise. The ones that chased you are more dangerous. They're Runners. You can't take chances with them. Others fit somewhere between Shamblers and Runners. The safe bet is to shoot all of them if they stray too close."

She nodded and raised the rifle to her left shoulder. At first, the barrel wavered in the air, but after a few moments, she took a deep breath and held it steady. He waited for the shot as the creature drew nearer. Nothing happened. Thinking she might have frozen, when the zombie was less than ten yards away, he raised his shotgun. Then she fired. Her first shot only grazed its shoulder, but she didn't panic. She quickly ejected the shell, slid a fresh cartridge into the chamber, and fired again. This time, she hit it in the head. A large hole appeared just above its right eye, exiting through an orange-sized crater in the back of its skull. It took two more faltering steps before tripping over its own feet and falling forward onto the dirt. She flinched in surprise but didn't turn and run.

He let out a sigh of relief. She had passed his first test. He didn't think he could have sent her packing even if she hadn't, but he didn't want her to know that. "Nice shot, but don't wait so long next time," he said, trying not to smile. "If you can't get a head shot, aim for the legs and cripple them. They're still dangerous, but only if you let them get too close."

"I didn't mean to frighten you. I wanted to make sure I hit it."

"A little more practice will take care of that."

"So, I can stay?" she asked, tilting her head and squinting at him.

This time he smiled. "For now."

She gave him a quick peck on the cheek and handed him the rifle. As she walked back through the gate, she flung over her shoulder, "Good. You can dispose of him."

Sassy. He liked that in a woman.

As he was getting ready to cart away the corpse, he noticed the sound of a dirt bike growing louder. He motioned for Jessica to hide. He loaded a round into the chamber of the rifle and waited beside the gate. It was another few minutes before the bike came into view. He relaxed when he saw the large frame of Alton Reed atop the little Kawasaki dirt bike, looking like a trained bear riding a toy clown scooter. He pulled up in a cloud of dust, removed his helmet, and said, "We've got trouble, Deputy."

Jake shook his head. "I told you I'm no deputy. What trouble? And how did you find me?"

Reed glanced at the ground. "I followed your tire tracks." Before Jake could comment, Reed continued, "A gang of eight or ten men came into Oracle last night in a five-ton truck and several motorcycles. They're going door to door, looting and shooting anything that moves. They're killing zombies, which I don't mind, but they're also killing people. I watched them murder an elderly couple just for the hell of it. We've got to stop them."

Jake frowned. Had the Ranger's badge he wore given Reed the idea that he made a habit of helping people? His days as a cop were long over. He didn't owe anyone anything. "Why should I interfere?"

"It's our duty as human beings to help."

Jessica appeared from behind the wall, startling Reed. He stared at her, as she said, "He's right. You can't just let them murder people."

"Of course I can. I have no intention of tackling ten armed men to save people I don't know." He looked at Reed. "My *duty* to society is finished. They're your neighbors. You save therm."

"It seems to me that anyone still alive is our neighbor," Reed countered indignantly. He glanced at Jessica, smiled, and asked, "Who are you?"

Jake made the introductions. "Jessica Hubley, meet Alton Reed, my new friend who's trying to get us killed. Jessica might hang around for a while."

"Lucky you. All I run across is murderous gangs. It looks like they're settling in to stay. It won't be safe to move around with them there."

"We have to do something," Jessica pleaded.

"You're doing nothing. You can barely shoot and your shoulder is still healing." He scowled at Reed, damning him with his eyes for involving him in things he had rather stay out of. Now, to refuse would make him look like a coward in Jessica's eyes. He was surprised that he cared what she thought of him, but he did.

And perhaps the small bit of cop remaining in him put in its two cents worth. "We can't just take on a dozen armed men," he protested. "We'll get slaughtered."

Reed rummaged in the dirt bike's saddlebags and produced a six-pack of beer. "I brought beer. Maybe it will help us come up with a plan. Got any chips?"

Jake dragged the zombie corpse away from the gate. He could deal with it later. *First things first.* It wasn't a Jake's Law, but he might need to incorporate it into the litany. If he did, it should rightfully become *Jake's Law #1*, but he didn't feel like re-doing the entire list. He could call it *#13*.

Jessica played the perfect hostess, placing Reed's warm beer in the refrigerator and setting three of Jake's ice-cold Budweiser long necks on the table, along with a bag of pretzels. She sipped her beer but didn't touch the pretzels. Reed could barely keep his eyes off her as he spoke. Jake couldn't blame him. She presented a lovely picture.

"They're holed up in a house near the Oracle Park Inn, mostly getting drunk and doing drugs. At least one of them sits on the balcony on guard at all times, usually guzzling whiskey. They don't look like militia or anything, mostly bikers or ex-cons, but they're well armed with rifles, shotguns, and pistols."

Jake nodded. He knew the type. "They released a lot of prisoners up in Florence when things got bad. They should have executed the lot of them." He slammed his beer down on the table. "We'll need a diversion." He looked at Reed. "Do they all go to the same houses when they're looting or do they split up?"

"Split up, usually two or three per house. They drag what they want outside, and the truck comes and picks it up."

Jake looked at Reed with new found appreciation. "How long did you watch them?"

"All night. I left before dawn. I found the dirt bike and pushed it halfway to San Manuel before getting up enough courage to hotwire it."

Reed flushed when Jessica reached out and patted his hand.

"Hotwired?" Jake asked. "How does a science teacher learn how to hotwire motorcycles and follow tire tracks?"

"Just something I picked up from books."

"Some books." He looked at Reed with renewed respect. "We'll have to take them on two or three at a time. If they're busy shooting up the place, a few more shots shouldn't alarm them, but one mistake, and we're both dead."

"I'm going too," Jessica said.

"No way," Jake said, shaking his head vehemently side to side.

She narrowed her eyes and glared at him. "You'll need someone to drive the jeep if you have to get away in a hurry," she insisted.

Before Jake could protest, Reed sided with her. "She's right. If we park too far away, we might not make it back if more of them show up." He patted his rotund belly. "I'm not exactly built for speed. We can devise a signal if we need her to come pull our chestnuts out of the fire."

Jake shook his head. Two against one. That meant entrusting his life to two people he wasn't completely sure of. He tried to think of another plan that didn't involve her, but couldn't. Reluctantly, he agreed. "Okay," he said to Jessica. She flashed him a smile. "But if anything happens, you come straight back here. We'll make our way back however we can."

She nodded.

"We wait until tonight," he said. "Maybe we'll get lucky and they'll be all liquored up."

He knew it was too much to hope for. Even drunks stayed somewhat sober around zombies, or they quickly wound up as food. At least they wouldn't expect armed resistance. Maybe. Reed produced a short length of metal pipe. Its purpose eluded Jake until he saw the fuse dangling from one end. Now, the discarded pipe he had seen in Reed's RV made sense.

"A pipe bomb?" he questioned.

Reed smiled and nodded. "I took the chemicals I needed for making gunpowder with me when they closed the school. I added a few chemicals to increase the explosive potential. I made two more. I thought it might level the playing field."

Jake knew a gun enthusiast who had blown himself up while making his own shotgun shells with homemade gunpowder. Black powder and gunpowder could be unpredictable and dangerous, especially for an amateur. He looked at the pipe bomb, a six-inch length of two-inch diameter steel pipe, capped at both ends. The fuse protruded from a hole drilled into one end cap.

"Have you tested it?"

Reed frowned. "No, but I followed the recipe closely. I studied chemistry, remember?"

"I don't doubt your ability, but I would like to see how much damage it produces."

Reed studied the pipe bomb in his hand. "Well, I suppose we could detonate it somewhere safe just to be sure."

"I don't want to frighten my livestock." Jake thought for a moment. "I know a place we can go."

They drove the ATV two miles down the valley to a canyon. When the terrain became too rough for the ATV, they continued on foot. Deep in the mountains, a series of small box canyons sprouted from Kielberg Canyon like tree branches. By the time they reached the canyon he sought, Jake was sweating profusely in the heat, and he considered himself to be in good shape, though he hadn't exercised much since E-Day. Reed was so exhausted he could barely lift his feet. He took puffs from his inhaler every few hundred yards, but he still wheezed like an out of tune pipe organ. Of the three, only Jessica seemed to handle the brisk hike with impunity. *Maybe there's something to this yoga business after all*, he mused.

At some point in the mountain's history, someone had tried mining the canyon for gold. They had found nothing of value, but the disintegrating mining equipment still rested where they had abandoned it half a century earlier. Soaptree yuccas, agaves, and horned toads were the only living things presently residing there. Jake chose a rusted steel ore carrier lying on its side beside a short set of rails leading to a collapsed tunnel. He buried the pipe bomb beneath the carrier, leaving only the fuse exposed.

"How long does the fuse burn?"

Reed looked sheepish. "I didn't test it, but I used black powder in a cloth wrapper coated with nitrocellulose for waterproofing. The book says it burns at thirty centimeters per sixty seconds. That's two seconds per centimeter or about five seconds per inch."

"About?" Jake replied. "Let's be sure." He snipped a small piece of fuse and held it up to a cigarette lighter. The one-inch piece of fuse burned for just over five seconds. "That's forty seconds for an eight-inch fuse, thirty-five for this one. Let's play it safe and call it half a minute."

He scanned the terrain. An outcropping approximately a hundred feet away would provide shelter from the blast. He had never been a fast runner, but he thought he could cover the distance in fifteen seconds, leaving fifteen seconds to grab dirt and cover his head. *Unless the damned thing blows up in my face.* "You two cover behind those rocks. I'll light the fuse and join you."

Jessica looked at him aghast. "Let me do it. I can run faster than you."

He didn't doubt it, but he wasn't about to let her make the attempt. "Maybe on a good day, but you're injured. I'll do it."

To prevent further arguing, he shoved her toward the outcropping. She left, but not before searing him with an angry glare. Reed followed her. He waited until they both disappeared behind the rocks, and then lit the fuse. He ran as fast as he could, praying that he didn't stumble. By the time he reached the outcropping, his heart was pounding. He hit the dirt and covered his head with his hands. Thirty seconds passed and still no explosion. He glanced at Reed questioningly just as the pipe bomb exploded. The noise was deafening. The ground shuddered beneath him. He covered his head again to protect it from flying gravel that settled over them in a cloud of dust.

The ore carrier now lay upside down fifteen feet away from the three-foot-deep hole marking its former position. A yucca plant five feet from the carrier lay in broken pieces scattered on the ground, its outer leaves still smoldering from the heat of the blast. The rusted steel carrier was split along one side, with splinters of steel embedded in the ground and in the nearby plants. Smoke and dust still filled the small canyon.

"It worked," Reed yelled as he danced a jig, his rotund belly bouncing like tapioca pudding.

"Damned if it didn't," Jake admitted, removing his baseball cap to scratch his head. "You say you have two more?"

Reed stopped dancing and adjusted his glasses. "I have enough chemicals to make more."

"Two should be enough with what I have in mind."

"Just what is your plan?" Jessica asked.

He had been considering that. "We'll gather a zombie army," he said, smiling.

7

June 10, 2016   Oracle, AZ –

The night was dark with only a sliver of moon. Jake and Reed clung to the shadows as they approached the house. Jessica had parked a quarter of a mile away. Jake had left her the shotgun with orders for her to leave if she ran into trouble. He hoped she heeded his advice. They had watched seven of the marauders leave their lair in two groups with the truck accompanying one group, leaving two or three men at the house. Even though they rode motorcycles, they weren't a biker gang; at least they wore no colors declaring their allegiance. They were just a group of men and a couple of boys in various dress riding motorcycles, probably stolen or salvaged.

He and Reed surreptitiously followed three men on bikes to a small house on the outskirts of town. A man with blond hair kicked in the front door. Once inside, the three ransacked the house in an orgy of wanton destruction, selecting a few items and carrying them to the yard, destroying everything else. The items they chose for their pile of loot were baffling – a lamp with no shade, several two-liter bottles of cola, an embroidered pillow from the Grand Canyon, and a television. There seemed to be no rhyme or reason to their plundering. Their frequent target practice on windows and other breakable crockery dismissed any fears Jake had of discovery. No one would notice their shots amid the random firing of the looters.

If Reed was squeamish about murdering someone, he didn't show it. His disgust with the trio was visible on his grim face. He may have known some of the victims. Jake had no close friends, but he imagined revenge was on Reed's mind. While the men were inside the house, he and Reed took up positions on each side of the small yard with a commanding view of the front door. He signaled for Reed to wait until all three were outside before opening fire. They had to kill them quickly. A long, drawn out gun battle would work in the gang's favor.

Finally, all three men emerged at the same time, passing around a bottle of booze and admiring their pile of loot. The blond kicked the lamp from atop a box of canned goods and crushed it beneath the heel of his boot.

"What the hell did you get this for?" he growled.

"A reading lamp," a boy that couldn't have been over sixteen replied. He puffed out his chest in a failed attempt to appear threatening.

The fair-haired one laughed and poked a finger in the kid's chest, throwing him off balance. "You can't read. And you don't need a reading lamp to jerk off to your tit magazines."

Jake shot the kid in the head before he could respond. Drunk or not, the other two rallied quickly, cowering behind their pile of stolen loot, shifting positions to search for their attacker. If he had been alone, they would have probably killed him, but Reed was on the other side of the yard. Jake took out the group's blond leader with two quick shots. The third man, a pot-bellied young Mexican wearing a pair of dark blue suit pants, a dirty white tee shirt, and a vest that matched the pants, made a run for the desert, dodging and weaving to avoid being shot. Jake put a bullet into his back when he ran between two saguaro cacti at the edge of the yard. He fell headfirst into the dirt and skidded to a halt.

"Help me drag these two into the brush," he yelled to Reed.

Reed stared down at the kid's corpse for a moment. His face was pale and he looked as if he were about to throw up.

"Get over it," Jake growled.

Reed nodded and grabbed one of the kid's arms. They hid the bodies out of sight of the road. The Mexican was already hidden by a row of cacti. Jake disabled the three bikes by removing the spark plugs and puncturing the gas tanks with his knife. Then they waited for the truck. A short while later, its squeaking springs warned them of its approach. It roared up the long driveway, followed by a pair of motorcycles. Jake planted the bomb in the pile of stolen goods, lit a cigarette, and jammed the fuse into the cigarette halfway to the filter.

"That should give us two or three minutes," he said to Reed. He pointed to the dead Mexican in the suit pants and vest. "I've got a use for this one. Help me."

Dragging the Mexican's body behind them, they retreated a safe distance to a low rise where they could observe the action. The truck pulled up in a cloud of dust. A tall thin man got out on the passenger side. He wore a straw Stetson over his long, stringy, reddish-brown hair and a leather vest over a white t-shirt. The driver remained in the vehicle. The cowboy tugged on his goatee, as he eyed the pathetic pile of stolen loot, and then shook his head.

"Where the hell are Whitey, Slant, and the kid?" he yelled at his companions on the two bikes, as they pulled up and stopped beside the truck.

One of the bikers shrugged. "I dunno, Levi."

The cowboy, Levi, stuck his head in the door of the house and yelled, "Hey! You assholes get out here. We're leaving."

After a few moments, he stepped inside the door, which saved his life. The pipe bomb exploded, lighting up the night sky and shattering the front windows of the house and the truck. The two bikers died instantly, as a fury of metal shrapnel and debris pelted their bodies. Flaming wreckage landed on the truck, setting it on fire. The driver screamed as he fell out of the truck's door, beating frantically at his flaming clothing. He rolled on the ground, but ignited a pool of gasoline draining from the bikes Jake had punctured. He exploded in a ball of fire. His screams lasted only a few seconds.

The cowboy peered around the edge of the door to see what the commotion was. He quickly surmised what had happened and remained just inside the doorway. Jake tried to center him in his scope, but the flames and smoke made it difficult to see. He took a chance and fired anyway. The bullet struck the doorframe, splintering the wood beside the cowboy's head. He dived for the ground, rolled, and came up running for the corner of the house. For a brief moment, as he glanced back, the flaming wreckage illuminated his face. Jake saw no fear, only a visage of pure hatred. He fired again, shattering one of the windows behind the cowboy's head.

"Damn! I missed him. Let's go. The others will come soon."

The explosion had been the signal for Jessica to return to pick them up. They dragged the dead man's body behind them to the road. Reed was huffing and puffing by the time the jeep appeared out of the darkness. He fell into the back seat and produced an inhaler from his pocket, taking a deep puff and wheezing. Jake tossed the corpse in beside Reed and climbed in the passenger seat.

"We managed to kill six of them. One survived, but he's on foot. The others in the house must know something's wrong by now." He smiled at Jessica. "Are our troops ready?"

She nodded. "They should be here any minute."

Before setting up their ambush, they had driven slowly around San Manuel dragging a pig he had slaughtered behind the jeep. He hated killing one of his animals for any purpose other than food, but the need was great. The smell of fresh blood coaxed the starving zombies from their neighborhoods. The trail of blood led straight into Oracle. Jake wondered what the thugs in the house would do when confronted by a small army of zombies, especially after hearing an explosion and seeing a large bonfire lighting up the horizon.

Right on time, the forefront of the zombie horde appeared out of the darkness, Runners leading the pack with dozens of Shamblers close on their heels. Jake flashed the headlights of the jeep to encourage them. The guard on the balcony saw the flashing lights, and then caught sight of the zombies approaching. He raced away to warn the others. As soon as he disappeared, Jessica gunned the jeep and headed straight for the house. When they were directly in front of it, Jake lit the fuse of the remaining bomb and hurled it at the front door. As they sped away, the explosion blew the door off its hinges and collapsed part of the front wall, crushing two of the three bikes parked against it. Now, the zombies would have no trouble gaining entrance through the gaping hole. To assure he had their attention, he had Jessica back up the jeep. He rolled the dead man's corpse out of the jeep. It landed in the rubble of the front door. Drawn by the sound of the explosion and by the smell of death, the zombies converged on the house. *Jake's Law # 8 – Use the tools you've got.*

"It's time to get out of here," he said to his companions.

They drove away slowly, enticing the zombies closer to the house. He smiled when the creatures stormed through the shattered front door. Shots came from inside the house. The gunfire lasted only a couple of minutes, followed by a loud piercing scream.

"They should have remembered *Jake's Law #9 – Always have an exit strategy.*"

One man still lived, the cowboy called Levi, but he was on foot, facing zombies revitalized by a meal of fresh meat. Like vultures drawn by the stench of death, they would quickly find the other dead men and feast on them as well. Unless he was a complete fool, the cowboy would flee the area. Jake doubted he was a fool, but also doubted they had heard the last of the cowboy.

"My bombs worked," Reed said with a broad smile.

"God help us if we have to murder everyone we meet," Jessica said as she stared at the carnage through the rear view mirror.

"I didn't murder two people I met," Jake reminded her. "Don't make me regret it."

Jessica didn't reply. Instead, she concentrated on driving.

8

June 10, 2016 Oracle, AZ –
Levi waited until he was certain the unknown shooters were gone before venturing near the house. The inferno from the burning truck and pile of looted goods had died down, but a cloud of acrid smoke from burning rubber tires and insulation hung in the air, along with the smell of scorched human flesh. All five bikes were trashed, either incinerated or twisted beyond repair by the explosion. Whoever ambushed them had been thorough. He stared at the burned bodies of his three companions and cursed. They never knew what hit them. He found Whitey and the kid's body in the brush nearby. He couldn't find Slant.

"Someone's going to pay for this," he vowed, as he removed his Stetson and wiped his brow with the back of his hand. He stared toward the crash house where the rest of his companions waited, wondering why they hadn't come to investigate. "Stupid-ass dopers," he cursed. "Can't they hear an explosion?"

He walked back through the desert to avoid the road. Before he reached the house, another explosion ripped through the night. He instantly knew it was the crash house.

"Son of a bitch," he snarled. Anger welled up in him at his unknown attackers.

Peeking through the brush alongside the road, he saw a horde of zombies pouring through the shattered front door of the house. Then he noticed the jeep parked down the road, the people inside watching the zombie attack. If he had his rifle, he could have killed them all, but he had only his pistol, and shooting would only have drawn the zombies to him. Something familiar glinting on one of the men's chest caught his attention. He watched the jeep leave, swearing he would find them and kill them. He didn't give a shit about the others, even Ax. They were trash, disposable, people he had picked up around the city, but the people in the jeep had inconvenienced him, had tried to kill him, and that was unforgivable.

Three stints in prison had taught him you had to defend yourself against all comers, redneck, white, Black, or Latino. If anyone thought you were weak, you'd wind up as their bitch or dead. After slashing one skinhead redneck ear to ear with a shiv, they had learned to leave him alone. Even the ADC guards didn't fuck with him, and that was just the way he liked it. He had been looking at another five years when the shit hit the fan, and the world rolled over in its stinking grave. As the cons died and came back to life around him, the guards finally opened the cells and let the prisoners fend for themselves inside the walls. It had been touch and go for awhile, but he had been one of the lucky ones, him and Ax. Now Ax's luck had run out.

His time in the slammer had taught him one more thing – how to smell a cop. The trap smelled like a police raid. The badge on one of the men's chest just sealed the deal. A cop. He spit the word out like it was acid on his tongue. He hated cops more than he hated zombies.

He stayed hidden and watched the house until morning. Finally, their grisly meal finished, the zombies left the house. He didn't much want to see what was left of Spence, Tall Dave, and Ax, but he needed his M16 and more ammo. The front door and part of the wall was blown inward by the explosion. Tall Dave had died instantly. That saved him from knowing he was being eaten. Most of his face and upper torso was stripped of flesh. Blood soaked his red beard. Only his long legs still buried in the rubble had been spared. Curiously, Slant's body was lying outside the front door. He had been with Whitey and the kid. What was he doing here? Had he run at the first sign of trouble? When Levi noticed the bullet holes in what was left of Slant's back, he smiled. The people in the jeep had shot Slant and dragged him to the house to use as bait for the zombies. Clearly the cop no longer took his official law enforcement duties seriously – no arrest, no trial, just an execution.

He found Ax in the kitchen, his usual habitat. He had never been the brightest bulb in the lamp. The fool former accountant had tried to barricade himself inside the small kitchen pantry, barely large enough to accommodate his rotund body. His remains lay in a bloody heap on the floor amid cans of food and opened bags of rice and meal. The compulsive eater had been eaten. He had escaped prison with Ax and had hung around with him for over a year. Seeing his friend's corpse should have elicited some emotion other than relief that it was someone else lying there and not him. It had been a hard year. Emotions were for the weak.

It took him a while to find Spence's body. The former bar bouncer had managed to take a few zombies with him. They lay in a small pile at the bottom of the staircase and along the stairs he had chosen to defend. He found what was left of Spence in a hall bathroom, lying in a pool of blood. He had saved his last bullet for himself. The neat hole in his head spoke to his desire of not being eaten alive. He had been eaten nonetheless. Zombies weren't finicky about their food. Fresh dead meat was as good as live meat.

Levi found his M16 untouched in the master bedroom. He grabbed several boxes of ammo, some canned goods, and a couple of bottles of water, and threw it all into a backpack. It wasn't safe around Oracle, but he would be back. Soon. He had unfinished business with the cop.

With a little work, he managed to repair one of the Harleys. He smiled when the bike cranked on the first try. As he rode off down American Boulevard, headed back to Tucson, he glanced east. A large cloud of dust clung to the horizon like a low-lying cloudbank. His new enemy was somewhere in that direction, in the mountains. He would find them and pay them back. But first, he had to round up a few more allies from Tucson. It wouldn't be difficult. There were hundreds of people who thought like him; people who had little in life and saw the end of the world as an opportunity to take what they wanted and maybe spread a little payback along the way. Right now what he wanted was to place some distance between him and the zombies. Then, he would be back with a vengeance.

9

June 11, 2016   Split Rock Canyon –

Morning brought its own new set of problems for Jake. Now, someone knew they were in the area. He didn't want to have to worry about a new threat. One man shouldn't present a problem, but the cowboy struck him as determined and vindictive. They had made a dangerous enemy. Against his better judgment, he asked Reed to park his RV at the farm. He was disappointed that Reed hadn't fired a single shot during the fight, but he had demonstrated his resourcefulness and his value as a chemist by creating the bombs. In spite of his lack of stamina and breathing problems, Jake was betting that Reed would prove his worth later on as well. If he kept adding people, the ranch was soon going to resemble a commune. All he needed was a few hippies and a guitar.

Jessica had surprised him. During the fight, she had remained cool and collected. In fact, she had looked on almost eagerly as the zombies attacked the thugs in the two-story house. She acted as if she were on speed or high on adrenalin, racing around the house recounting the night's adventure like it had been a scavenger hunt. After Reed left to collect his RV, she had directed her storehouse of energy toward him. He thought it odd how danger made some people horny, but he didn't complain. It was difficult to argue with great sex.

His past experiences with women had jaded him. He couldn't place all the blame on them. He was no catch, but his opinion of women had suffered greatly over the past few years to the point that women had become more trouble than they were worth. Jessica was wearing down his resistance. She was everything he had hoped the next woman in his life would be. Had the planets swung around into perfect alignment? Had God decided he had suffered enough and sent an angel? Maybe he had just learned to trust others a little more.

He heard the banging and scraping of the RV long before he saw it coming up the trail with a billowing cloud of dust following it. He wondered about the excessive dust. Then he smiled as he noticed the tree limb dragging behind the RV. Reed was covering his tracks. *Smart man.* The RV gave one final shudder as it drove through the open gate. He was surprised it had survived the trip over the barely passable road. He directed Reed to park near the cliff below the house. Reed popped out of the RV wearing a broad smile.

"Made it," he said.

Jake pointed to the tree branch. "Nice job covering your tracks."

"I watched a lot of western movies growing up."

"We'll get you connected to the electric grid and water shortly."

Jessica leaned over the balcony and waved down at them.

"You found a good woman there," Reed said. "I liked the way she jumped into the fracas last night." He glanced away, an uneasy expression on his face and said more quietly, "You didn't say anything about my not firing my gun last night."

Jake sighed. He could see that Reed was condemning himself. There was no need for him to exacerbate his guilt. "It's hard to murder a man, even animals like them. It wasn't easy in Afghanistan, and they were killers."

"I wasn't scared, at least not too badly. I just …" he paused. "I won't freeze again."

"If I thought you would, you wouldn't be here."

That seemed to ease Reed's discomfort. "Thanks. I can tell you feel uncomfortable around people."

"It's just that I just lived alone a long time. All this …." He brought his hands together to indicate confinement. "It's getting to me. I'm a loner. Trust comes hard for me."

"Not me. I need people around. I've been going crazy the past few months. I'm surprised I haven't been talking to zombies, trying to teach them high school physics. Some of them probably would learn as much as some of my former students."

Jake shrugged. "I'll get over it. I think we need each other right now."

"We could find more survivors," Reed suggested. "Band together. There are thousands of them out there."

"Let's see how we three gel before adding to our entourage," he cautioned.

Jessica raced down the path and skipped down the steps. She wore a pair of his blue jeans pinned at the waist and one of his oversized shirts, looking like the youngest child wearing hand-me-downs. They would have to go clothing shopping for her soon.

"I'm glad you're back," she gushed at Reed.

Reed smiled so broadly that Jake thought it might split the corners of his mouth. "Glad to be back."

She glanced at Jack. "We make a good team. I have eggs and bacon cooking, and coffee brewing."

Reed rubbed his belly, said, "I'm ready," and headed toward the house.

Jake smiled as Jessica hooked her arm through his. It was going to take some time to get used to the added company, but he found that he enjoyed it.

After breakfast, while they finished their coffee, Reed tried to explain the Staggers to them. Jake had watched the news reports and listened to the experts, but most of their explanations were way over his head. Reed promised to keep it simple.

"Tens of thousands of years ago, a tiny protozoan, a single cell organism transported by mosquitoes and flies, helped wipe out the Ice Age mammoth herds and probably killed a great deal of the human population of North America and the northern latitudes. The protozoan died out as the weather changed, frozen in the northern permafrost. Now, climate change has thawed large areas of permafrost. Tusk hunters in Siberia inadvertently reintroduced the parasite to modern man, who because of all the antibiotics we consume and the practically germ-free environment in which we live is highly susceptible to it.

"When the first cases of what later became known as the Staggers appeared in Hong Kong in February of 2014, it was considered just another particularly virulent form of Avian Flu. It spread at an alarming rate, reaching dozens of cities within weeks. The first symptoms struck the victims within twenty-four hours. Then, the initial irritating cough and mild temperature the patient experienced rapidly escalated into a hacking, lung-wrenching cough and severe fever of the brain. Within days, a loss of motor function culminated in a deep coma. A few days later, all life functions ceased, but the corpse wasn't dead, at least not to an observer. Whatever humanity had once existed within the former flesh husk disappeared, replaced by a mindless, savage creature craving flesh and blood.

"A hundred centuries ago, man kept to closely defined areas, limiting the disease's range. With today's rapid global transportation, it spread quickly. In spite of the World Health Organization's best efforts, no cure was discovered, no drugs proved effective. Spread both by human contact and airborne insect vectors, within a year, the populations of entire cities were decimated. Governments toppled, and petty border bickering flamed into full scale wars."

"But how does it work," Jessica asked.

"It acts like malaria on the body. In fact, the first symptoms are malaria-like – high fever, chills, the sweats. Unfortunately, nothing in our modern arsenal of medicines proved effective against it. It spread initially through insect hosts, then by direct contact."

Jake nodded. "I know all that. That's why the barricades didn't work. That's why so many people fled west thinking there were no mosquitoes in the desert." He laughed. "They forgot about flies and fleas and dust storms."

Reed, looking slightly annoyed by the interruption, continued, "After a few days of high fever, the body slowly succumbs as the adult parasite destroys the brain and shuts down, like during a coma. Thirty-six to forty-eight hours later, the infected awaken, not quite human, driven to an insane rage and hungry for flesh and blood, human or otherwise. At first, they're slow and disoriented, thus the name Staggers, after the similar disease affecting a horse's mind. After that, they become quick, nimble, and deadly. Their scratches and bites spread the disease. Some of us have a natural immunity, probably a gene inherited from our ancestors who survived the disease. Most don't. Eventually, the resurrected die if they don't eat, but that takes months, as their bodies slowly consume its own muscle mass."

"Didn't anything show promise as a cure?"

Reed took a sip from his coffee cup before answering Jessica's question. "A few drugs did, but they worked too slowly. Once the parasite begins destroying brain cells, the body is doomed. Even if they don't become zombies, they die eventually of the symptoms. No one ever recovered from the Staggers."

"No one?" Jessica asked.

He set his empty cup on the table and pronounced, "No one."

"What about the worms?"

"The worms are the adult parasite. They feed on the brain and produce sporazoa capsules that spread by contact or through insect hosts."

"They're disgusting," Jessica said.

Jake agreed with her. Something about the wrigglers gave him the shivers. "Why didn't the winter weather kill the parasite?"

"It may have killed some, but it's warm inside the human host body. The cold killed tens of thousands of people in the cities, as gas and electricity shut off, but the disease spread south to warmer climates, even to Central and South America. There's no place on Earth that the disease can't reach. Flying insect vectors live everywhere."

Silence descended over the table as all they digested Reed's information. The rattle of his cup on the saucer, as Jake finished his coffee, was unnaturally loud. To break the nervous silence, he said, "But we're immune, right?"

Reed nodded. "I hope so. I'm fairly certain I've been exposed, and I haven't succumbed. I expect you two have been exposed as well. Either we're immune, or something about our body chemistry prevents or slows down the rate of infection."

Jessica leaned forward with a look of horror on her face. "Slows down? You mean we might catch it?"

Jake silently damned Reed for alarming her. Reed waved his hand in the air in dismissal. "Oh, it's a remote possibility. Odds are very good that we're immune."

This seemed to satisfy her, but Jake wasn't as certain. However, now was not the time to air his doubts. "How about some target practice?" he suggested to get Jessica's mind off the disease.

Jessica rolled her eyes in mock surprise. "Oh, goody."

* * * *

Though her right shoulder still bothered her, Jessica's accuracy improved with each shot. She displayed a natural talent for shooting and a good eye. She now seemed more relaxed around firearms, as if she was finally coming to grips with their necessity. Reed was proficient, but somewhat lazy, shooting before taking careful aim. It was important that each shot counted, something

Jake couldn't seem to drill into him. His lack of a sense of urgency concerned Jake.

"I might not hit the target the first time, but I do hit it," Reed protested when Jake brought up his accuracy.

"If the target is shooting back, like last night – a brief flicker of shame crossed Reed's face –you might not get a second chance. Hitting a zombie in the shoulder won't work. You have to hit the head or place several rounds into their chest to be effective."

"You were a deputy. You're used to shooting people."

Jake tensed at the remark; then relaxed. "In all my years as a deputy, I didn't shoot a single person."

Realizing he had spoken out of turn, Reed made light of his remark. "Maybe we should find some machineguns. Then, being accurate won't matter as much."

Jake shook his head. "Machineguns are harder to aim and fire too many bullets too rapidly. It wastes ammo. Accuracy is the key. It's better to carry a pocketful of ammo than a lug around an ammo case."

Reed replied with sarcasm, "Okay, Sarge. Set up another target. Let's see. Take a breath. Hold it. Release gently as I slowly squeeze the trigger. Right?"

Jake smiled. "Right. Then reload quickly. Always keep your weapon loaded until you're safely at home."

"Why are you driving us so hard?" Jessica asked.

He stared at her. What could he say? That he was certain Levi would return with more friends? That he was afraid that zombies would locate them? That he didn't trust the military? That there were people in the world who would kill them for what they had?

"Guns are tools. You need skill just like an artist or a mechanic. Shooting and hitting the target has to become second nature. Someday, it will save your life."

She stared at him for a moment before nodding. "If you say so. I trust you."

Jake swallowed. He didn't want people to trust him. He didn't have all the answers. He knew how to survive, maybe how to build, but he didn't know people. He was pretty sure about Jessica and Reed, but what about any others they might meet? Would they be potential friends and allies, or like Levi, taking what they wanted at the point of a gun? The wrong decision could kill them all.

He picked up a handful of paper targets and marched off to the posts he had driven into the ground to create a makeshift shooting range. As he tacked them to the posts, his gaze climbed the side of the cliff, taking in the rock formations and the desert plants clinging tenaciously to precarious ledges. *That's us,* he thought. *We're hanging on by our fingertips. It wouldn't take much to send us tumbling down into oblivion.* Surviving was hard enough. Now he was certain they had made an enemy.

As he scanned the sky, he noticed a jet contrail to the northeast, then another. *Military.* Most people would try to attract the jet's attention. He wanted to remain invisible, or as close to it as possible. The military had their agenda. He had his. He wasn't sure they were the same. *If the rumors were true.*

They spent another hour at target practice. Longer would be better, but he had a limited supply of ammunition. He had a Lyman cartridge prepper, a Dillon reloading machine, and lead bullet casters, but his powder supply was limited, and making bullets took time. It was a precision process unless you wanted to blow your hand off. For now, at least, it was easier to salvage ammunition from local gun shops or Sportsman Warehouse. Later, it might become necessary.

As they walked back to the house, Jessica summoned up the courage to discuss the previous night's escapades.

"It was horrible," she said.

"It was necessary," he replied. "They were murderers. They would have killed us if they had the chance."

"I know, I know, but … it was so horrible. The zombies …"

"We were outnumbered and outgunned. It's the best idea I could come up with. I suppose we could have thrown bombs through the windows while they slept, but it didn't seem sporting."

Jessica whirled at him. Her eyes had narrowed and her jaw twitched. "Sporting? You think killing men is sporting?"

He knew he had made a poor choice of words, but he didn't back down. "Look. I've shot Taliban terrorists I had more sympathy for than that lot. They would have killed Alton and me for sure. You, they would have kept around for a while for their own private sport. Then they would have killed you when they were through. You're wasting your sympathy on the wrong people. If you want to feel sorry for someone, feel sorry for the people they murdered."

"What we did was murder," she insisted.

Jake stopped walking and grabbed her arms. She tried to pull away, but he gripped her too tightly. "Murder plain and simple," he said. "I'm not making excuses for anything I do, not to you or anybody. They were a threat to you, me, and to any other survivors out there, and I killed them, gladly. I won't lose any sleep over it. I'll handle any other threat in a similar manner. You'd better get used to it." He stared into her eyes. "The danger excited you last night. You felt the adrenaline surging through your body. Now, you've had time to think about what we did and you feel guilty. Don't. Thinking too hard can get you killed and maybe those around you."

He released his grip on her and continued walking. Reed had gone on ahead. If he had overheard the conversation, he gave no indication, as he went inside his RV and closed the door. Jake knew he shouldn't have responded so vehemently, but her accusation had struck a raw nerve. She was right. It had been murder, intentional murder. They might be forced to murder again to save themselves. She had better get used to the idea that not all survivors deserve to live. *Jake's Law #6 – Bad people deserve bad ends.* He knew that if it came down to him or someone else's life, he would choose himself.

He gave Jessica the space she needed to think. He made himself scarce by feeding the animals and doing small jobs around the farm. He inspected his crops, hoeing the weeds that seemed to grow better than the crops in the summer heat. It was a constant struggle. The corn was almost ripe, as were the melons. He picked a few tomatoes, cucumbers, and basil for a salad, and some okra to fry. The green beans and peas would be ready in a week or so. He had a pressure cooker and jars ready for canning. They would provide needed nourishment during the winter.

He was so absorbed in his crops that he failed to see the jet returning until it was almost upon him. The noise of the A-10 Thunderbolt's GE turbofan engine rumbled down the valley as it passed overhead at a height of less than nine-thousand feet, barely clearing the mountains. It was too late to hide. The slow moving

Warthog would have noticed the sun reflecting off the solar panels from miles away. He resisted the impulse to wave at the pilot to prove he wasn't a zombie. He tensed and waited for the Warthog's GAU 8 Gatling gun to cut loose, spewing uranium depleted 30 mm bullets down the valley at 3,900 rounds per minute. Nothing happened. It didn't even make a second pass, instead gaining altitude and flying off toward the northwest. A sense of dread swept over him. Why had the jet chosen his canyon to inspect? Was it coincidence or something more ominous?

Davis-Monthan Airbase in Tucson had been abandoned for almost a year, but somewhere within flying distance, enough military personnel survived to maintain jet aircraft. It might be from Luke Airbase west of Phoenix. Undoubtedly, the pilot had been taking reconnaissance photos. He hoped no one decided to make use of them.

Jessica heard the jet as well. She stood on the balcony staring up at it. To her, it probably meant possible rescue. To him, it meant trouble. In other regions, the military had rounded up survivors into FEMA camps. Last he had heard, conditions in the camps were appalling, akin to survivors tales of the 2005 Hurricane Katrina aftermath in New Orleans. He wanted no part of military intervention. After the jet left, she looked down at him but made no attempt to wave or talk to him. She went back inside. He resumed his gardening.

He had broken a new record. In less than forty-eight hours, he had managed to allow evil to insinuate itself into his Garden of Eden.

10

June 11, 2016   Split Rock Canyon –

Jessica watched the jet fly away with a sinking feeling in her stomach. She didn't really expect rescue, but the jet meant that someone somewhere was still alive. She had almost given up hope on humanity. She was one of the lucky ones, though she had not yet come to terms with her good fortune. So far, her life after the apocalypse had been a cascading series of poor decisions. Had she made another one by staying with Jake? Only time would tell.

Before the Staggers, she had been happy and content with her job as a nutritionist and yoga instructor at the Foothills Spa. Her boyfriend was a caring man whom she deeply loved. When the plague struck and people all around her began dying, she had thought it providence that both she and Lloyd were immune. They bought a pickup load of supplies and barricaded themselves in their condo to wait for help. After three weeks, no help came and their store of supplies ran out. They ventured to several stores searching for food, but found most of them already looted. Against Lloyd's advice, she had insisted on one last store. When the zombies cornered them in an office, he had shoved her out a window and remained to fight them off while she escaped. His screams still echoed in her mind.

Later, she had encountered two more people, and together they managed to survive. Not learning from her previous mistake, she had insisted that Ben go out for supplies, even though Liz had been vehemently opposed to the idea. Zombies had followed him back, and both he and Liz had perished. If not for Jake's providential appearance, she would have died as well. Her decision to sleep with Jake had been born both by desperation at the thought of facing zombies alone, and by her physical need. He was a good lover, though strangely cold and withdrawn.

Her moral compass had changed considerably since the apocalypse. At first, it had been little things. Even taking food from an abandoned home had felt like stealing. Now, she had participated in cold-blooded murder. The blood on her hands this time was deliberate. It didn't wash off with soap and water. It left a stain that reminded her of the world in which she now lived. Jake was a survivalist. He had anticipated how bad things could get. He had considered what he might have to do to survive and had come to grips with it. Could she become as hard and as cold as him? She had made mistakes, but she was learning quickly. If sex could keep her alive, she wasn't opposed to using it, but now she wondered if teaming with Jake was another big mistake.

Jake had been right about one thing, and she despised him for pointing it out to her. Though the idea of murder was abhorrent to her, the danger had excited her. Not the killing itself, but the thrill of the operation. For once, she had been doing something other than running or hiding. She had been acting rather than reacting. The shame had come came later. Jake was a hard man. Maybe that was why he had survived. She didn't want to become a hard woman, ruthless and uncaring, but she knew that if she didn't follow his rules, Jake's Laws, he might kick her out.

She sighed. She had never been so calculating before the plague. She had considered herself a strong, single woman; a professional with reasonably attainable goals. The collapse of her world had left her frightened and alone, thrown her into a world of chaos and confusion. She knew now that survival meant more than simply staying out of the hands of zombies. It meant developing the proper skills. If that meant selling herself to Jake, so be it.

Jake returned to the house carrying an armload of freshly picked vegetables. She decided to ignore their earlier encounter. She smiled and took them from him. His lips moved, as if he wanted to say something, but he turned away abruptly, leaving it unsaid. She hoped it had been an apology, but he was a stubborn man. If an apology from her would help soothe his ruffled feathers, she would swallow her pride and offer it.

"You're right," she said.

"Being right doesn't make it any better," he said, surprising her with his candor.

"What do you mean?"

"Killing people is never going to be easy or right, but it is necessary at times. Zombies are easy. They're no longer human, but what about the infected? They can kill you as quickly as a zombie. We may be immune, or we might just be lucky. Can you kill someone that isn't a zombie, someone who can speak and reason, but by his or her very presence can kill you?" He shook his head. "It's a hard choice to make, but you may have to make it.

"I once had the responsibility of upholding the law. I believed it was the only way to maintain order and stability. In Afghanistan, I saw firsthand what lawlessness looked like. People died every day with no one to turn to for justice or protection. The Afghan Army couldn't or wouldn't do anything. We couldn't do anything without risking political repercussions. I wrote my own set of laws and tried to live by them. I did the same thing here. I could see the writing on the wall for us. I became a survivalist. I still tried to do some good as a deputy, keep our laws in effect, but I knew something was going to happen in my lifetime." He chuckled. "I never suspected zombies. When the President declared Martial Law, it broke my heart. It meant our laws were finished. That just left my laws. I kept them few and simple, easy to interpret. They keep me straight, at least in my heart. They might not be nice laws, but they are effective. Someday, when things get better, I'll set my laws aside, but not yet."

She nodded, puzzled but strangely shaken by his sincerity. "I think I understand."

His face became grim. "You think I'm a cold, heartless bastard. You may be right. It's my choice, and I'll live with it. You don't have to. You're a good person, and that works against you now, but you're the kind of person the world needs. Simply surviving isn't enough. You have to think beyond the plague, beyond all the death and destruction. When that time arrives, I'll be superfluous. If you survive and keep your humanity, you can rebuild the world. I can teach you survival. That's all I'm good for."

His admission touched her deeply. In his own way, he was apologizing, not for killing the men, but for scolding her for condemning him. "I'll try." She paused. Was her next question too personal? "Tell me, what's with the badge?"

He reached up and touched the badge on his chest. "It's a long story."

She laughed. "We've got nothing but time."

"My great-grandfather, Cody Blakely, was an Arizona Ranger. The Rangers originally formed in 1860 to fight Indians but disbanded in 1861 when the Confederacy took over the territory.

In 1882 when the Indian raids and the Mexican border troubles grew worse, the Rangers were reformed under Captain John H. Jackson. My great-grandfather lied about his age and joined up when he was sixteen. He was a lieutenant by eighteen. The Arizona Rangers were a bad ass bunch of hombres. They took on gangs of outlaws, Mexican border bandits, and renegade Indians. In most cases, they were judge, jury, and executioner. I wear the badge to remind myself that the only law now is my law, Jake's Law."

She looked at him and caught him smiling at her.

"You're wondering if you've made a bad decision hooking up with me. Maybe you did."

She tried not to let her agreement show on her face. He turned to walk away.

"Jake," she called out. Had she been too hard on him?

When he turned to look at her, she couldn't read his expression, but his jaw was clenching and unclenching, as if he dreaded what she might say.

"I'm sorry I tried to be your conscience. I owe you my life. I'm … not sure how I feel about things, but I won't second guess you again."

"No, you be my conscience. I need one."

He had surprised her. He was a deeper person than she had thought. He just had difficulty expressing himself to others. If she was wrong about one thing, she might be wrong about others. She wouldn't underestimate him again.

Later, they sat on the balcony with the heat rising from the canyon floor in invisible currents that shimmered and danced at the edges of her vision. The balcony was still in shade, making it comfortable. She relaxed, leaning back in her chair, enjoying the day. Jake sat stiff-backed, staring out across the canyon, as if keeping an eye on his domain. Music drifted up from Reed's RV. She recognized a few strains of one of Handel's organ concertos and smiled. Reed's classical musical tastes mirrored her own. The eighteenth-century German composer's music was perfect for yoga meditation. She wondered what type of music, if any, Jake liked. She considered a person's choice in music to be very telling about their character. She smiled at a fleeting mental image of Jake cleaning his rifle while listening to Bach.

Near sundown, Reed joined them. He brought along a bottle of wine.

"This Pinot Grigio should go with whatever we're dining on," he said.

"A fresh garden salad and venison for you two. Salad and cheese for me," she said.

As she rose to get started on the meal, Jake stopped her. "We should all prepare the meal."

"The kitchen's too small. We can take turns. Tomorrow, you cook."

"Fair enough," he said.

She could hear the pair talking about the previous night's escapade as she chopped veggies for the salad. A package containing several cured venison steaks sat in a refrigerator drawer next to slab of bacon. She chose two and tossed them in a frying pan. She sliced some carrots and potatoes and placed them around the venison. The smell of cooking meat almost nauseated her, but she endured.

"Why are you so sure Levi won't just go away?" Reed asked. "Hell, maybe the zombies got him."

Jake's answer gave her pause. "He had the look of a lone wolf killer."

"He's only one man."

"He found those lowlifes. He'll find more. Dirt attracts dirt. The promise of food, booze or women will be enough to rally them. He's methodical, ruthless, and determined. That makes him dangerous."

"So what do we do?" Reed asked. After a moment, he added, "I can rig some security cameras along the road and outside the fence for early warning if they find us."

"That's a good idea. We need to become more proactive in our defense. Life is dangerous. Sooner or later, someone will find us here."

"Who are you ..." Reed paused. "Oh, the jet. You're talking about the military."

"Or the militia. Either way, their goals might not mesh with ours. I don't intend to be cooped up in some FEMA camp like breeding cattle."

Jake's anger seethed just below his words. What did he know about the FEMA camps that she didn't? She, Ben, and Liz had discussed finding a FEMA camp, but decided the journey was too dangerous. As it turned out, not going had been even more dangerous. If the army offered safety, what was Jake's objection – his innate distrust of authority, or was he just afraid of giving up control?

"You seem pretty certain about the military," Reed said. His expression at the mention of the FEMA camps betrayed his disgust.

Jake didn't answer.

"I think you're hiding something from us," Reed continued. "I don't appreciate it. We're all in this together."

"The military has their own agenda. To them, it's all in the numbers – the number of dead versus the number they can save. Who can contribute, and who is a drag on resources? To me, it's more personal. I trust me more than I do them."

"I think you're wrong," Reed responded, but he didn't elaborate.

Jake's answer baffled her. If they couldn't trust the military, who could they trust? Were his own prejudices and resentment of the military clouding his judgment?

As soon as the steaks were ready, she brought them to the table. The tension between the two men was palpable. As she set a plate in front of Jake, she deliberately brushed her hip against his shoulder. As she hoped, his anger dissipated as he reached out to fondle her waist. She smiled down at him, but she was thinking, *"My life is my own. I'll decide who to trust and how to live it."*

11

June 16, 2016   Oro Valley, AZ –

By ones and twos, Levi slowly found the kind of men he needed. Some had always been cold and cruel – thieves, gang members, ruthless businessmen. Others had become that way after the plague when wits and weapons were all that stood between death and deliverance. All were barely eking out an existence, anxious for more. Levi attracted the desperate to him like a hooker attracts customers, by displaying his wares, what he had to offer them.

With the seeds of his new army in tow, he scoured the city, choosing only those he deemed capable of accepting him as leader, killing the rest and taking their supplies. By week's end, he had gathered twenty men and five women who shared his ideas of survival of the fittest. Most would have been at home in the cell next to him in prison. He trusted none of them, but knew they would follow him. Each of them had a basic character flaw that assured this – they sought approval in others they considered superior to them. They each needed and wanted to belong to a group with a leader that made all of the decisions and accepted all of the responsibility. Two years earlier, he would have been one of them, meekly accepting his lot in life. Now, post-apocalypse, he was a changed man – harder, colder, more sure of himself. As long as he produced for them, they would follow him.

He selected a school in Oro Valley surrounded by a high wall and a gate as a base of operations for scavenging the area for weapons and supplies. To keep them occupied, he often made zombie killing runs for fun and target practice. Choosing three of the hardest and cruelest who showed an innate knack for leadership, either through example or by the simple expediency of pummeling all opposition, he divided the group into three teams.

One of these three was a woman. The other women were simply camp followers, a bit of fluff for the men to enjoy. This one was different. She was almost as hard as he was and held within her a barely controlled rage against everyone and everything. The plague had taken her family, but she couldn't extract her revenge on a parasite. Instead, she was at war with the world. She intrigued him. In the classroom he had commandeered for his quarters, he called her to him.

She sauntered in, unafraid, allowing no emotion to show on her face. She stood before him, a few inches shy of six feet, her short-cropped hair dyed jet-black, with a crudely-inked tattoo of a red-tailed hawk on her right forearm. She wore tight jeans that hugged her hips and sculpted her buttocks. She wore no shirt. Her two-button denim vest barely contained her ample breasts. She would have been pretty,except for the livid scar running diagonally along her right temple. That she chose to expose the scar rather than cover it with longer hair spoke volumes to him about her. She was defiant and proud. He forced her to stand before him for several minutes before speaking. She didn't flinch from his gaze.

"What's your name?" he finally asked.

"Hawk."

He smiled. "Your real name?"

Her lips quavered slightly, and her eyes grew colder and darker, as she repeated, "Hawk."

He nodded. "Okay, Hawk it is." Her name didn't really matter. He was sure many people had chosen new identities after the apocalypse. He found it interesting that she had chosen a predator bird for her totem. "What do you want out of life?"

She stared at him for a moment, as if she had never asked herself that question. "Want?"

"Yeah. Are you looking for an honorable death, revenge, a new spring wardrobe? What the hell do you want to do?"

Her face went rigid. "Kill zombies."

That brought a smile to his face. Her hatred for the creatures matched his own. As long as he provided targets, she would stay with him. "Are you opposed to killing a few people, for survival purposes of course?"

She paused before replying. Her rigid stance relaxed slightly, but only slightly. "No."

Her answer was short and sweet, just the way he had expected her to answer. He liked her more and more. "You're not bad looking, not that it would matter to these assholes. They'll fuck anything. They're going to be all over you. You'll have to fight them off and sleep with one eye open."

Her right hand dropped to the hilt of her knife, a massive Jungle Master with a ten-inch stainless steel blade and rubberized grip. Judging by the nicks in the handle and scratches on the blade, it had seen considerable use.

"There's an easier way," he said.

She stared at him for a moment before a tight smile flickered across her lips. "Be the boss's bitch."

He stood and walked over to her. He pushed his face to within inches of hers and inhaled her muskiness. She didn't bat an eyelash. "It won't be that bad. They'll leave you alone, and maybe I won't be such a bastard all the time. Who knows, you might even grow to like me."

Her face resumed its original hardness. "I'll fuck you, but I won't like you."

He backed away and laughed. "I like you. You're me with a set of nice tits."

"Is that all?" she asked.

"Move your shit in here and let the others know about our arrangement. Tonight … well, we'll see."

He could feel the chill of the room dissipate after she left. He would never break her or own her. He didn't know what lot in life had turned her so cold and bitter, and he didn't care. She would submit to him for her own reasons, and that was enough for him. However, he would sleep with a knife under his pillow just in case. She would turn on him in a heartbeat if she felt he had passed whatever line she drew between them. He licked his lips. Probing that line would be exquisite.

12

June 16, 2016   Split Rock Canyon –

In his secluded little canyon fortress, Jake was pleased to see their living arrangement settle into a daily routine. Disorder was an anathema, and order was an island of stability amid a sea of insanity and chaos. The tension eased between him and Reed, or seemed to. Reed cherished his privacy, keeping to his RV most of the time, taking only dinner with him and Jessica. Sharing this last meal of the day gave them all the opportunity to talk things over and discuss plans for the future, and establish a division of chores. Reed proved less than enthusiastic about feeding the animals. He and animals didn't seem to see eye to eye. After one of the goats butted him in the ass as he bent over to pour feed into their trough, he refused to go near them. However, his surprising skills as a mechanic soon had the water pump working more efficiently.

Jessica's attitude had changed, as if she had reached some kind of a decision. She became a willing pupil, eager to learn all she could about weapons and survival. He showed her how to disassemble the .45 and the rifle, and the proper way to clean and oil the parts. Her sudden change in attitude mystified him, but her enthusiasm pleased him. Soon, she would become a dependable third member of their group instead of someone he would have to watch over. To his surprise, her metamorphosis from frightened caterpillar to bold butterfly took only the best part of a week.

"What changed your mind?" he asked early one morning, as they gathered vegetables before the heat of the day made the task uncomfortable. The air was still and warm in prelude to the one-hundred-plus degree heat that would come later in the day.

Jessica still wore his cut off jeans shorts and a too large t-shirt with no bra. The sweat-dampened shirt clung to her breasts like Saran Wrap, hiding nothing from him. He found it difficult to concentrate.

"You did," she replied.

He didn't know what he had said or done that had finally gotten through to her, but he was satisfied. "That's good. For a while, I was afraid for you."

She smiled. "Not now?"

"Maybe a little, but you're learning quickly." A dark thought crossed his mind. "Are you in a hurry to leave?"

Her composure broke just slightly, not enough for him to decide if he had hit upon the answer or if the thought of leaving disturbed her. "No."

Maybe it was just his ego, but his heart quickened at her answer. Being alone for so long, even at his choosing, had created a distance between him and other people's problems. Now, a small portion of the human race had entered his small world, and he found that he liked it. He didn't kid himself by calling it love. He appreciated Reed's help and certainly enjoyed sex with Jessica, but he knew it could all disappear in a dark instant, leaving him back where he started. He didn't want Jessica to leave, but he wouldn't force her to stay. He had known her for less than a week, but the thought of losing her sickened him. He hadn't invested as much of himself in another person in a long time. He felt exposed and confused by the inrush of feelings to which he had thought himself immune. It wasn't love, but it was close enough.

"Good," he replied. "You're not ready yet."

She placed a handful of beans in the basket she carried draped from her arm, wiped her forehead with the back of her arm, and said, "I can shoot. You taught me well."

"You can hit a target, and you can hit a zombie. You know zombies aren't the only threat out there. Killing a person takes some … I won't call it courage, but it takes deliberation. It's not something taken lightly. They might think they have the same right to kill you as you do them. "

Her face clouded for a moment. Then she replied, "I'll defend myself if I have to."

He believed her. "Good." He decided to leave it there. There was no use in pushing her further until the need to prove herself arose.

As they were talking, Reed joined them, perspiring profusely. His bold-print shirt lay sweat-plastered to his body. He looked decidedly uncomfortable in the heat. "I've been thinking about our conversation about bigger weapons. They have weapons at the WATTS Army National Guard at Pinal Air Park. Why don't we get some?"

"How do you know they didn't take them with them when they evacuated?"

"They didn't," he said, and then added, "I'm willing to bet on it."

Jake stared at Reed. Reed's certainty confused him, but life was a gamble. "It's worth a shot."

"When do we go?" Jessica asked.

"Now is as good a time as any," Jake said, snipping one last tomato from its vine and placing it in the basket.

* * * *

The Pinal Air Park was just north of Marana off I-10. By sticking to the back roads most of the way, they avoided areas infested with zombies. While passing through San Manuel, Jake noticed Reed staring at the wisps of smoke still rising from the school he had torched. Luckily, the wind blew from the northwest, taking with it the stench of burnt flesh and decay. He wondered how Reed felt about his act of arson. It was obvious the former schoolteacher had acted out of frustration and anger. Did he now regret burning down the school? If so, he said nothing about it.

South of Oracle, they doubled back north along Highway 79, passing a few abandoned vehicles along the way, but spotting few zombies in the sparsely populated area. Cutting west across the desert using dirt roads, they soon reached I-10. Here, they found long lines of cars and trucks choking the Westbound and Eastbound lanes, contributors to the last great traffic snarl before the Interstate was closed. Even the access road was blocked. They weaved through and around cars, shoving a few off the road, stopping long enough to cut a gap through the chain link fence separating the Interstate from the side roads. They crossed over I-10 on the Pinal Air Park exit.

The Air Park was long abandoned. Lines of mini sand dunes swept in from the surrounding desert like waves on the beach, burying much of the tarmac beneath layers of sand and a year's growth of weeds and shrubs. Mounds of dry tumbleweeds piled against the undercarriages of the museum airplanes like kindling for a bonfire. A zombie wearing tattered army fatigues stood near the open front gate like a forgotten sentry. He was barely more than skin and bones. Even in his starved stupor, he sensed fresh meat nearby. As the creature staggered toward the jeep, Jake shot him in the head with the crossbow to avoid attracting more of the creatures with gunfire.

Only two Apache AH-64 helicopters remained at WAATS, the Western Army National Guard Training Site at the Silverbell Army Heliport. Upon closer inspection, he saw the reason for their abandonment. Both had been cannibalized for parts, including their GE-T700 turboshaft engines and 30mm M230 Chain guns. Jake would have loved to get his hands on one of the chain guns for some real firepower.

They located the armory quickly enough inside one of the barracks buildings. The steel vault door of the armory was locked. Reed placed his last pipe bomb where the lock met the door jam. He seemed confident the gunpowder explosive could open the door, but Jake had his doubts. The door looked too solid and heavy. He and Jessica took shelter outside while Reed lit the fuse, rushed outside, and squatted against the wall. The explosion shook the ground and rattled the building. Inside, amid a cloud of smoke and dust, the vault door was swinging free.

"It worked!" Reed yelled. He seemed as surprised as Jake at the bomb's effectiveness.

The vault contained a locked cabinet and a fenced area stacked with crates of ammunition and a rack of weapons. In their haste to evacuate the base, the Guard had left much of their armament behind. Jake felt like a kid in a candy store as he stood in the open doorway. He immediately grabbed two M 4 carbines from the wall.

"These babies fire 5.56 mm NATO rounds and have excellent range." He also stuffed two M9 Beretta 9 mms into his belt.

"Where are the explosives? This is mostly ammunition." Reed asked in disappointment, as he pulled out crates and read labels. "I thought there would be grenades and Claymore mines."

"The Guard doesn't keep things like that around. We'll take what we can get," Jake said.

He forced open the cabinet with a pry bar he had brought along. Inside, he spotted an AA-12 full-auto twelve-gauge shotgun still in its case. He wondered why the Guard had left the experimental automatic assault shotgun behind but didn't question his luck. The eight-shell magazine was attached, but to his delight, he found a thirty-two-shell drum magazine in a separate box on the bottom shelf. He held the shotgun in his hands, marveling at the light weight. Now, he could retire his old Versa Max.

He entered the wire cage with Reed and began ferrying boxes of 7.62 mm ammunition to the door. Reed stopped him.

"What's that for? There's nothing here that fires that caliber."

Jake smiled. "Oh, I might find a use for it."

Reed scowled as he realized Jake was keeping another secret from him, but said nothing.

After a few minutes, Jake stopped and mopped his sweaty brow with his sleeve. "I think we've got all we can carry," he said, staring at the growing pile of weapons.

Reed didn't look convinced, but he reluctantly agreed. He dropped a case of smoke grenades he was carrying on the floor. "I guess we really don't need these."

As they loaded the jeep, zombies began appearing from a few of the nearby buildings. He had hoped to get away without firing a shot, but that now seemed unlikely. He broke open a case of 12-gauge shells and began loading the AA-12's drum magazine. By the time the jeep was loaded, a dozen zombies had noticed them and began lumbering in their direction.

"Let's go," he said.

"Do we really want to leave the rest of this ammunition for someone else to find?" Reed asked.

Jake looked at the building and then at the approaching zombies. It would be close. "Okay." He grabbed a road flare from the glove box and hopped out of the jeep. "Crank the jeep and be ready to go," he told Jessica. She slid over to the driver's side. She looked worried but said nothing.

Jake raced through the dormitory ripping sheets from the beds. He piled the sheets around cases of ammunition, struck the flare, and dropped it amid the sheets. Within seconds, the sheets began smoldering. As he exited the barracks building, a zombie stood between him and escape. He raised the AA-12 and fired low so he wouldn't hit Jessica or Reed. The 12-gauge pellets took the zombie's leg off below the knee. Jake leaped over it as it fell. The jeep was moving as he climbed in.

"Go!" he yelled.

Jessica floored the pedal, heading directly toward a crowd of zombies. Jake glanced back at the armory. Several zombies gathered near the door, drawn by the earlier explosion. The first pops of ammunition exploding was disappointingly small. Before Jake could express his frustration, several larger explosions quickly followed. Smoke and flames spilled out the open door, igniting the zombies. Flaming pyres, they turned toward the sounds of the explosions just as the entire building disintegrated with a flash and a thunderous boom. The zombies disappeared, along with most of the building. The concussion and a wall of heated air and dust rolled along the tarmac and slammed into the jeep. Jessica swerved but kept the jeep upright.

As they plowed into the crowd of zombies, bits and pieces of wreckage began raining down on them. Jake brushed away a hot piece of metal, noticing absently that it was a spent 5.56 mm round, leaned over the side of the jeep and began firing. The twelve-gauge pellets ripped through the creatures like baby buzz saws, separating heads from shoulders and punching fist-sized holes through chests. He fired as quickly as he could pull the trigger. The zombies paid no heed to the carnage around them in their need to reach the jeep. Jessica hit one head on. It crumpled and rolled beneath the jeep. He quickly dispatched the remaining creatures.

Patting the still warm barrel of the shotgun, he said, "I like this."

Reed stared at the remains of the armory beneath a large cloud of black smoke. Bullets still shot into the sky like fireworks. He turned to face Jake and said, "We should stop at a Radio Shack so I can round up some cameras and wiring for alarms," as if he were suggesting a shopping trip to the corner market.

Jake smiled and glanced at Jessica. "You'll have to talk to our driver."

"As long as I can pick up some decent clothes," she replied. "I'm tired of your cast offs."

13

June 16, 2016   Oro Valley, Arizona –

The explosion had been loud enough to rattle windows and awaken Levi from a sound sleep. He rolled a still sleeping Hawk off his arm and padded to the window naked. A billowing black cloud rose above the horizon to the north. The unmistakable popping sound of ammunition exploding brought a smile to his lips. Someone somewhere was having some fun. He had no doubt that it was the trio who had wiped out his previous companions, the cop. Behind him, Hawk stirred. He turned to stare at her. One breast with a thimble-sized nipple protruded from beneath the covers. Their lovemaking had been vigorous, a tug-of-war between two strong-willed people, each bent on dominating the other. Despite her obvious hatred of him, she had seen to his satisfaction before allowing him to minister to her needs. He could tell that she was awake.

"You're not curious?" he asked.

She rolled over on her side and propped herself up on one elbow. In that position, the scar on her temple made her look like a fierce Amazon warrior. "Should I be?"

He shook his head. "No. It's enough that I am. I think my cop friend is consolidating power."

"You hate him, don't you?" She smiled as she spoke, delighting in tormenting him.

"He tried to kill me, so yes, I'm a little miffed." He flashed her a tight-lipped grin. "I don't forgive easily."

She rolled out of bed, giving him a quick glimpse of her shaved pubes, pulled up her jeans, and grabbed her shirt from the floor. She slid it over her head and sat on the edge of the bed, as she donned her socks and laced her boots. Levi stiffened when she reached for her pistol and knife. He was naked and unarmed. She noticed his look of concern and smiled.

"Don't worry. If I decide to kill you, I'll tell you first."

She walked out of the room, slamming the door behind her. Levi relaxed.

"Someday I'll have to kill that bitch."

He dressed and went downstairs. The smell of burned bacon filled the kitchen from an untended skillet on the stove. He grabbed the handle, burned his fingers on the hot metal, and grabbed a rag from the counter. He turned off the flame and slid the smoking skillet to the side.

"Which one of you fucks is trying to burn down the house?" he yelled.

One of the women, a mousey young thing who called herself Flicker, rushed in, saw the mess, and cursed. "I was …"

Levi slapped her across the mouth hard enough to draw blood. She staggered against the counter, staring at him in fear. He pointed a forefinger at her. "Don't ever leave stuff cooking on the stove while you go do drugs. Do you want to burn us out?"

"I was …" she began.

He raised his hand in the air to strike her again, and she cowered. "I don't mind the drugs, but when they interfere with business, I put my foot down. If you don't want to become zombie bait, you'd better straighten your shit up." He looked at the ruined bacon, noticed there was no coffee brewing, and growled, "Make some coffee, goddamn it! Do something useful."

He left Flicker massaging her split lip and walked into the living room. Empty beer cans, plates of half-eaten food, and dirty clothes lay scattered across every surface. Half a dozen men in various states of undress and drunken stupor filled the room with the stench of unwashed bodies and farts. Weapons, some as filthy as their owners, lay discarded on the floor. He could tolerate lousy personal grooming habits, but not a blatant disregard for good weapons.

"Get off you asses and clean those weapons before they blow up in your faces the next time you use them."

People glanced up with dazed expressions, but they began moving, if slowly, gathering weapons. A secret thrill coursed through his veins that he could motivate such men through fear and intimidation. Almost any one of them could have broken his back in a fair fight, but he had no intention of fighting fair, and they knew it. None had the temperament to be leaders. Each one had already submitted himself to the leadership of others since the end of the world. Levi had simply become the latest in a long line of cruel bosses.

"Did any of you notice the explosions to the north?"

They glanced at one another uncomprehendingly.

"I thought not. Does anyone know what might be burning north of here?"

One raised his hand. "A house?" he said.

At Levi's scowl, he backed away. "The only thing north of Marana that could blow up like that is the National Guard Armory at the Pinal Air Park. I know because I intended for us to go there yesterday and raid it, but you assholes were too busy partying. Now, someone else has beaten us to it. Now, they have machine guns and explosives, while we have these." He kicked a .38 Smith and Wesson pistol lying on the floor into a corner with the toe of his boot.

"I know where we can get some machine guns," one of the group said.

Levi stared at him. He thought the man's name was Justin or Justice. He wasn't sure which. "Where?"

"A gun shop on the south side," Justin said.

"No, fool, I want something good, not more hunting rifles and pistols."

"No, no. This guy keeps a few goodies locked up in back. You know, AK47s, M16s, the good stuff."

"You're sure of this?"

Justin smiled. "I brought a load across the border from Agua Prieta once. He showed me."

"Take four men and bring back something nice. If you do, you become one of my lieutenants."

Justin almost fell over himself getting his friends up and moving. Most were still suffering from hangovers, but a few judicious kicks and shoves got them dressed and out the door. A truck cranked and pulled away squealing tires. With his offer to advance Justin for a successful run, he felt confident they would find weapons somewhere.

To two of the women still lying on blankets he yelled, "Get off your asses and clean this pig sty. It stinks in here."

They glared at him but said nothing. One, a skinny blonde, began walking around the room naked, picking up dirty clothes and discarded plates of food. When she bent over in front of him, purposefully giving him a close up view of her narrow ass, he said,

"Get that thing out of my face. Save it for the others. They're less discriminating than I am." The second girl, barely out of her teens, chuckled. To her, he snapped, "Shut the hell up or I'll feed you to the zombies."

Satisfied he had inspired them to work, at least until he disappeared, he went outside.

The explosions had quieted, but a cloud of black smoke still billowed in the north. If Justin managed to find automatic weapons, all was well and good. If not, there were other places to obtain weapons, other arsenals. The thought of having .50 caliber machine guns or even an armored half track to play with gave him an erection. He reached down and rubbed his crotch.

"Isn't that my job," Hawk said, as she walked up beside him.

Damn, she walks light. He wanted to throw her to the ground and fuck her, but he couldn't spend all his time in bed. "Not at the moment. I've got things to do."

"Here?" she asked. Her eyes were on the two sluts visible through the window still picking up garbage in the living room.

"No, I feel like scouting around a bit."

"Need company?"

He stared at her. What was behind her offer? Did she want to get him away from the others to kill him? He decided that she didn't, at least not yet. "What's it to you?"

Her eyes returned to the two girls. "If they see that you need me, they'll leave me alone. Otherwise, I'm going to kill the blonde bitch. She bad mouths me behind my back."

As much as he would like to see a fight between Hawk and the blonde, he knew who would win, no contest. "Sure, tag along if you like."

He had chosen a new white Ford Explorer from a dealership for his vehicle of choice. It still had the dealer's sticker on the side window. It gave him a thrill each time he saw the MSRP of twenty-nine thousand dollars. He turned west onto Tangerine Road and drove to I-10. Heading north on the access road, weaving through a sea of parked cars, he got close enough to confirm that it was indeed the National Guard Armory on fire. He was certain it was the group in the jeep. They were becoming an itch he longed to scratch. If Justin came through for him, he would even the score.

"You look like you're contemplating something nasty," Hawk said.

He jerked his head to stare at her. He hadn't realized he had let his anger show. "It's time to start a war."

"With whom?"

He nodded at the column of smoke. "The ones who did that."

"Why do they matter so much? You've got twenty men."

"Because they're smart. I've got clowns to work with."

She pursed her lips, stung by his comment. "Am I a clown?"

He shook his head and grinned. "You might be the only bright spot in my otherwise dreary life, if I thought I could trust you not to kill me."

In response, she set her weapon on the rear seat and began stripping off her clothes. When she was completely naked, she lay back on the seat and said, "Do I threaten you now?"

Forgetting where they were and throwing caution to the wind, he dropped his pants and crawled over to her. She accepted him inside her eagerly, rising to meet his thrusts. This was not lovemaking. It was release, pure and simple. He pounded her until he came, and then moved back to his side of the SUV.

As he zipped his pants, he said, "Not as much."

The intimacy lasted only a few minutes. Zombies clambered over car hoods and crawled from ditches toward them. Any other time he would have stopped to kill them for fun. This time, satisfied, he cranked the SUV and sped away.

14

June 16, 2016   Marana, AZ –

To avoid the clogged interstate and congested access road, Jake directed Jessica to a dirt road leading to Red Rock, a small town a few miles north of Pinal Air Park. Backtracking on dirt roads would require a roundabout approach to reach their destination but would avoid built up areas and the risk of more zombies. He had had enough of zombie killing for one day. The community of Red Rock had almost completely reverted to the desert upon which it had been built. A fire had leveled many houses in the major neighborhoods. Entire streets were lined with ash-filled ruins. Wind-blown sand reached window high in those houses remaining unconsumed by fire. The boulevard running between neighborhoods was now a flat ribbon of brush-filled desert with patches of asphalt showing through.

As they forded the Santa Cruz River in a shaded stand of trees, Jessica stopped the jeep in the middle of the shallow river.

"What are you doing?" Jake asked.

Laughing, she removed her shoes and jumped into the water, wading downstream, kicking and splashing in the water like a child in a puddle.

Exasperated by her actions, Jake called to her, "We don't have time for this."

She stared at him. "What? No time to wade a river on a sweltering summer day? Let's *make* time."

"She's right," Reed said, removing his own boots and socks.

Outvoted two-to-one, Jake relented. "All right. We splash awhile."

He removed his boots and socks, rolled up the legs of his jeans, and climbed out of the jeep. He kept his AA-12 with him. The water was cool and refreshing on his feet. Spying the cow piles along the bank, he warned, "Don't drink the water. It's not clean." He scanned the trees, hoping to spot a stray cow for dinner, but saw nothing.

Jessica sat on a boulder in the middle of the stream and let the water circle her legs. She dipped her cupped hands in the water and poured it over her head. "That feels good."

Reed did her one better by plopping down on his backside in the water and rolling in it. Jake watched on with muted anger at his inability to relax long enough to enjoy a simple wade in the river. Where they saw cool flowing water, he saw a disease-laden stew. Where they saw a thick copse of trees along the sandy banks, he saw hiding places for zombies. Where they saw an opportunity to relax, he saw wasted time.

After ten minutes, he herded them back to the jeep. "We still have shopping to do," he reminded them.

Passing through downtown Marana, they attracted the attention of several zombies, but Jake did his best to avoid them. Even Reed, perhaps made tranquil by his dip in the river, seemed uninterested in killing them. A small tendril of smoke rose from a window in the elementary school. As they neared the building, he caught the aroma of soup cooking. Someone was still alive and taking refuge in the school. The parking lot sun shelters were topped with solar panels providing power. The steel fences were an effective barrier to roaming zombies, but not against human predators. For a moment, his eyes locked with Jessica's, and he knew she wanted to check on the survivors. He shook his head. She turned away disappointed.

"If they have weapons, they might shoot first and ask questions later," he explained in a futile attempt to justify his decision.

She turned back to face him. The track of a tear ran down her cheek. "And if they don't? Shouldn't we help them?"

"They've got a good location. It seems secure enough."

"You don't care if they live or die," she accused, crossing her arms across her chest in that millenniums-old gesture of rejection and denunciation.

"Yeah, that's it," he replied harshly.

He didn't feel like trying to explain to her that whoever was inside, whatever their condition, he didn't want to risk a confrontation. It was difficult enough to cope with his two current wards. Adding more strangers would upset the dynamic of their little group. In the backseat, Reed coughed.

"What?" Jake snapped, staring at him.

He looked surprised at the question. "Nothing."

They continued down the road for several minutes in silence. He could feel Reed's gaze on the back of his neck. If they were trying to induce guilt, it was working. Finally, he said, "Turn around."

Jessica swung the jeep around in the road and headed back the way they had come. At the entrance to the school, he said, "Pull in here."

At the chain gate across the entrance, Jessica stopped the jeep. He fished out the Maxim Versa shotgun, filled a bag with shells, and pushed them beneath the gate where they would be plainly visible. He no longer needed the Maxim. He had the AA-12. The shotgun might make a difference to whoever was inside. It was the best he could do without taking on their problems.

"Let's go."

Jessica smiled at him. Reed chuckled with delight. He ignored them both.

The Tractor Supply store in Marana was just off the expressway on the access road between Cortaro Farms Road and Ina Road. Of all the area stores, it would have durable clothing, tools, and oil and filters for the vehicles and was far enough away from any neighborhoods to be zombie free. The nearby buildings were businesses and unlikely to harbor zombies. The parking lot was empty of vehicles. He directed Jessica around the side of the building, past the ten-foot-high wrought iron fenced enclosure containing rolls of barb wire, fence posts, and plastic water tanks for cattle. A side door and a roll-up garage door were both closed and the windows unbroken, which was a good sign that the store hadn't been plundered. They continued to the rear of the building. A second roll-up door was partially open and boxes lay scattered across the asphalt parking lot. His first assumption had been wrong. Someone had been there before them. His first thought was to leave the area, but the building was still their best choice to find what they needed, and the boxes looked weathered, as if they had been there awhile.

They parked out of sight behind the store in the empty parking lot near the fence's iron gate. Jake pushed the rear roll-up door higher and led the way inside with the AA-12 shotgun. He winced as the squeaky wheels of the door echoed loudly in the cavernous room. The interior was dark, musty, and stifling hot. The windows were dirty, allowing in very little sunlight. A thermometer on the wall read 118 degrees. Jake didn't doubt it. Each breath of hot, stale air was a challenge. He clicked on his flashlight and played it around the darkened interior.

"Reed, you stay here and keep watch." To Jessica, he said, "Stay close to me."

The looters had been haphazard in their pillaging, damaging more items that they took. Jessica zeroed in on the clothing section. While she shopped, methodically rummaging through every shelf, he quickly picked out two pair of jeans, underwear, and tee shirts for himself and tossed them into a shopping cart. He added a case of oil and wiper blades for the jeep, extra paper targets, and arrows for his bow, and a case of mason jars for canning. By the time he had the cart full, Jessica had picked out her wardrobe, including a wide brimmed straw hat and rugged work boots. She pushed the hat onto her head and modeled it for him.

"The perfect thing for gardening, don't you think?"

"Very chic," he replied. "That reminds me. I need to pick up fertilizer and work gloves."

"Why not a rototiller?"

"Rototillers need gas. Besides, hoeing is good exercise. If you've got what you need, go relieve Reed so he can shop."

Before she could leave, two quick rifle shots from the rear of the store reverberated like thunder in the metal building. Jake glanced at Jessica, motioning her to remain where she was, and then rushed to check on Reed. His heart was pumping, his mind racing through different scenarios, expecting trouble. The last thing he expected was to see a smiling Reed proudly displaying a headless six-foot rattlesnake dangling from the barrel of his rifle.

"Bastard almost got me. He was curled up in a coil of rope near the corner of the building. If he hadn't rattled, I might have stepped on him."

"Why did you shoot it?' Jake demanded, relieved to learn that Reed was all right but angry that he had resorted to shooting the snake.

Reed stared at him. "What did you expect me to do, adopt it?"

"Your shots might draw zombies." He looked at the snake. "You could have just left it alone. It was inside trying to get out of the sun."

Reed flung the snake down the aisle away from them. "Well, excuse me. I thought I was doing us a favor. Besides, it was clear outside."

Jake glanced toward the door. "You're sure?"

Irritated by Jake's questioning, Reed answered, "Yes, I'm sure. Do you think I'm blind?"

"Okay. Okay. Just be more careful next time." Jake glanced down at the new belt buckle around Reed's waist. "Where did you get that?"

Reed pointed to a rack against the side wall, well away from the rear door. "Over there." He fingered the buckle. "Do you want one?"

Jake tried to keep his voice even, but his frustration at Reed's lack of concern irritated him. "I thought you were watching the door. How long were you gone?"

Reed frowned. "Just a few minutes. What's the problem?"

"The problem is I depended on you to guard the door." He shook his head. "Go get Jessica to relieve you while you get what you need. I'll start loading the jeep."

Still pouting from his dressing down, Reed marched to the front of the store. After a few moments, Jake followed him and called to Jessica. "Bring the shopping cart when you come." He was disappointed by Reed's lackadaisical attitude. He was a big believer in *Jake's Law #7 – Trust yourself first; others seldom.*

As Jessica approached, she said, "Reed's pissed. What did you do?" She handed over the shopping cart.

By the tone of her voice, she agreed with Reed. "He left his post," he growled. "We need to know if someone shows up. Keep your eyes open."

"Is it a firing squad if I don't?"

He glowered at her. "Don't tempt me." He took the cart and rolled it toward the door before she could say anything more.

Between the ammunition and weapons from the National Guard armory and the goods from the store, the jeep would be loaded down. He was pleased that they had made a good haul. They would have to make fewer trips for supplies. As he neared the door, a shadow fell across him, catching him by surprise. Glancing up, he saw a Runner rushing through the door. He barely had time to warn Jessica and raise his shotgun before the creature was upon him. He shoved the cart in the zombie's path with his foot to slow it down, as he fired from the hip. With the loaded cart in the way, few of the pellets actually struck the creature, doing more damage to the case of motor oil in the bottom of the cart. The creature changed direction and lunged at Jessica, its teeth bared for the bite. She backed up until a storage rack blocked her retreat. Thinking quickly, she pulled the rack over and jumped out of the way as it fell. The rack pinned the Runner to the floor. Jake placed two quick shots into its head, killing it.

The creature wasn't alone. Two more entered, both dangerous Runners. By then, Reed had joined them, looking confused by the presence of the zombies. He brushed off Jake's angry stare and said something unintelligible, as a quick, short burst from Jessica's M16 drowned out his words. Now, only one zombie remained. Jake charged it, aiming for the head. *Jake's Law #1- Aim high; shoot straight*. The creature swerved at the last second and his shot went wild. It was too late for another shot. He lowered his shoulder and dove into the creature like a line backer, lifting it from the ground and slamming it back down again on its back with him atop it. Unlike an opponent in a football game, the zombie was unperturbed. Instead of stunned, it was angry, hungry and angry. Jake fought off its frenzied attacks with one arm, while trying to remove his knife from its scabbard with the other.

After what seemed an eternity, the knife was in his hand, but the creature's mouth was inches from his throat. Its fetid breath sickened him. The smell rising from its unwashed body made his eyes water. The starving animal gleam in its mad eyes made him redouble his efforts. He jabbed the knife into the creature's neck until his hand was slippery with blood, but it didn't diminish its attack. He placed his forearm under the creature's throat and pushed its head backwards.

Jessica stood just inside the door staring at him with a frightened expression.

"Shoot it," he yelled. He hoped her aim was true, but it would be better to die by a stray bullet than at the hands of the zombie.

She hesitated, but then raised her rifle and fired. The bullet struck the zombie in the back of the head, ripping a large exit hole in the right temple. Spurting blood drenched him, but the creature went limp beneath him. He spit out some of the disgusting foul liquid that splattered into his mouth and wiped his face with his sleeve. He rolled the zombie off him.

Jessica had recovered from her shock and was pointing out the door. "More zombies," she yelled, "dozens of them, coming from behind the store." She fired a short burst through the open door.

Jake wiped the gore from his face and rushed to her side. One creature lay dead on the ground just outside the door, but many more were crossing the rear of the lot, half concealed by the dense undergrowth. At least a dozen of the creatures appeared from around the corner of the building, between the store and the road, blocking their exit. The wails as the creatures recognized potential food sent chills down Jake's spine. It was the sound of starving animals.

"We can close the door," Reed suggested, "barricade ourselves inside."

"No, we'll be trapped. We have to leave now."

The pair stared at him dumfounded. He knew he presented a ghastly picture, drenched in zombie blood, suggesting they fight their way through a zombie horde. He probably seemed mad to them, but he knew he was right.

"If we stay, more will come. It's better to get away now." He turned to Jessica. "Do you have the keys?"

"They're in the jeep."

"Good. You and Reed go out the side door into the enclosed area. I'll draw them inside the building after me. Open the gate when they're past and crank the jeep. Don't shoot unless you have to."

Reed stared at him shocked. "Are you kidding?"

Jake pointed to the group blocking their escape around the side of the store. "We don't know how many more are around the other corner. I don't know where they came from. This is a business district. The safest way out of here is past the theater in the Arizona Pavilions." Reed continued to stare. "We don't have time for this. Move! Take the cart."

"The cart?" Reed moaned.

"Yes, we need the supplies. We can't come back after it."

Jessica and Reed sprinted for the side door with Reed pushing the cart. A trail of black, viscous oil dripped from the cart. Jake walked to the door and showed himself to the zombies. They wasted no time coming after him. When both Reed and Jessica were safely through the side door, he began backing inside the store, shooting zombies as he retreated. He killed almost a dozen of the creatures but more came in. Where were they coming from? There were no houses nearby. He couldn't hold them off for much longer. When he heard the jeep crank, he raced for the side door. Outside, just ahead of the Runners, he began toppling stacked rolls of barbed wire in their path. The first ones became entangled, but the ones behind them went around. He cut the rope holding together a bundle of fence posts and pushed it over to slow them down.

"Come on!" Jessica yelled to him.

He abandoned trying to contain the zombies and ran for the jeep. Reed was still emptying the contents of the cart into the rear. Jake grabbed an armload of clothing, tossed it into the jeep, and shoved Reed in on top of it. They would have to abandon the rest. Reed fell into the rear of the jeep huffing and puffing, reaching for his inhaler. Jake cursed under his breath. Reed would be useless for a few minutes as he caught his breath.

"Go," he called out to Jessica, as he leaped across the jeep and slid into the passenger seat. He fired two quick blasts of the shotgun as two zombies came through the gate

Jessica floored the jeep and slammed him back into the seat. She clipped one creature with the front bumper, sending it rolling across the asphalt. Jake began shooting into the mass of zombies in front of them as fast as the automatic AA-12 would fire. The triple-ought buckshot cut a wide swath through the creatures, but sensing food, they continued to press forward. Most were Shamblers, too slow to present a major problem, but their numbers were increasing. A few were Runners. These nimble creatures seemed to know where the jeep was headed and attempted to cut them off. Jake marveled at their ingenuity even as he fired into their midst.

"That way," he said, pointing to a road leading toward the Pavilions Center, an area shopping and restaurant district.

Jessica drove straight through a chain link fence and across a parking lot. The jeep skidded as she turned down Arizona Pavilions Boulevard. After they passed the KOLD TV station, more zombies appeared from the movie theater parking lot, blocking the road and surging toward them. Jessica stepped on the brakes. The jeep skidded to a stop.

"Which way?" she asked.

He pointed to an open lot their left. "That way, toward the river."

Jessica started the jeep, cut across an empty lot, and dove over the river embankment. The jeep caught air as it went over the edge. The wheels touched only momentarily on the lower slope. The vehicle bounced wildly as it struck the sandy river bed bumper first, almost throwing Reed from the jeep. The wheels spun in the loose sand before finally finding traction. She pointed the jeep north along the river, dodging large mesquite and brittle brush plants that proliferated in the sandy bottom, slowing down only when they had left the horde of zombies far behind.

Ahead, scores of zombies stared down at them from the Cortaro Road Bridge over the Gila River. The starving creatures were moving like migrating herds of bison from the neighborhoods at the foot of the Tucson Mountains toward the city seeking food. It now seemed no place in the city was safe from their threat.

Reed puffed from his inhaler, but his eyes revealed the guilt he felt at letting them down while on guard. Jake saw no reason to further exacerbate the situation by accosting him again. He had learned his lesson the hard way, by almost dying. Jessica had proved her mettle behind the wheel. They had come through alive. That was a plus in Jake's book.

15

June 20, 2016   Split Rock Canyon –

The wind picked up late in the afternoon, howling down the canyon like a pack of raging wolves. Sudden gusts birthed dust devils that careened drunken-sailor wildly until they crashed into the stone wall and dissipated. The animals became restless, pacing nervously in their pens. Like Jake, they could smell the ever-increasing moisture in the air. A storm was brewing. The sky was mackerel-streaked with cirrocumulus clouds, foreshadowing an early onset of the monsoons. The prospect of rain pleased him, but a flash flood could damage his garden. In spite of all of his preparation, he was entirely at the mercy of the unpredictable weather. He blinked as windblown sand stung his eyes.

"Will it rain?" Jessica asked. There was a tinge of hope in her voice.

Jake glanced up at the darkening sky. Already, dense mushroom-shaped cumulonimbus clouds were peeking over the mountain tops to the southwest. By nightfall, they would sweep in with a vengeance, bringing heavy downpours. "Fast and hard. Soon, I think."

"You're certain?" She stared at him, but then she glanced away. "At least it's cooler."

Jake pulled her close and hugged her. At first, she stiffened in his arms, but then pressed against him. He thought it odd how contented he felt. The world was in its death throes, and yet, he was at peace for the first time in years. It was a strange turn of events. A loner by choice, he now had friends and a lover. It had taken the end of the world to force him to see the error of his solitary ways.

"Cooler but with a higher humidity," he pointed out. "It's a trade off."

It was dark enough that the lights were on in Reed's trailer. His shadow passed in front of the window, as music blared from his stereo, a waltz.

"Is he dancing?" he asked Jessica, incredulous that the non-athletic Reed could dance.

She smiled. "Probably. He's a romantic at heart."

He looked at her, frowning. "Really? And I'm not?"

"You're trying," she said after a short pause that left him wondering.

"You're helping. I don't know what I would have done without you."

She winced and blinked rapidly, as if sand had gotten into her eyes as well, and then nodded.

A drop of rain splashed his face, presaging the deluge to follow. "I guess it's time to close the windows and enjoy the rain from inside."

Night fell over the valley like a hand smothering a candle flame. Peals of thunder shook the windows, as rapid-fire lightning flashes cascaded across the sky, creating a mosaic of light. The rain came down in torrents, a solid sheet of water that reduced visibility to near zero, deafening in its fury. Gusts of wind drove the raindrops almost horizontally onto the windows, tapping an unreadable Morse-code message. The lights flickered. Jake worried that his solar panels might be ripped from their frames.

Sipping a whiskey while Jessica read, Jake couldn't shake the sense of gloom that enveloped him. A storm even of this magnitude shouldn't trouble him so much. He had survived many Arizona monsoons. The hairs on the back of his neck were standing on end, and he didn't think it was from static electricity. He rose from his chair and began to pace the room.

After a few minutes, Jessica set aside her book and asked, "What's wrong?"

Jake shrugged and took another sip of whiskey. "I don't know. Maybe I'm getting paranoid."

She smiled up at him. "Maybe you just need another drink."

He downed the remains in his glass. "No, I think maybe I'll go talk to Reed. See if the monitors show anything."

"In this storm? Don't be silly. You'll get soaked. Besides, it's as dark as the inside of a paper bag out there. The rain is like a veil. The cameras will be useless."

Jake nodded. "Yeah. That's what worries me."

He didn't bother with a raincoat or umbrella. The wind would have ripped the latter from his grip, and the former was useless against such a downpour. He pulled his baseball cap tighter on his head. Muddy water cascaded down the slope and over the ledge, making the path slick. He almost lost his footing on the wet wooden-plank bridge. Only his grip on the rope railing prevented him falling off. The roar of Split Rock Falls grew louder, as water funneled down from higher up the slope and into the narrow creek. The wash was running swiftly. He hoped it didn't overflow its banks.

He knocked on Reed's door. Reed answered the door clad only in his underwear. He saw Jake's soaked condition and frowned. "What's up?"

Jake brushed Reed aside and stepped into the trailer. He scanned the bank of monitors they had installed in a cabinet against one wall, studying their hazy, dark screens. Even the infrared camera positioned along the road showed nothing.

Noticing the direction of Jake's gaze, Reed said turned down his stereo. "It's raining too hard to see anything."

"That's what bothers me. I didn't consider a storm."

Reed shrugged. "It'll just last a few hours."

Jake shook his head. "A lot can happen in a few hours."

Reed started to reply, but Jake cut him off. "I've got a bad feeling about this storm. I'm going to patrol the wall, maybe walk down the road a bit."

"Do you want me to come along?" he motioned toward his pants and shirt thrown across the back of the sofa.

"No. Go stay with Jessica. You remember where I stored the ammo?"

"Sure. You buried it beneath the chicken coop."

Jake nodded. "Just outside the north-facing chicken coop wall, I buried another crate. If things go badly, dig it up."

Reed began dressing. Jake went back outside. It was impossible to see if any Staggerers or anyone else lurked outside the wall. He would just have to trust to luck. He pulled his pistol, opened the gate, and stepped through. Immediately, he knew he had made a huge mistake. Shadows rushed at him from the darkness. He raised the pistol, but something hit him across the back of the head. He went down, coughing up a mouthful of mud as he tried to rise. A foot pressed down between his shoulder blades, forcing his face back into the mud. He was drowning in a mud puddle. He sputtered out his last breath just as the boot eased its pressure. Hands rolled him over onto his back. He gasped to take in air. Illuminated by a flash of lightning, a face grinned down at him. Water dripped from the brim of a Stetson. It wasn't a Staggerer, but he wished it was.

The Cowboy!

"Last time we met, you tried to kill me."

Jake spat out a clump of mud. "I regret missing."

Levi stared down at him. "You'll soon regret it more."

With a defiant tone, he said, "Levi, right? Get it over with. It's wet out here."

"Oh, I think I'll take my time. Why don't we go visit your friends?"

"What friends?" Jake regretted sending Reed to stay with Jessica. Now, they would have no warning. He had failed them all.

"The fat guy and the chick," Levi replied.

Two men grabbed him by the arms, stretching them to their limits, almost wrenching them from his shoulder blades. They half-dragged, half-carried him though the open gate and up the path. Six men broke away from the large group. Two went to check out Reed's RV. The others headed toward the smokehouse and work shed. In total, Jake counted fifteen men. He suspected more lurked in the shadows outside the gate. Levi had a small army.

To his astonishment, one of his soldiers was a woman. She stared at him for the entire journey. Her eyes were as dark as her cropped black hair. They were cold and calculating. She seemed amused at his plight. The scar on her forehead lent her an air of fierceness. When he smiled at her, she jabbed him hard in the stomach with the butt of her AK47.

"It's not polite to stare," she said.

"My pardon," he gasped.

They were on Jessica and Reed before the pair knew what was happening. Two men slammed Reed to the floor. The woman pointed her AK47 at Jessica. Jessica wisely tried nothing foolish, but she continued to stare at the woman with the gun. Levi plopped down the couch and shook out his Stetson, sending water flying everywhere.

"Nice place you've got here. I'll bet you're wondering how we found you."

Jake was, but he wasn't going to give Levi the pleasure of asking. "I suppose you floated here down the wash like all the other trash."

His captors tossed him to the floor. One of them delivered a swift kick to his ribs. The pain radiated through his abdomen and chest like a fire brand.

"Okay, bad guess. The Yellow Pages?" He waited for another blow.

"I watched the jets. They seemed to favor this area. I wondered why. Yesterday, one of my men found fresh jeep tracks. I knew it was you."

"Now that you know where we live, why don't you drop by sometime? Leave your cell phone number. We'll chat."

This time the blow landed near the base of his spine, sending a spasm of pain racing up his back and radiating out into his arms and legs. His lower body went numb. He hoped it wasn't a permanent disability. He decided that his barbed remarks were serving no useful purpose and might hasten his demise.

"Oh, I think we'll stay. It's a nice place. You've done a good job." Levi picked up a University of Arizona throw pillow. "Though I think your taste sucks." He tossed the pillow into the corner, knocking over and breaking a lamp. He covered his mouth with his hand and arched his eyebrows in mock regret. "Oops. Never mind. I'll do a bit of shopping."

Jake couldn't resist one more jab. "Just when I had it the way I liked it."

This time, Levi raised his hand before he received another kick. Jake was grateful for the brief respite of pain. "Be careful with our guest," he said to the two men standing above Jake. "Mustn't damage him too badly. There's no sport in mercy killing."

Great, Jake thought. *They want to play games with me before killing me.*

Levi's gaze strayed toward Jessica. The tall female with the AK47 noticed the direction of his gaze and frowned. "She can stay," he said.

"I'll take whatever you're going to do to him," she snapped, nodding her head in Jake's direction.

Don't be stupid, Jake thought. *Play for time.*

Levi shook his head. "I don't think you really mean that. I owe him and he'll pay dearly. You … might be useful." Several of Levi's men laughed. Fear flashed on Jessica's face. He turned to Reed. "You, fat man, what do you do?"

"I'm a science teacher," Reed answered. He tried to keep his voice calm and even, but failed miserably. "I built the bomb that almost killed you."

Levi stared at him a long moment before pronouncing, "You might be useful as well." He turned back to face Jake. "I'm not sure just how to deal with you. I've contemplated this moment many times in my mind, but the reality is much sweeter. Oh, don't worry. Your death won't be quick. That's too easy. I have something extra special in mind for you, Copper."

"I can't wait," Jake replied. "I love surprises, and I'm not a cop."

Levi reached down ripped the Arizona Ranger's badge from his shirt. He stared at it a moment before saying, "The badge says otherwise."

"It's a souvenir."

"You act like a cop, so either you're a cop wannabe, or you're an ex-cop. I hate cops."

He tossed the badge across the room. It struck a photo of Jake standing beside a hunter kneeling over a trophy elk and shattered the glass. He turned to his men.

"Take the fat guy and the girl to the shed. Check it good for anything they might use to escape, and then post a guard. I'll deal with them later."

"You want us to tie them up, Levi?" one of the men asked.

"Duh! Of course I do, you dimwit. I said I don't want them to escape."

The dimwit and two others forced Jessica and Reed's hands behind their backs and tied them with rope. Reed cried out in pain as the rough cord bit deeply into his flesh. Jessica said nothing, but the tall woman smiled as the ropes were tightened. Jessica cast one last forlorn look in Jake's direction before they were forced from the room with guns jammed in their backs.

I'll get you out of this, he promised, *just as soon as I figure out how to save myself.*

Levi nudged Jake with the toe of his boot. He winced as the boot touched a sore spot near his ribs. "When the rain stops, I'm going to stake you out like a scarecrow and watch you die slowly." He smiled. "Unless a Staggerer gets to you first."

He jerked his head and two men grabbed Jake roughly by the arms, tied his hands behind his back, and then dragged him from the room. He fought his way to his feet and staggered between them on numb legs, biting his tongue to keep from crying out as the feeling slowly returned. They escorted him down the path and across the canyon floor, applying a liberal amount of blows to urge him to move faster. The stream, fed by heavy rains higher up the slope, was now a raging river lapping hungrily at the top of its banks. The roar of water echoed down the canyon, almost drowning out the claps of thunder that accompanied the fireworks coloring the sky. At first, he was afraid they were going to ignore their leader's orders and toss him into the raging waters to die when the water slammed him into the narrow drainage pipe running beneath the wall, but after standing him at the edge of the crumbling bank for a few minutes and laughing, they marched him to the smokehouse and locked the door.

His side ached and his head pounded, but he was still alive. He was glad Levi wanted revenge more than immediate satisfaction. Dead men can't escape. Maybe Levi believed in *Jake's Law #10 – Serve revenge in big doses*. He hoped so. He needed time to decide on his next move. Weary, but not defeated, he collapsed on the floor to rest.

* * * *

Jessica hadn't had time to react as the armed intruders pushed into the house. Too late, she realized her pistol was across the room out of reach. Resisting would serve no purpose, only hasten her death. Two of the men slammed Reed to the floor, knocking off his glasses. He groaned in pain, as he groped the floor for them. A tall fierce woman with a scar on the right side of her forehead leveled an AK47 at her. Water dripped from her wet, dark hair onto her face, but she didn't blink. Her cold stare was more frightening than the gun she held. Jessica held her breath, believing she was about to die, as the woman's finger toyed with the trigger for a few seconds.

A man wearing a Stetson entered the room. She knew immediately it was Levi, the cowboy. He glanced at the woman, and she withheld her fire. Jessica released her breath but stood rooted to the spot, afraid to move. They tossed Jake to the floor beside Reed. Her heart sank.

Jake's stoic refusal to give an inch to Levi strengthened her resolve. She had rather die with Jake than become a plaything for the lowlife characters filling the room. To her disappointment, Levi had other plans for her. She trembled as he pronounced Jake's sentence of death. She and Reed would remain prisoners for as long as they remained useful. Reed was resourceful. She didn't doubt he would find ways to prove his worth. To such a bunch of animals, she had only one thing of value they were interested in – her body. If the look of hatred from the tall, dark-haired bitch were any indication, she might not live long enough for even that humiliation.

Their captors locked them inside the old ranch house, now a work shed. They stripped the shop of anything sharp that might sever their bonds, unceremoniously dumping the items outside in the rain to rust. Reed collapsed against a wall, wheezing. She joined him.

"Jake will get us out somehow," she said. In spite of their predicament, she found that she believed Jake would survive. Her mind refused to picture him dead. It gave her an iota of hope. However miniscule it might be, hope was the key to survival. She could endure whatever Levi's men did to her, but she couldn't survive if she gave up hope.

Reed glanced up at her frowning. "You have a lot of faith him. We're trussed up like Thanksgiving turkeys with no weapons, surrounded by a couple dozen of Levi's men. I don't see our chances as very good."

"If we were the type to give up, we'd have been dead a long time ago. We survived the plague. We'll survive this, at least long enough to come up with a plan."

Reed stared at her for a minute. "Maybe you're right. The alternative is to die. I don't much feel like dying."

She leaned back against the wall, taking comfort from its cool adobe brick. Her words were meant to buoy her spirits more than Reed's. Inwardly, she didn't hold out much hope. It was obvious that Levi desired her, and that the dark-haired bitch didn't much like the idea. She could play one against the other, but she would be treading a razor's fine edge. She didn't see that she had much choice. She was helpless, tied up, and didn't know what tomorrow might bring. She closed her eyes and let the sound of the rain lull her to sleep.

16

June 22, 2016   Galiuro Mountains, AZ –

True to his word, Levi wasted no time extracting his revenge. Two days later, as soon as the sporadic monsoon rains had run their course, two men dragged Jake from his smokehouse cell and deposited him at Levi's feet. His body felt as if it had been used as a piñata for a baseball team fiesta. His legs and hands were numb from being bound so tightly for two days, and he was weak from hunger. Though his captors had come in to check on him several times, each time removing armloads of his smoked meat, no one had bothered feeding him or bringing him water. He had staved off thirst by sipping water from a dirty puddle on the floor, but the remaining smoked meats dangled enticingly just out of reach. He had not seen or heard from Jessica or Reed during his captivity, but he guessed they were still alive.

"I hope you've been contemplating your fate," Levi said.

"I've been busy wondering how to increase the energy output from the solar panels. I've been thinking of putting in a bowling alley, and I need more power for the pin setters."

"I'm glad you still have your sense of humor. You'll need it."

One of the men approached him with a knife. Jake braced himself for death, but the man grinned, as he waved the blade in his face. After slicing away Jake's shirt and pants, he tossed the shredded clothes on the ground. Next, he removed Jake's shoes and socks, leaving him clad only in his underwear. Then he cut the rope binding his legs. Jake bit his lip to keep from screaming aloud from the pain of blood returning to his numb limbs.

"Take him out into the desert and tie him to something, a rock or a tree." Levi grinned. "A cactus will do."

The man with the knife laughed.

"Let's see how good your survival skills are when staked out naked for the predators to chew on," Levi said. "Before you go, what's your name? Maybe I'll put up a marker if we can find anything left of your bones."

"Jake Blakely, but don't bother with the marker. I won't need it, and I don't give a shit what your name is. I'll leave your bones lying on the ground for the buzzards to pick clean."

"Bold talk from a corpse."

"Oh, I don't know. Look around you. Dead men are coming back to life all over the country."

"After the animals get through with you, there won't be enough left to turn Staggerer."

As they marched him down the path on wobbly legs, Jake surveyed his ranch, which had undergone a vast transformation since his capture. While he had been locked away, Levi's men had moved in and taken over. Several motorcycles, an SUV, and a large truck sat by the gate. Tents covered the space between the trailer and the cliff. His vegetable garden had been trampled. Motorcycle tire tracks crisscrossed the once productive patch of ground. His goats were roasting over a spit. The chicken coop was empty. Jake regretted their loss more than the loss of the ranch. With all the smoked meat and canned goods he had available, their deaths seemed useless and cruel. His invaders were like a horde of locusts, devouring everything in their path and then moving on.

Two men tossed him into the back of his own jeep and drove through the gate. He watched his ranch disappear behind him, doubting that he would never see it again. So much of his life had gone into his fortress, but in the end, it had failed him, just as he had failed Jessica and Reed, the only two people in his life he could call friends.

The San Pedro River was deep and running with muddy water. Trees and brush floated downstream in the swift current. Most of the year the river was either dry or contained a trickle of water. Now, it drained the entire west slope of the Galiuros. The jeep's tall exhausts allowed it to ford the river, but the current shoved the jeep downstream until the wheels caught traction. Farther from the river, the Riparian river growth of trees, reeds, and brush changed to mesquite, saguaros, and prickly pear cactus. The saguaros were swollen with stored rain water.

The journey over the rain-washed San Pedro River Road was torture on his already stiff and bruised body. He slammed into the rear seat with each wash they crossed, each rock they struck, and every cattle guard they rumbled over. The driver took special delight in seeking out the deepest ruts.

His gaze fell upon a sliver of broken hacksaw blade amid the trash covering the floor of the jeep and felt a glimmer of hope. He grasped it between his hands and shoved it inside the waistband of his underwear. If they didn't strip him naked or decide to beat him senseless before staking him out, he might have a slim chance of escape.

They took a left on the Cascabal Road cutoff, continued for another half an hour, and then pulled over.

"This is good enough," one of them said.

Jake checked his surroundings. He recognized the area as being south of Alder Wash. A lone Palo Verde tree, surrounded by young nursery cacti growing in its shade, thrust from a patch of sand between two large boulders. A dozen yards away, a twenty-foot saguaro loomed over it. Jake gulped, hoping they didn't decide to truss him to the saguaro. The sharp spines would kill him before he got the chance to escape. Luckily for him, they had brought only a short length of rope. The girth of the water-swelled saguaro was too great. Instead, they chose the Palo Verde tree as his execution spot.

"He's not in the sun," one of them said, as they lashed his chest and feet to the Palo Verde's main trunk. "The tree will shade him."

"What difference will it make? The coyotes or a mountain lion will get him soon enough." He stared at Jake. "Or maybe a hungry wolf." He tilted his head back and howled several times.

The other man chuckled at the other's antics. "Right. Wish we could watch."

"I can leave you here and come back later," the first said.

The second glanced around and said, "Nah. I ain't staying here."

Jake watched his jeep drive away before testing his bonds. His captors had done a thorough job. He could barely move his arms. The ropes bit deeply into his naked flesh of his chest and ankles. After the rains, the ground was damp. The heat licked up the moisture like a thirsty dog, creating a layer of hot, humid air that clung to the ground like an invisible fog. He was sweating profusely by the time he managed to lift the sliver of saw blade from his underwear. It took him almost an hour more to saw through the tough ropes binding his hands. He almost dropped the blade, as the pain of blood circulating again hit him. He gritted his teeth and continued cutting.

Finally, his chest was free. He untied the knot binding his feet with clumsy, numb fingers and collapsed onto the sand exhausted. He was free, but he was almost naked with a sliver of saw blade as his only tool. He had no weapons, no food, or water, but he was survivalist. It was time to put his training to the ultimate test.

Night would fall soon. As quickly as the heat rose during the day, it fell just as rapidly at night. He might not freeze to death, but he would burn a lot of precious calories he didn't have to stay warm. He needed food and shelter. Shelter wasn't as difficult as food. There were caves and deep crevices in the rocks in nearby Kielberg Canyon. He could find water still pooled in hard-packed earth or in natural stone tanks, but with no weapons and no string for snares, game might be difficult to obtain. Jojoba nuts, yucca fruit, mesquite pods, cactus fruit, elderberries, Palo Verde seeds – the list of edible desert plants was long, but finding them was sometimes a scavenger hunt. He began by collecting the seeds from the Palo Verde that had been his cross. Now, it could save him. The green pods were tough to peel, but the peas inside were sweet and nourishing. He ate them almost without chewing, eager to satisfy the knot his empty stomach had become. He was still hungry when the last pod was devoured, but he was no longer starving.

The heat baked his exposed skin, and his feet found every burr, every cactus spine, every sharp stone buried in the sand. Some type of foot covering was his next challenge. The tough outer leaves of a yucca plant proved just the thing. After sawing the leaves from the plant with his blade and tying a folded bundle around his feet with tough fibers pulled from the leaves, he took a few experimental steps. What his footwear lacked in fashion they more than made up for in durability.

He grazed from the few berries and edible plants, like chia, that he found along the way. His destination was not random. He had a plan. The canyon where the abandoned mine lay, where they had tested Reed's explosives, had scraps of metal. From metal he could make crude weapons and tools, not enough to take back his ranch from armed intruders, but enough to survive, and survival itself was a blow to Levi's carefully crafted plan for revenge. The mine was in a side canyon of Kielberg Canyon

He couldn't help Jessica or Reed. Their fates rested, for the time being at least, in the hands of the cowboy. He tried to dismiss their plight from his mind. He had enough problems without allowing his guilt of failing them to move him along foolish paths. However they suffered, Levi wouldn't kill them, at least not for a while. A while was all he needed.

Twice, he passed small puddles of muddy water. With nothing with which to carry water, he drank his fill, hoping he didn't get dysentery from the dirty water. He gathered prickly pear fruit, gouging holes in them and squeezing them to force out the sweet nectar. He startled some mourning doves, quail, and roadrunners in his passing, but had nothing with which to kill or trap them. He threw rocks at a pair of fat quail but missed by a margin of which he was not proud. His skills as a primitive hunter were sadly lacking. He had relied too much on guns and technology. Now, he would have to rely on his wits.

He passed several small *Sobaipuri* Indian ruins, no more than piles of stone excavated in the '70s. The *Sobaipuri* were related to the *Pima* Indians and perhaps descendents of the *Hohokam* who once inhabited the region. He sifted through the sand with his fingers and dug up two small flint arrowheads that might prove useful both to start a fire and as a cutting tool. Flint was hard to find in the area. Quartzite was more plentiful. In fact, an entire Arizona town was named for the mineral.

It was dusk by the time he reached the mine canyon. The damp air was already growing chilly. He needed fire. Using the last rays of the dying sun, he finally found a piece of steel from the shattered ore cart. Tender was another matter. After the rain, everything was still wet. Luck was with him, as he found a few scraps of wood beneath the overturned ore cart. He rubbed a piece of wood on the edge of the cart, carefully collecting the dry powder in his hand. When he judged he had a sufficient quantity, he squatted out of the wind beside the same boulder behind which they had sheltered from the explosion, laid out his meager pile of tender, and patiently began striking metal to one of the flint arrowheads, showering the wood with sparks. It took much longer than he anticipated, but the tender at last began smoldering. He gently blew into the smoking tender until he coaxed a miniscule flame to life. Gradually feeding bits of wood to the precious flame, he soon had a glowing blaze. It was a tiny fire, producing more psychological comfort than true warmth, but it sufficed.

He curled up naked beside the fire and tried to sleep, but sleep wouldn't come. Anger and guilt in equal proportions troubled his mind – anger at what had been done to him, and guilt at how he had let his friends down. He wanted to strike back at Levi, but knew now wasn't the time. He abandoned thoughts of sleep and paced back and forth in the dark slapping his arms to keep warm.

* * * *

June 23, 2016   Kielberg Canyon, Galiuro Mountains, AZ –

Morning's first faint light creeping over the mountain tops lifted his spirits, but didn't warm him. He sifted through pieces of metal from the mine cart, finally locating one that was long enough and sharp enough for his purpose. Further diligence was soon rewarded with an old coffee pot half buried in the sand, refuse of the old mine site. With it he could collect water and store it, if he could find it. He searched along the cliff until the steady drip of water falling reached him. A trickle of water dripped from the rocks, as it found its way down the mountain from the recent rains. It was only a few drops at a time, but he was patient. He knew the best place to store water in a desert was inside your body. After the pot was half full, he drank it, relishing its slightly salty wetness, and placed it back beneath the slow drip to fill while he saw to his breakfast.

His stomach growled to announce its emptiness. He thought of the smoked sausages in his smokehouse and yearned for just a taste of one. He would have to settle for what he could forage. He recognized the arrow-shaped leaves and red stems of greenthread plants. They grew in abundance above the four-thousand-foot elevation. With them and a handful of elderberries, he brewed a pot of Navajo tea. What it lacked in flavor, it made up for in satisfying the gnawing hunger in his belly.

From a length of tree branch washed down by the rains, he fashioned a crude spear with the metal he had salvaged, attaching it with heavy fiber thread ripped from a yucca plant. He hefted it in his hand to test the balance. The Native Americans would laugh at it, but it would serve its purpose. He now had a weapon. Next, he needed clothes. He knew of two places to obtain clothing. One was his ranch, which was out of the question. The other was one of the local ranches, and that meant facing zombies. *Better zombies than men with guns*. With spear in hand, he set out. The miles wore on him, sapping his little remaining strength. His beating and near starvation had weakened him. He leaned more heavily on his spear for support.

He found a spot where a tree whose roots the current had eroded leaned over the river. He could climb the tree, cross the swollen river, and descend via the trees branches dangling over the other side. He performed a balancing act as he climbed the tree, using the spear as a balancing pole. The cold water rushing by beneath him didn't look inviting, especially with the boulders protruding from the current. He almost made it. Just over halfway across, the roots loosed their grip on the wet earth. The tree and he fell. He went to his knees, clasping the tree with both arms. The tree shuddered to a stop inches from the water. He resumed his crossing on hands and knees, the rough bark digging into tender flesh.

The first ranch house was a blackened ruin. The shattered shell of a propane tank lay splintered beside the house, either the cause of the fire or as a result of it. He fared little better at the next ranch. The owners had time to pack everything before vacating, leaving the doors wide open for vandals and the wildlife. Piles of animal scat stained the carpet. Each house he came to had been thoroughly looted, meaning that he wasn't the only survivor in the area. The corpses of a couple of zombies meant the survivor was armed.

His makeshift sandals were ragged strips worn through by the time he stumbled upon the next ranch house. As he clambered over the fence, a rifle shot forced him to the ground. Someone still lived there. A male voice called out.

"Get off my property."

"I just need water and something to wear," he replied.

"I'll hit you next time. I mean it. Git!"

Jake decided a naked man with a crude spear couldn't win an argument with a rifle. He left.

He abandoned the idea of nearby ranches. They were few and scattered across the valley, taking too much time to search, and time was another thing he didn't have. Levi's men could discover he was missing at any time. His best hope lay in San Manuel.

He avoided the road, following the river until it began to curve away from the town, and then cut cross country. He went up and down washes and arroyos and over ridges, trying to avoid teddy bear cholla, prickly pear, and saguaros with his naked body. The sun beat down on him unmercifully. He focused his attention on the direction in which he was going and plodded onward. His yucca sandals disintegrated along the way. He continued barefoot. His feet touched asphalt before he realized he was on the outskirts of town. He immediately spotted zombies prowling the streets. Normally, he would have left them alone, especially in his haggard condition, but now he didn't have that option. It was almost dark and food and clothing might be in one of the houses. He had to reach them. The creatures' emaciated condition and slow gait encouraged him. They were Shamblers, not Runners. He hoped they were weaker than he was. If he moved quickly, he could subdue them silently without alerting other creatures, perhaps stronger ones, of his presence.

Gripping his spear with both hands, he raced across the open ground toward the first one, a man who might have once been a cook or butcher wearing a bloodstained apron. Jake didn't have time to wonder if the blood had been from its profession or from its prey. It noticed him when he was less than twenty feet away and lurched toward him, a low wail rising from its throat. He jabbed the spear through the creature's eye and into the brain, yanking it free before the zombie could fall and wrench the spear from his grasp. The second zombie, now alerted, closed on him just as a third lumbered into view, saw him, and growled. Outnumbered, he had to act fast. Using the spear as a vaulting pole, he rammed the second zombie in the chest with both feet. It stumbled backwards and fell. Before it could rise, he stabbed it through the skull.

The third creature was in better condition, faster than a Shambler, but not as strong as a Runner. It moved swiftly and was upon him before he could recover his spear from the second creature's head. He kicked at it to keep it at bay, while he struggled to free his spear. Just as he thought he would have to abandon his only weapon and run for his life, he managed to yank it free. He stabbed it into the third zombie's heart several times. Even injured, perhaps fatally, it continued its pursuit. Jake spun on his heel and rammed it into the back of the creature's skull, just beneath the occipital ridge. He yanked the blade sideways, severing the creature's cervical vertebrae, but the haft of the flimsy spear snapped, leaving his precious steel blade embedded in the creature's skull. He tossed the piece of useless wood to the ground and fought to catch his breath.

The long walk into town and the battle with the three creatures had sapped his strength. He couldn't face more of the creatures, especially weaponless. Still breathing hard, he stumbled to the nearest house. The door was locked, but he broke a window and crawled inside, careful of the broken glass beneath his already bloody bare feet. He was relieved that no irate homeowner with a shotgun confronted him for his act of breaking and entering. In the post-apocalyptic world, justice was often swift without trial or explanation.

In the kitchen, he located two cans of peaches, the only food not devoured by invading pack rats and hordes of insects. His hand trembled, as he used the can opener to get at the can's contents. The syrup was sweet and satisfying. He drained the first can, letting juice dribble down his chin and onto his chest, before devouring its contents using his dirty fingers. Satisfied, he tossed the empty can aside and began searching the kitchen for anything useful. He smiled when he saw an eight-inch chef's knife lying beside the sink. He picked it up. Its weight felt good in his hand, and the balance was superb. On impulse, he also took the six-inch vegetable knife from the knife block. With weapons in hand, he inspected the rest of the house. The bedroom was a shambles. Clothing was strewn over the bed and floor from the hasty departure of the former homeowners. The only articles of clothing he found that fit were a pair of denim jeans two inches too short and a black tee shirt with a list of Van Halen tour dates and cities for their 2012 tour. It would have to do.

Digging beneath the bed, he found a pair of work boots. They were a size too big, but with two pairs of socks, they sufficed. He found no weapons other than the two kitchen knives, now tucked into his belt. He had better luck in the garage. He pocketed a Bic lighter and a case pocketknife with a file and two blades. A collection of yard tools hanging from a rack on the wall caught his eye. Most were useless as weapons – an electric hedge trimmer, a jig saw, a hoe, a shovel, a rake – but one had potential. He picked up the pair of large hedge shears, admiring its twelve-inch blades and sixteen-inch wooden handle. Using a wrench from a toolbox, he dismantled the shears, testing the feel of one of the blades in his hand. It was heavy enough and sharp enough to be an effective machete. He gave the blade a few minute's attention with a rat-tail file to hone the edges to a razor-sharp finish. As an afterthought, he removed the tines from the rake and kept the handle to use as a walking staff.

Now, clothed and properly weaponed, he set about gathering any small items that might prove useful, including the remaining can of peaches, and dropped them in a child's SpongeBob Squarepants backpack he found hanging from a hook by the door. He felt foolish carrying it, but beggars couldn't be choosers. He couldn't ignore *Jakes' Law # 9 – Use the tools you've got.* He tried not to dwell on the fate of the child that had owned the bag or its parents. Too many people had died to make it personal. There were just three people he cared about, and two were prisoners. He had to do something about it, but not yet. He wasn't ready for a confrontation with Levi.

His exhaustion overwhelmed him as he was planning his next move. He made certain the doors were secured and curled up on the bed. He was taking a chance, but he couldn't continue without rest. He fell asleep almost immediately.

* * * *

June 24, 2016   San Manuel, AZ –

He awoke just before dawn, better rested but sore. One by one, he examined the nearby houses, gathering what items he deemed necessary or useful – a ball of twine, a flashlight and extra batteries, a cheap compass, a light jacket for cooler nights, a small mirror, a few bottles of water, chlorine tablets for an RV water tank. The water purification tablets would make drinking water from springs and creeks safer. The home's former occupants had been camping enthusiasts. An all-season tent was tempting but too bulky to transport. A roll of plastic tarp was lighter and would serve the same purpose, as well as catch rain water. A canteen, a collapsible plastic five-gallon water bag, a sleeping bag, and camp cookware went into backpack, followed by two rolls of duct tape. Its myriad of uses would come in handy.

He coiled a length of climbing rope he found hanging from a rafter around the outside of the pack. Fate seemed to favor him as he came across a pair of leather hiking boots in his size. He discarded the old boots but kept both pair of socks. Most houses had already been thoroughly ransacked, but one pantry produced several cans of beans and soup. His child's backpack was full. He added items to a pillow case and suspended it from his belt. The one object he most desired he couldn't find – a pistol or rifle.

He glanced out the window at the sound of a trashcan being overturned. His search had attracted unwanted attention from zombies, not all of them as slow and emaciated as the first three. He decided it was time to leave. He knew remaining near San Manuel would be dangerous. If the zombies didn't get him, some of Levi's men would eventually discover his escape and search him out. His best bet for safety lay in the mountains with which he was familiar.

The Galiuro Mountains were a maze of canyons, washes, ridges, and peaks. He decided on the upper elevations east of San Manuel where water, game, and trees for firewood were more abundant. Hefting his brightly colored backpack, his rolled up tarp and sleeping bag, his makeshift machete, and his rake handle walking stick, he started out.

Escape wasn't as easy as he hoped. He avoided most of the zombies by dodging in and out of houses and through backyards, but one persistent creature, an extremely large specimen, continued to dog his trail. Finally, realizing that the zombie's untiring pursuit would outlast his remaining store of energy, he stopped to fight at the edge of the river. In his weakened condition, it was a risky move. He dropped his pack and gear, and allowed the creature to catch up. Part of its lower jaw was missing, but it still retained enough teeth to cause considerable damage. Its size, over two hundred and fifty pounds, would work in its favor. When the zombie saw Jake, it wailed and quickened its pace.

When it was within striking distance, he faced it with his makeshift machete. He fended off the first attack with the blunt edge of the blade to judge the creature's strength, which proved to be considerably more than his. He realized he could take no chances. As the creature raced at him the second time, he backed up, and then leaped aside and brought the blade down on the side of creature's neck. The sharp blade sliced deeply into the tender flesh above the collar bone. When he wrenched the blade free, blood sprayed from the wound in rapid pulses as the artery drained. The creature continued to lumber toward him while the last of its strength slowly ebbed. Jake kept backing away until the creature finally collapsed to the ground at his feet, dead. He wiped the bloody blade on the creature's shirt and rolled its corpse into the river. The current swiftly sped it downstream and out of view.

He was still bruised and sore from his beating and exhausted from his journey into San Manuel and his fight with the zombies. He wanted nothing more than to rest, but he knew he couldn't linger in the area. He was too exposed. If he didn't reach his destination before he collapsed, he never would. The lure of sleep nagged at him with every step, but he ignored it. Each foot in elevation he gained meant safety. He followed one of the canyons northeast of San Manuel because it was easier hiking than the Copper Creek trail that ran higher along the ridges. In places, the runoff from the rain was deep and swift, channeled by the narrow canyon walls. Fording the streams was dangerous, and the cold water drained his energy. In spite of his condition, he made good time, reaching Bluebird Mine Road just as the last light of day was failing.

He gathered what dry brush he could find and built a small campfire. Sitting down to a dinner of hot soup, followed by half the can of peaches, he finally allowed his weariness to overcome him. He stripped off his wet clothing, hung them to dry beside the fire, and collapsing on top of his sleeping bag naked. He ignored the voice inside his head telling him to secure the area and trusted to luck that he would see the sun rise again. He rolled up in the sleeping bag and slept.

17

June 22, 2016   Split Rock Canyon, AZ –

Jake was gone. Through a window in the work shed, Jessica watched in horror as two of Levi's men dragged him to the jeep and drove away while Levi stood on the balcony of Jake's seized house smiling down on the proceedings like a vengeful judge presiding over a hanging. She didn't expect to feel as she did. After all, Jake was just a man with whom she had traded sex for a safe place to stay and training in how to survive in the new world. She didn't love him. She felt something for him, some emotion just beyond gratitude, but she wasn't certain what it was. It was certainly less than she had felt for her boyfriend. Whatever emotion coursed through her veins, she still didn't want him to die.

"Don't give up on him yet," Reed said.

She turned to him. "He's tied up and naked. What do you expect him to do?"

Reed's brow furrowed as he stared at her. "What's with the sudden concern? He doesn't care about us."

She found herself in the awkward position of defending Jake. "He's a loner. Being around people was something new to him."

"Now you're making excuses for him?"

"I'm not … Oh, shut up."

When one of the guards walked by the window, stopped and made lewd gestures at her, she walked away from the window and sat on a stool by the workbench. They had been prisoners in the one room house for two days. Food and water was brought to them sporadically, but going to the bathroom was a humiliating experience, as she was forced to squat beside the building with her guards standing over her watching and smiling. She knew it wouldn't be long before Levi decided her fate.

She had seen the way he had looked at her, like he was staring through her clothes. She couldn't use him like she had Jake. Levi was a hard, dangerous man. Besides, the black-haired bitch that orbited him like a moon wouldn't allow that to happen. He would use her like a whore and discard her with the trash. She would become like one of the other girls around the camp, doing drudge work and keeping the men happy. It was fate she didn't wish to contemplate.

"Do you have a plan?" she asked.

"I'm going to try to be as useful to Levi as I can. It's the only thing I've got to offer him."

His veiled reference to her sex didn't amuse her. "I don't know. I don't think his men would shy away from anal sex with a cute fat guy."

Reed fumed and glared at her.

"I'm sorry," she said. "You didn't deserve that."

His features softened. "Jake will find a way to come after us." He nodded his head as he spoke, as if he were trying to convince himself.

"I thought you said we were own our own."

"He'll never give up this ranch. Freeing us will be … collateral."

"They're going to kill him." The truth left a bitter taste in her mouth.

Reed ignored her. He looked around the workshop at Jake's reloading machines. "I've been studying these machines. I think I can use them. If I can make myself useful …"

Jessica shook her head. "Levi will never trust you. He doesn't trust his own men. He only allows two or three of them around him, and the bitch, of course. He keeps the rest at a distance. Oh, if they had only left something to use as a weapon. I'd rather go down fighting than wind up one of Levi's whores."

"Jake mentioned something buried on the north side of the chicken coop wall. I'm figuring it's weapons of some sort. That's the kind of secret he liked to keep."

Jessica perked up. "If we could get to them …"

Reed guffawed. "Fat chance of that. They've already slaughtered the goats and chickens. If they saw either of us around there, they would suspect something was up."

"The water pump is nearby. Couldn't you make up an excuse to check on it?"

While Reed considered her proposal, she returned to the window. One of the men grabbed a young girl, barely sixteen, and dragged her into one of the tents. The girl struggled as best she could, but it was futile. Her fate was sealed. Was that her future, a whore for Levi's army? She made up her mind that she would die before she let one of the creatures calling themselves men touch her.

"I can try, but not too soon or he'll be suspicious."

"Don't wait too long," she warned. "Levi doesn't strike me as patient."

Two armed men came for them an hour later and escorted them to the house, shoving Reed in the back with the butt of a rifle when he moved too slowly for them. She noticed that Levi had already made himself at home. He sat in Jake's favorite leather chair with a bottle of whiskey beside him. His raven-haired angel hovered near him like a faithful dog. She sneered when Jessica entered the room. A vein throbbed beneath the scar on her temple.

"I hope you've been comfortable," Levi said.

"As comfortable as your guards would allow," Reed answered, "Though a bed would have been nice."

Jessica ignored Reed and his attempt at chit-chat and snapped, "What did you do with Jake?"

Levi stared at her for a moment, and then smiled. "We staked him out for the mountain lions to gnaw on. As a hunter, I'm sure he appreciated the irony."

A rage she couldn't control swept over her. "Fuck you!" she shouted and lunged at him.

The dark-haired woman took a menacing step toward her, growling deeply in her throat, as her hand fingered the long knife at her hip. Levi stopped her with a wave of one hand, grabbing Jessica by the throat with the other. She pulled at his hands as he squeezed the breath from her, but his grip was too strong. Just as she was passing out, he released her. She collapsed to her knees gasping for breath.

"Don't try that again, or I'll let Hawk slice you up. Now, you two can join our little group or die. I leave the choice to you, although I'm sure Hawk here would love to gut you both just for practice."

Reed stepped forward. "I apologize for Jessica. We've both been under a lot of stress lately. I for one am willing to join you. I vote for surviving."

Jessica glared at Reed, unable to speak. She had made a foolish move that had almost cost them their lives. She studied Reed's face. If he was lying to get in Levi's good graces, he was hiding it well. Taking a deep breath she said, "I don't for a minute think you'll let us live long, so go ahead and kill me now."

Levi shook his head slowly. "You have courage, if not wisdom." He looked at Reed. "As a science teacher, you might prove useful, but if you screw with me, I'll hang you outside the wall as zombie bait." His gaze returned to Jessica. The intensity of the look in his eyes made her shudder. "You, however, bear watching. You know how to hate. I like that. You're like me."

At this, Hawk again fingered her knife and paced the room, clearly agitated at the attention he was paying to Jessica.

"I'm nothing like you," Jessica replied. "You're a murderer."

"Murderer? I seem to remember you three killing several of my men. We were no threat to you, yet you took it upon yourselves to become judge, jury, and executioner. By what expediency do you claim that right, yet withhold it from me. I intend to survive. I'll help as many as I can of my choosing to survive with me, but I'll tolerate no slackers or enemies. You must choose."

Quietly, Reed whispered to her, "For God's sake, Jessica. Don't ruin this. He'll kill both of us."

As much as she wanted to drive a knife into Levi's heart, she knew that opportunity wouldn't come without a price. "Okay, I'll play along. I guess I have no choice."

"Kill her," Hawk cried, stepping forward. "Kill her now!"

Levi scowled at her and snapped, "Shut up."

Hawk continued, "She's lying! They both are. Look at her. She'll kill you the first chance she gets."

"Then don't give her the chance. Keep a close eye on her, on both of them, but if you hurt her, I'll make you pay for it."

Hawk fumed as she paced. Her dark eyes focused on Jessica with so much rage and hatred that Jessica feared they would burn her skin. *It's not loyalty*, she thought, *and it's not love. What thread binds her to Levi so tightly?* Jessica knew without a doubt that one false step and Hawk would kill her in spite of Levi's orders. Slowly, she rose to her feet, rubbing her throat where Levi's fingers had dug in so deeply. She backed up and stood beside Reed. Reed's hand pressed into the small of her back trying to reassure her.

He whispered, "Thank God, Jessica. You scared me to death."

Levi stared at them. "My men have removed anything dangerous from the RV. You two can share it for now." He nodded to Reed. "I will allow you limited access to the workshop under guard. I want a few of those bombs you used so effectively against me." He smiled at Jessica. "I advise you to cause no trouble. My people are stupid and a bit ornery. They might act before thinking. Later, we'll discuss your roles in my little society. You may both go now."

Beside her, Reed released his breath. Her anger still simmered just below the surface. She fought to keep it under control. To Reed, Levi's pronouncement had sounded like a reprieve. She had watched Levi's not-so-subtle body language and the way his eyes lingered on her and knew that he wasn't finished with her yet.

* * * *

June 24, 2016 Split Rock Canyon –

However restricted their movement, life in the RV was better than confinement in the workshop. They had beds, a bathroom, and a kitchen to cook their own food. They avoided the other residents of the ranch as much as possible. Reed maintained the solar panels and produced ammunition. She repaired what remained of the vegetable garden, tended to the remaining pigs, and washed clothing for everyone like a camp follower. Everywhere she went, she felt the men's eyes on her. She knew that only their fear of Levi kept them from treating her like they did the other women. She didn't know how long that would last.

Of the five women, two were pregnant, but she doubted they knew who the fathers were or that the fathers cared. Once, when she tried to help one of the pregnant women, heavy with child, as she carried a heavy load, Hawk appeared from nowhere and shoved her to the ground. Looming over her, she smiled down on her.

"Let her do her job."

"She's pregnant," Jessica pointed out. "Look at her. She's weak."

"The weak die."

"What kind of monster are you?"

Hawk's cheek quivered in anger, as she narrowed her eyes at Jessica. She pulled her knife from its scabbard. The sun gleamed off the long steel blade. Fear rose in Jessica's throat, bringing with it the sour taste of bile. For a long, breathless second, she thought she was going to die. Then, to her horror, Hawk slashed out at the pregnant woman instead. The tip of the blade left a long slice along her cheek. The woman screamed in pain, dropped the load she was carrying, and ran off holding her hand to her bleeding cheek. Hawk pointed the bloody blade at Jessica.

"That is what I will do to you if you look at Levi."

Jessica was aghast. Did Hawk think she wanted that animal? "I want to kill him," she replied.

"He is mine," Hawk said. She shoved the knife back into the scabbard and left, leaving Jessica relieved but confused. Had Levi been discussing her with Hawk? What did she know that upset her so?

She discovered the answer sooner than she wished. The next day, Levi paid her a visit. After sending Reed away on the pretext of checking the engine in one of the vehicles, he sat at the table ogling her. She wore a pair of cut off shorts and a t-shirt with no bra, and his lecherous gaze made her decidedly uncomfortable.

"What do you want?" she asked.

"Take off your clothes."

Now I know. She fought the impulse to try to rush past him and remained motionless. She said nothing. Frowning, he rose and walked toward her. "I said take off your clothes."

She stood defiant. "If you want me, you're going to have to rape me, and to do that, you'll have to beat me into submission."

The slap came so quickly that she didn't see his hand move. Her right cheek stung from the heavy blow. He followed the slap with a punch to the abdomen, forcing the air from her lungs and almost doubling her over with pain. He was on her before she could fight back, pinning her right arm behind her back and throwing her to the floor. White hot sabers of excruciating pain lanced up and down her arm and through her injured shoulder, bringing tears to her eyes. Her flailing left arm soon joined the right beneath her. She was unable to move either arm. The sour odor of whiskey was on Levi's breath, as he pressed his face into her neck. With his full weight on her, he ripped away her shirt and tugged down her shorts. She struggled and succeeded in biting his ear, but he ignored the pain, even seemed to enjoy her fighting back. With one hand, he unzipped his pants. She bucked wildly to throw him off, but he was too heavy. Wedged in the narrow hallway of the RV, she couldn't roll over to topple him. Pushing her panties aside, he entered her with one painful thrust. She cried out in pain, but that just emboldened him. He thrust harder, leaning forward to bite her nipples. Unable to resist, she turned her head away and sobbed.

He was finished in a few short minutes. He rose and stared down at her. "That wasn't so bad, was it?" He laughed. "I bet you didn't fight so hard with Jake."

She opened her eyes and looked up at him. "Jake didn't take anything from me," she replied in almost a growl. "I gave it freely. As for you, you took nothing either with all your animal rutting. You could have gotten as much from one of your stinking men or that black-haired whore. Rape is an assault, not sex. You might have gotten off, but to me, it was just a brutal beating. If you expected anything more, I'm sure you were disappointed."

He stared at her for a moment, and then grinned. "It doesn't matter. It won't matter to my men. By the time they get through with you, you'll wish you were nicer to me."

"I'll kill them if they try to touch me. I'll kill you next time."

He laughed at her. "Good luck with that."

He zipped up his pants and walked out. She lay there sobbing for a few minutes. Then, afraid to let Reed see her like that, she pulled up her shorts, threw away the torn shirt and put on a clean one. She wasn't the first woman to be raped and wouldn't be the last one, but it was the last time it would ever happen to her. At her first opportunity, she would kill Levi, even if it meant her death. Such men didn't deserve to live. Now, she understood Jake better. She had thought him unnecessarily callous and cruel, but she had been wrong, or at least his reasons had eluded her until now. She remembered *Jake's Law #6 – Bad people deserve bad ends.* She would see to it that Levi got the end he so richly deserved.

18

June 24, 2016 Galiuro Mountains, AZ –

Jake's camp slowly took shape. Choosing a location in a saddle between two red rhyolite ridges overlooking Rattlesnake Canyon gave him a commanding view of the lower slopes on each side. At about five-thousand feet in altitude, the nights were cooler, but copses of juniper, pine, and oak provided wood for his fire. The plastic tarp draped over a tree limb and secured by rope produced a serviceable shelter against the wind and sun. A bed of pine needles beneath his sleeping bag provided a comfortable resting place. He had gathered prickly pear fruit, chia for tea, wood sorrel for greens, yucca fruit, and ripe elderberries in the lower altitudes as he climbed. These, along with the few canned goods he had scavenged provided his nourishing but lean meals. A small pool of potable water had collected in a nearby natural rock depression from the rains. He filled the collapsible water jug and purified it with the chlorine tablets. If he used it sparingly, the water would last him six or seven days. After that, he would have to search for more.

On his second day in the mountains, he supplemented his meager store of food by catching a rabbit with a twine snare. Two fat quail soon followed. Removing the wooden handle of the eight-inch knife, he mounted it in a slit he laboriously cut in the end of his rake handle. Securing it with heavy twine, and then wrapping the twine with multiple layers of duct tape, he eyed his spear with the judgmental eye of a hunter. It lacked the aerodynamic qualities required for good flight, but as a jabbing weapon, it passed his muster. He was eager to try it out on some of the larger game whose spore he had crossed on his scouting forays.

His most cherished possession was not his weapons, his tent, nor his food, but two rolls of toilet paper he had carefully packed. Removing the cardboard cores had made them compact enough to fit into the backpack. He didn't mind roughing it. In fact, it felt good after so long confined to his ranch to once again be out in nature, but some habits were hard to break, and wiping his ass on leaves was not one he looked forward to.

The key to survival in the wild was conservation of energy. Every calorie burned was one he would have to replace. Even a cheetah pursued its prey only so far before abandoning the chase. He had killed elk, white-tailed deer, mountain goats, and even the occasional javelina, but always through the sight of his rifle. Stalking a deer on foot, getting close enough to stab it with a spear, required more skill than he had ever considered. He had spotted deer tracks the previous day while foraging.

Before sunrise, he set out with his spear in hand, his knife, backpack, and a canteen. He had rubbed mesquite sap and prickly pear juice into his clothes and skin in hopes that the mélange of scents would mask his own human scent. He moved as silently as a shadow through the sparse thicket of brush and trees, stepping cautiously over brittle dead branches, careful to remain downwind of the deer. The deer led him on a winding trek up and down the slope for most of the day. He finally spotted a magnificent buck in a meadow standing knee deep in a patch of yellow Mexican poppy, grazing warily on the tender growth.

He climbed into the lower branches of a pine tree and waited. His hunger begged him to take a chance and attack, but his training stayed his hand. The deer would soon eat its fill and return to the safety of the woods. It's only path led back in his direction. He ignored irritating insect bites and the heat, watching the animal with the intensity of a hawk. He shifted his body occasionally to prevent stiffness but remained vigilant. At last, the buck began moving back toward him, stopping at times for another mouthful of grass. He inched the spear into position, hoping his inexperience with a spear wouldn't betray him. As the deer passed almost directly beneath him, he fell on it, careful to avoid the dangerous antlers. His aim was true. The eight-inch blade pierced the heart, killing it almost instantly.

He took a moment to regard his trophy before removing his smaller knife and gutting the animal. He reluctantly discarded the heart and liver. They would have been nourishing, but his fear of parasites won out. The deer was too heavy to carry to his camp intact. With no way to preserve so much meat, he would have to take what he could easily transport. He hacked off the two rear legs, carved out the loin, and a section of rump roast. These he could slice into thin strips and smoke or roast whole. He regretted wasting the rest of the carcass, but he knew the smell of death would soon draw scavengers. The deer would not be wasted. Already, a crow cawed at him from a nearby treetop, eager for its meal.

He secured the legs with a length of duct tape. He wrapped the loin and rump in a piece of plastic and stuffed them into the backpack. He donned the backpack and slung the legs over his shoulder and around his neck. Loaded down by his heavy burden of meat, the journey back to his camp was exhausting. Only the thought of a thick steak cooking over an open fire kept him going.

He could hardly contain his hunger as the aromatic smoke drifted through the camp. With a little salt he had brought along and some fresh sage gathered from the slope to season it, it tasted as good as any steak he could have produced at home. He followed it with the remainder of the peaches for desert. As his meal settled, he sliced most of the meat into thin strips and hung them from a wooden rack near the fire to slowly smoke and dry. The rest he cooked to serve as his next few meals. He realized he could stay in the mountains until winter, stealing back to San Manuel occasionally for supplies and hunting for meat, but that wasn't in his game plan.

He had worked for ten years to create the perfect retreat. It had sufficed to keep him safe and in reasonable health during the apocalypse. If it had been destroyed by an act of nature, he thought he could have dealt with the loss, but to be taken by force … that he could not allow to go unpunished. He wanted his ranch back, but more than that, he wanted Levi dead. He didn't bother trying to justify his desire as an attempt to rescue his friends or to eliminate a very bad man from society. His reasons were not as altruistic as that. He wanted revenge, pure and simple. He wanted Levi dead, and his band of thugs with him.

Of course, he hoped Reed and Jessica were still alive. He clung to the thought that if Levi wanted them dead, they would have joined him in the desert staked to the Palo Verde tree. Reed would find a way to be useful to survive. Jake didn't hold that against him. Surviving was surviving, and Reed had the instinct for it. However, Jessica was another matter. He had noticed the lecherous stares Levi had leveled in Jessica's direction. He had also noticed the reaction of the dark-haired woman, probably his whore. The thought of Jessica in Levi's bed sickened him. He hoped Jessica would find the idea of being Levi's woman as repugnant as he did, but she had traded sex for security with him. Why not Levi?

No, he thought, deriding himself for underestimating her. She wasn't that kind of woman. She had made a bond with him. There might be no love involved, but at least they had a mutual respect for each other. As he thought about Jessica, her image swam before him – cute but not beautiful; slim, but not waifish; confident, but not overbearing. Whatever the relationship between them, she held nothing back, whereas, he had. He had kept his secrets, not because he didn't trust her or Reed, but because it was in his nature to be secretive. He was glad now that he had revealed the location of the buried crate to Reed. If nothing else, he could use its contents to mollify Levi in a difficult situation.

With Levi searching for him, he would have to keep his cook fires small to avoid detection. That night, satiated by the fresh meat, sleep still eluded him. Jessica's plaintive face haunted him. The wind through the trees was her voice whispering for him to save her. He arose before dawn, his mind made up. He would take back his ranch and free his friends or die in the attempt.

19

June 26, 2016   Split Rock Canyon, Galiuro Mountains –

Levi surveyed his new domain not with the pride of a man who had wrestled it into existence with his bare hands, but with the satisfaction of having taken it by force. In the new world, force trumped all. Might truly did make right. With no laws, the lawless need fear nothing. His men were not farmers or ranchers. They didn't appreciate the effort that had gone into creating the ranch they so callously set about destroying. He had been forced to beat senseless two men who, in a drunken frenzy, began shooting and damaging solar panels on the roof. His object lesson in brutality had halted further wanton acts of destruction, but he realized that he could never change them into anything more than simple scavengers.

Since his unsatisfying encounter with Jessica, Hawk had been cold and distant to him. She followed his instructions but spoke only when he demanded a reply. He didn't mind. Her constant cloying presence annoyed him. She clung to him as if she owned him rather than the other way around. Her rage seethed just below the surface and would soon erupt like a volcano. The likely target would be Jessica, and he wanted to keep her alive, at least for a while. Raping her and threatening to turn her over to his men had humbled her if not cowed her. She refused to meet his gaze the few times they were near one another. He almost quivered in anticipation at the change in her. Before, she had been aloof, looking down on him as a spoiler, a taker. Her admiration for Jake Blakely had slanted her view of the new reality. Now, she understood the meaning of real power, his kind of power, raw and unbounded. Presenting her with Blakely's rotting corpse would break what remained of her spirit. Whatever hope she clung to would vanish. She would come to him, subdued, humbled, and eager to survive under whatever terms he demanded.

He motioned to two of his men. They came over and stood beneath the balcony. "Go get the jeep ready. We're going to pay our former landlord a visit."

He would bring back Blakely's rotting corpse or any remaining parts to show Jessica. That would remove the specter of his presence and show her what fate awaited her and the fat man if she didn't cooperate.

On the journey, his mind was preoccupied with bold matters – killing off the zombie populations of San Manuel and Oracle, looting the entire town for supplies, and expanding his territory to include Oro Valley and Marana. He could build a small army, offer protection to survivors at a price. They would swear allegiance to him or die. He would carve his own little empire from the ashes of the dying world. He would be Lord Levi.

The jeep skidded to a sudden stop, bouncing him back to the present. The driver stared at him, trembling, as he eyed the empty Palo Verde tree.

"He was here," the driver said. "Right there. We tied him to that tree."

"He's not there now," Levi growled.

"Maybe a mountain lion got him," the driver suggested.

Levi got out of the jeep and sauntered over to the tree. He was in no hurry. He knew exactly what he would find. There was no blood, no remains, just pieces of rope lying on the ground, the ends cleanly cut. He shook his head.

"Honest, Boss, we tied him real tight. Just ask Smitty."

"Oh, I will." Before the driver could react, Levi pulled his pistol and shot him between the eyes. The driver slumped over the steering wheel, lying on the horn. Levi jerked him from the seat to silence the horn, dumped him on the ground, and then slid into the driver's seat. The remaining guard trembled in the back of the jeep, the driver's blood splattered across his face. "Round up a couple of men and scour these mountains."

The guard sighed and nodded, glad to have escaped Levi's wrath.

"Blakely is very resourceful. Even naked, he managed to escape."

He knew that word of Blakely's escape would bolster Jessica's resistance and create panic among the men. The last thing he needed was a ghost challenging his authority.

"I should have put a bullet in his head."

A day of searching produced nothing. Blakely had simply disappeared into the wilderness, naked and weaponless. Yet, Levi knew he wouldn't die. Blakely was a survivor. He would find the means to overcome the overwhelming obstacles facing him, and focus on regaining his lost kingdom. One part of Levi yearned for such an encounter, a personal battle to the death. He should have faced Blakely when he had captured him, but he had thought a slow death would serve as a warning to the others. Now, Blakely's resurrection placed a strain on his reins of power. It was a mistake he would not repeat.

Slowly, word spread through the camp of Blakely's escape. That night, men slept with one eye open, their weapons beside them. Every sound, each sudden appearance of someone set men's nerves on edge. *Soon*, Levi thought, *they'll be shooting each other in blind panic.* It was time he assumed personal charge of the hunt.

* * * *

June 27, 2016   San Manuel, AZ –

Knowing that Blakely would head for some place to obtain food, shelter, and a weapon, Levi split his men into groups and began a search of the nearby ranches. They found nothing until one group encountered rifle fire from one of the homes. Certain they had found his quarry, they sent for Levi. His men cowered behind tree watching the house. He strode out into the open and stood there, daring Blakely to shoot him.

"Give up, Blakely," he shouted at the ranch house.

"Name's not Blakely. Name's Albertson. Get off my land."

Levi swore under his breath. It wasn't Blakely but some pissed off rancher. Still, he couldn't allow anyone to oppose him unpunished. Beside, Blakely might be hiding inside.

"Surround the house," he ordered his men. "Burn him out."

The fire spread quickly, but the owner refused to come out, sending pot shots in their direction as the flames consumed the house. After part of the roof caved in, he ran out the door yelling and firing. Levi's men cut him down. No one else escaped. Levi knew Blakely wasn't there.

"Spread out. Search every building but find him."

They were reluctant to begin the search. Already Jake had gained almost legendary status. They feared him. To spur their interest, he needed to offer a reward comparable to the challenge. He had the perfect prize.

"The first one to bring me Blakely alive gets the girl."

Her presence was a constant challenge to his manhood. He wanted her, but not as a slave, an unwilling participant in sex. She was the one thing he couldn't fully take from Blakely. She was proud and unbending. She would have to watch Blakely die in front of her before she gave up hope. He had another problem. Hawk was becoming truculent because of Jessica's presence. To her, the girl was a constant threat, one she would have no qualms about eliminating. She wanted him for herself with no challengers, however reluctant, waiting in the wings. Frankly, he was surprised that she hadn't already taken matters into her own hands.

"Women," he chuckled to himself. "Only a handful left in the world and they're still a pain in the ass."

The men vented their fear and frustration on zombies, killing dozens and wasting ammunition, but Levi knew better than to try to stop them. They could find more ammo later. An hour into the search of the town, they discovered the decapitated zombie corpse. As soon as he saw it, he knew it was Blakely's handiwork. By its condition, he judged it to be less than two days old.

"By now, Blakely will have food and weapons." He scanned the surrounding town and dismissed it. Blakely was too smart to remain among zombies. He looked up at the nearby mountains, and then raised his hand and pointed at the ridge. "That's where we'll find him."

He dispatched three teams on motorcycles and in the ATV into the mountains to search for Blakely. All were heavily armed and eager to prove themselves. However, his faith in his minions was limited. Blakely was smart. He would hear the search parties coming for miles and hide. If he had a weapon, the first sign of him would be when one of his men died. It would be a small price to pay to learn of his location. Levi sniffed the air. The breeze was picking up and the smell of moisture rode the wind. A monsoon storm was coming soon. The chances of finding Blakely before nightfall were slim.

He waited at the edge of town throughout the long hot afternoon, his eyes glued to the mountains, his ears tuned for a gunshot. One by one, each team returned empty-handed. He pointed to the two men in the ATV.

"You two find a spot along the river and keep watch. If Blakely makes it past you, I'll tie you to a cactus."

He knew Blakely was coming. He could feel it in his bones. The man was too stubborn for his own good. He would die for that obstinacy. Levi still had one ace in the hole – the girl.

* * * *

Hawk said nothing as she kicked in the door of the trailer, grabbed Jessica by the arm, and roughly escorted from the trailer. Each furtive glance, every muscle in Hawk's body revealed her hatred for Jessica. For the first time since her capture, Jessica feared she was about to die.

"Where are we going?" she demanded, coughing from the dust the wind was lifting from the canyon floor. She needn't have asked. She knew where they were going. Hawk was propelling her toward the path to the house on the ledge to Levi.

"You'll find out," Hawk replied, squeezing her arm.

Jessica hadn't failed to notice the frenzy that had fallen over the camp over the past two days and suspected it had nothing to do with the approaching storm. Groups of men had left, returning later with no loot or supplies, as if they had been searching for something but had not found it. The answer could be only one thing. *Jake!* He was still alive. Only his escape could induce such panic in Levi. Her heart swelled at the thought. As long as Jake was alive, he would come after Levi and her.

"He's alive, isn't he?" she said to Hawk.

In answer, Hawk slammed her into the side of the trailer and shoved her forearm tight against Jessica's neck. Jessica felt the power beneath the muscle and quailed in spite of herself. Hawk hated her and would kill her in an instant.

"No matter what happens, you're a dead woman," Hawk snarled. "Levi is mine."

Jessica laughed at the absurdity that Hawk considered her a rival. "You can have the fucking bastard. I'll kill him if I get the chance."

Hawk bounced Jessica's head against the side of the trailer, rattling her brain. "He's got you under his skin, like a goddamned disease."

Jessica grinned. Hawk couldn't kill her for fear of Levi's wrath, but she couldn't allow another woman to take her place. Her position was all she had left. To lose Levi would kill her.

Hawk released her neck but shoved her forward. "Keep moving."

The gusts of wind that had been pounding the canyon all afternoon had reduced visibility to a few yards. Men huddled inside their tents out of the dust storm, but the wind's eerie moans as it poured through the rock formations made them jumpy. They sat with weapons close at hand, weapons they would not need against the storm. Two guards patrolled the wall inside the compound. Levi was taking no chances.

Levi was waiting for them. By his dour expression, he had not found Jake. She pressed the point home, hoping to see him squirm.

"You'll never find him," she said.

"Oh, he'll show up sooner or later. I have something he wants," he said, staring at her.

His answer surprised her. "Me? I'm just another survivor. This ranch is all he has. He'll be back for it, and he'll kill you for taking it."

"I think you underestimate your value to him." He glanced at Hawk. "A man needs a woman. It's a curse. Blakely is a romantic. He sees something in you that elevates him from a loner to a human being. He's tasted love. He can't spit that out of his mouth so easily. Your vaunted deputy will come for you, and I'll be waiting for him." He motioned to a chair. Stunned by Levi's words, she sat. To Hawk, he said, "Leave us now."

Hawk didn't budge.

"Damn it!" he snarled, slamming his fist into the chair arm in fury. "I said leave."

Hawk tossed one last deprecating glare at Jessica before entering the bedroom and slamming the door behind her like a petulant child.

"Moody girl," Levi said. "I think she's jealous of you."

"Maybe she's afraid I'll kill you."

Levi chuckled. "You might, if I allowed it, but I won't. You'll sit quietly until Blakely joins us, or I'll give you more reason to hate me."

She knew his threat was not an idle one. She had tasted his savagery. She settled back in her chair to wait. She closed her eyes, but she could still feel Levi's hungry eyes roving her body and shivered with revulsion. The ugly memory of him on top of her as he raped her rose like a black specter and wouldn't go away. She gripped the arms of the chair so tightly her fingers ached. He said nothing, simply sat in silence, but his vile thoughts were like hands groping her beneath her clothing, leaving her dirty and defiled. She bit down on her lip until the pain focused her thoughts. Jake was coming. Even if he was coming for his ranch, he wouldn't forget about her and Reed.

Levi said nothing, but the room was anything but silent. The dust became rain with no transition between dry and wet. Great muddy drops hammered at the windows and rattled the panes. A cacophony of thunder ripped the air as if a distant army was blitzing an enemy, and the small canyon was target zero. Jessica opened her eyes at the sudden fury. Flashes of lightning cast ghostly shadows across the room.

"I love storms," Levi announced

She faced Levi. His Stetson was pushed down over his eyes and his cowboy boots crossed on top of an ottoman. He looked relaxed, but she knew it was a façade for her benefit.

"In the slammer, storms kept the bulls inside. I could walk the yard free, letting the rain soak me to the skin, washing off the stink of prison. I dared the lightning to strike me dead." He opened his eyes and glanced at her. "It didn't."

"Too bad," she answered. "You'd look good dead."

"Only the good die young, as Billy Joel so famously sang."

"You certainly don't fit that description." She didn't know why she bothered talking to him. It was what he wanted, but she couldn't stop herself. She wanted to hurt him, wanted her words to slice away his flesh and pierce his black heart. She wanted to inflict pain on him so badly she could taste it.

"The good died in their beds, and then rose from the dead and started eating people. The good tried to help family and friends and wound up as food. The good ..." He stopped and swallowed, his Adam's apple rippling the skin of his throat. "No one ever bothered to help me. I learned a long time ago that you can't fight what you are. I embraced myself whole-heartedly, and I'm much saner for it."

"Saner?" she shot at him with enough venom to stop his heart. "You murder people for food and for trinkets."

He laughed. "I survive. It's that simple. I gather those around me who are as eager to survive as I am. There is no more civilization. It's just winners and losers now. I intend to be a winner."

"At what cost? Society …"

He snarled and half rose from his seat. He dropped his feet to the floor and sat forward. "Society? Society locked me away and forgot about me, as the world was dying around them. What did a thief matter to the righteous when their welfare was at stake? Don't talk to me about society." He waved his arms around. "Society is what I want it to be, whatever fills the void left by the old. This is the new society."

She shook her head, dismayed by the depths of his rejection of his fellow human beings. Whatever in his past had hardened him had done a thorough job. "I feel sorry for you."

It was exactly the wrong thing to say. Levi leaped from his seat and propelled himself across the room. Before she could react, he grabbed her by her shoulders, lifted her from her seat, and shoved his face to within inches of hers. His fingers dug into the tender flesh of her barely healed dislocated shoulder. His breath reeked of alcohol and disappointment.

"Don't ever feel sorry for me. Feel sorry for your friend Blakely. He'll come here soon because he's a stupid, stubborn fool. When he does, he'll die, this time in front of you so you can witness it. You're mine to do with as I please. Maybe you had better make a decision. You're mine, or you're dead. There isn't another choice."

He released her. She collapsed back into her chair. She shrugged her shoulders to shift her bruised muscles. "You should kill me now. If you don't, I'll surely find a way to kill you."

He stared at her for a moment, and then laughed. "You've got guts. I'll give you that. Too bad you tied yourself to Blakely."

He resumed his seat, chuckling to himself every now and then, peering out the window into the dark void beyond. She suspected he wasn't watching the storm unfold. He was waiting for Jake. She smiled and watched him frown when he saw her reflection in the glass.

An hour passed before Hawk re-entered the room. Jessica glanced up at her. Something had changed during that time. The hatred in her eyes had been replaced by something else. *Pity?* No, not pity. She couldn't imagine Hawk pitying anyone, but there was no mistaking the redness in her eyes. She had been crying. Was Hawk seeing herself in Jessica's plight? Had she also made a conscious decision to sell herself for comfort and safety and was now regretting her judgment?

Jessica considered her own circumstances. When Jake had rescued her, she had been at her lowest point since the Apocalypse. Injured, without his help, she would have died. Even so, he hadn't demanded sex to nurse her back to health. In fact, he had warned her against trying to use him. Had she surrendered herself to him because, as a man, she knew he expected his reward for rescuing a damsel in distress, or because she was simply tired of being alone? She hadn't been lying when she had told him it had been a long time between men, but why had she chosen him? If she didn't care for him, why was she so concerned about him, so glad that he was still alive?

It hit her like a blow to the head. She thought herself a fool for not realizing it before. As much as Hawk hated Levi, she needed his approval, not his love. She had made mistakes in her past that had forged her into the killer that she was now, but she wasn't proud of it. Levi used her like the weapon she had become. He gave her a reason to continue. *Am I she so much different from Hawk*, Jessica wondered? *Do I want Jake's approval?* Was there a chance she could reach Hawk?

"I need to go to the bathroom," she announced.

Levi frowned at her. "So go."

As she walked into the bedroom, Hawk followed close on her heels. Jessica turned to face her half-expecting a knife in the ribs.

"Let me go," she pleaded.

Hawk stared at her.

"Let me go," she repeated. "Let us both go, me and Reed. We'll slip out of here and disappear. No one need know it was you. Your problem will be solved. You can't kill me, but you're afraid to keep me around." The words tumbled out of her mouth quickly before Hawk had time to consider their source. "Help us escape. Tonight. If we stay here, Jake will come for us. He'll kill Levi. If you let us go, we'll find him. All three of us will leave the area."

She knew she had no right to speak for Jake. After all, it was his ranch that had been taken. In all probability, his reasons for coming back had more to do with reclaiming his property than in rescuing her or Reed.

"If I stay here, I'll either kill Levi or force him to kill me. You want him and I don't. Let me go."

Hawk hesitated. A frown of confusion crossed her face as she considered Jessica's proposal.

"You'll have him all to yourself," she added.

Hawk drew her knife and brandished it in her face. "I could just kill you. Say you tried to escape. Then I'll have him to myself."

"He'll hate you if you do. No, your only hope of keeping Levi safe and for yourself is to let me escape."

Hawk sneered. "Shut up."

Jessica sighed inwardly. It wasn't going as she had hoped. She opened her mouth to try again. Hawk's backhanded blow caught her by surprise.

"Go to the bathroom or pee in your pants. I don't care which."

Jessica rubbed her stinging cheek and went into the bathroom. She tried to shut the door, but Hawk's foot in the door stopped her.

"Leave it open."

Jessica stared at the window. It was dark outside. The rain was so heavy that she couldn't see the cliff face less than five feet away. If she could escape, she could slip away into the darkness. Hawk followed her into the bathroom. At first, she thought she was going to have to pee with Hawk watching, but Hawk picked up a screwdriver lying on the window sill, the one Jake had used to install the shower curtain. She turned the screwdriver over in her hands a few times before setting it back down. Her gaze locked on Jessica, and then fell to the screwdriver.

"You need more toilet paper. I'll get some from the hall closet," she said, as she left the room.

Jessica glanced at the nearly full roll of paper on the dispenser and smiled. Hawk was giving her a chance. She immediately went to the window and tried to raise it. The paint-sealed window hadn't been opened for years. She ran the blade of the screwdriver along the edge of the window seal and pushed. It finally popped open with a loud creak. She held her breath but no one came. She was running out of time. Screwdriver in hand, she slipped out the window and into the night.

She inched down the narrow space between the cliff and the wall of the house, silently praying that Levi didn't catch her. If she could reach the canyon floor before anyone noticed her escape, she would be free. The rain was coming down hard, drenching her, but would mask her escape. As she neared the end of the house, a figure slipped out the window behind her silhouetted by the bathroom light – Levi. The blade of the knife he held in her hand gleamed in the lightning flashes. With a malicious grin on his face he started toward her. She ran, but he was faster. He caught up with her before she reached the plank bridge, slamming her against the cliff face.

"No you don't," he whispered in her ear. Water from his Stetson poured over her face. He pressed the tip of the knife into her right cheek until it broke the skin.

She swung the screwdriver at him, grazing his side. He winced, knocked the screwdriver from her grasp, and kneed her stomach. She doubled over in pain.

"Close," he said, "but no cigar."

He jerked her to her feet and dragged her back to the house. She was in too much pain to resist. Inside, her gaze fell upon Hawk, lying bleeding on the floor. Her expression was one of disbelief. Levi nudged her with the toe of his boot.

"The bitch thought I wouldn't catch on. Toilet paper! I put a new roll on the dispenser this morning. When I confronted her, she lied to me. No one lies to me."

"You, you stabbed her," Jessica said in disbelief and horror.

"No big loss. I've still got you." He grinned.

She punched him in the face with all her strength, willing her hatred into the blow. He staggered backwards, almost tripping over Hawk. He recovered quickly, this time pulling his pistol and aiming it at her head. The gun didn't waver, as she stared into the black abyss of the barrel.

"Don't make me kill you," he snapped. "A bullet will make a nasty mess of your pretty face."

She hesitated. A bullet to the head might have been quicker and cleaner than what he had in store for her, but she couldn't bring herself to, in effect, commit suicide. She had to wait for Jake. Her shoulders drooped in defeat.

"Come on. It's time to check on the guards. Blakely should be here soon. I wouldn't want to miss him."

He stepped over Hawk as he would a dying dog, devoting no more attention to her. Jessica felt a twinge of sorrow for her. In the end, she had tried to help if only for her own convoluted reasons. But there was nothing she could do to help Hawk. She had to concentrate on remaining alive until Jake came.

20

June 27, 2016   Galiuro Mountains, AZ –

Jake wasn't a patient man. He was eager to extract revenge on Levi, but he knew his patience would soon be rewarded. The winds grew steadily stronger from the southwest. The flinty taste of dust was in the air. The unmistakable smell of moisture presaged another monsoonal downpour. The clouds grew heavy and gray, their bottoms sheered by wind. The storm would be preceded by a *haboob*, a massive dust storm. Dust would provide the perfect cover to infiltrate his ranch. He knew the guards, unable to see more than a few feet in front of them, would seek shelter from the biting dust. Once inside his compound, he would find weapons. If possible, he would free Reed and Jessica. If not, he would kill Levi first.

Levi's death would break the other's spirits, making them easy to deal with. It would not be a one-on-one challenge or a long, drawn out killing. He would sneak into his house and slit the bastard's throat in his sleep if necessary. Such men deserved no elegant ending. A quick death was efficient and less dangerous.

The western skies grew dark well before dusk, laden with tons of fine dust, sand, and pea-sized gravel. As the *haboob* approached, it was a wall of dust five miles wide, its top towering almost a mile into the sky. It would sweep across the Avra Valley from Casa Grande to Marana, engulf Picacho Peak and Eloy, and plunge down the narrow San Pedro River valley at fifty to sixty miles per hour. By the time it reached his ranch, visibility would be near zero. He was taking a foolish risk in attempting to use the dust storm as cover. He would have to hike to Split Rock Canyon and climb the surrounding cliff to approach the ranch from the rear, all with a strong wind blinding him and trying to sweep his feet out from under him with every step he took. He would have to reach his ranch before the monsoon rains. Travel would be impossible during a deluge.

With reluctance, he abandoned his camp, taking only the rope, his spear, a knife, the machete, and a canteen of water. He doubted anything would remain of the camp after the storm. If he failed and survived, he would be back to square one. He didn't want to face that challenge again. He had cheated death once. He wasn't eager to make a second attempt.

Descending the mountain was a test of wills, his versus the wind. Sudden gusts of wind threatened to rip loose his grip from precarious handholds. His hands and legs were swollen from fluid buildup, and his muscles were stiff and achy. He was weak from a near starvation diet. His blood sugar was low and he had no medicine. The blinding dust made finding the path down the mountain difficult. Once he reached the lower canyons, he was protected from the wind and the going was better for a while, but the San Pedro River valley was a funnel, channeling the wind between the Galiuros and the Catalinas like water flowing from a fire hose. Only his innate sense of direction kept him headed southeast toward the ranch.

The hike was long, but his anger lent him the strength his body lacked. He ignored the wind and the blinding dust. He ignored the innumerable times he stumbled and fell or slammed his head into or tree limbs. He ignored the pain. He focused his mind on the coming fight and on Levi's death.

He knew he was no Superman, no Delta Force super soldier. His army days were long behind him. He was a hunter. His normal prey were deer, mountain goats, and elk; not men. Even as a deputy, the worst he had handled were drunks or domestic brawls, usually a combination of the two. The first attack on Levi's men had been achieved through surprise and with guns and explosives, not to mention the zombie army. Now, the odds weren't in his favor. His enemy was well-fed on his food and well-armed. They were in a fortified position and expecting him, and he had a makeshift spear and a homemade machete as weapons.

If one of the men in the ATV hadn't coughed to clear his throat of dust, Jake would have stumbled blindly into them. Two men sat in his ATV on the leeward side of a thicket of trees watching the trail along the east side of the river. Only the thick dust had saved him. They were so confident that no one could see that they had become lax in their vigilance, more intent on their comfort than in guarding the road. They passed a bottle of booze back and forth to wash the dust from their mouths. He could go around, sneak past them in the storm, but they had the weapons he needed for any chance of carrying out his plan.

He waited. Eventually, as he knew they would, one of the men stirred from his seat.

"I gotta take a piss," he said, shouting into the wind to be heard.

"Piss downwind," the other warned, "Or you'll fill your boots."

The man took a few steps from the jeep and stood facing a large boulder. Jake edged around the boulder, keeping low. A steady stream of urine arced onto the face of the boulder. Jake hesitated. Shooting a man from a distance was one thing. Killing him face-to-face with a knife was another. Then he reminded himself that these men were murderers, had stolen his ranch, and had tried to kill him. *Jake's Law #6 – Bad people deserve bad ends*. He let the anger inside rise like water filling a bucket until it overflowed. He raised the machete in the air and stepped around the edge of the boulder.

The man glanced up in surprise at the shadow suddenly materializing from the dust. He backed up frantically, still urinating. Jake struck savagely before his opponent could react, letting his rage spill out through his arms. He attacked like a madman. The machete separated head from body. Blood sprayed from the ragged wound, mixing with dust and urine, forming clumps of wet dirt that fell to the ground like rain. The body toppled onto the boulder and slid to the ground. He had not made a sound. Jake removed the dead man's pistol and shoved it into his belt. He would have to eliminate the other guard silently. He couldn't risk a shot being heard over the roar of the wind.

As he crossed behind the vehicle and stepped to the driver's side of the ATV, the driver handed him the bottle without glancing up. "One last slug, Deke. You'll need it after your piss."

He looked up. His eyes widened, as he realized it wasn't Deke. Jake thrust the tip of the machete into the man's throat. He gurgled once, reaching in vain for his rifle. Jake slapped down his groping hand and yanked him from the vehicle. By the time Jake was settled in the driver's seat, dust was beginning to cover both bodies. Soon, they would vanish beneath a layer of dirt, as if they had never existed, the desert erasing them from its memory. Now, he had a rifle, a shotgun, and a pistol to add to his arsenal. He felt considerably better about his chances.

There was no real sunset because of the storm. Dusk became night with little transition. The sandstorm ended almost as abruptly as it had begun. Large, muddy raindrops fell for a few minutes, splattering the windshield and Jake, and then the rain came down in sheets almost as thick as the dust had been. In the darkness and the blinding rain, he fought to keep the ATV on or as close to the narrow trail as possible, praying he didn't crash into a boulder or tree or drive off into the river. He didn't know if Levi had placed more guards around but suspected he would have men on the main road across the river. Levi was a cautious man.

Jake abandoned the ATV at the foot of Split Rock Canyon and continued on foot. He left his makeshift spear and machete in the vehicle, as well as the rifle to travel light. He kept the shotgun and pistol. Hugging the canyon walls for cover, he crept toward the gate. He knew the placement of the cameras and avoided them. He wanted no warning to reach Levi until he struck. The roar of the falls covered any sound he might have made splashing through puddles or wading through shallow washes. It delighted him that he was using the cover of the storm just as Levi had done when he had taken the ranch from him. It seemed appropriate somehow.

A single guard stood in front of the gate, looking miserable in the rain with a plastic garbage bag draped over his clothing as an ersatz rain suit. His attention was focused on the inside of the compound, wishing he was dry and drunk with his confederates. He never noticed Jake creeping along the wall; never saw the knife near his throat. He made no sound except a short grunt of surprise, as Jake swiped the blade quickly across his throat. He fell face first to the muddy ground, drowning in his own blood. Jake dragged him to the wash and rolled him in. The body quickly disappeared beneath the churning brown water pouring down the mountain from rain higher up.

In spite of the storm, there was considerable activity inside the compound. He would not catch them asleep. Men hurried from tent to tent in groups of two or three. Flames danced beneath a large open canopy, a cook fire. *Feeding time at the zoo.* As he watched, a figure passed in front of the gate patrolling inside the wall. Even if he managed to crawl over the wall through the wire, he would be seen. He would have to use his backdoor.

A hundred yards back down the canyon, a narrow trail ascended the cliff, a shelf of rock just wide enough for mountain goats and pumas. It was a dangerous, difficult path for a man on a good day. In the rain and wind, it was almost impossible, but it was his only option. He dropped everything he was carrying except his rope, his knife, and the pistol. He regretted the loss of the shotgun, but he would need both hands free for climbing.

There was one problem. The trail was on the opposite side of the canyon. To reach it, he had to first cross the wash. With it now a raging torrent, there were only two ways to cross it – backtrack several miles or negotiate the narrow twelve-inch wide ledge built into the wall to reinforce the metal grate through which the water poured. He didn't have time to retrace his route. Someone could discover the missing guards at any moment. He eyed the six-foot long ledge and the wild, raging spillway beneath it with trepidation. He had no choice.

He hugged the wall trying to will his flesh to meld with stone, as he placed his boot on the ledge and took his first step. The wall shuddered against his body from the force of the water striking it. His fingers sought holds in the narrow crevices of the wall, as his feet inched across the ledge. Water erupted from the narrow opening in a spray, drenching him and licking at his feet. Halfway across, the wall shook violently as something struck it from the other side, a tree or boulder carried by the current, jarring one hand loose. For a death-defying moment, he teetered over the precipice, his weight pulling at the numb fingers of the one hand holding him above the raging surge. His fingers tore at the stones for another hold, finally finding purchase in a small niche between rocks. He hugged the wall for a moment, resting his cheek against the cold wet stone, trying to catch his breath. After the initial effort, the last few steps were anticlimactic, and he once again stood on solid earth.

He almost missed the trailhead in the pouring rain. He took the first few dozen yards standing, hugging the cliff as he had the wall crossing the ledge. After that, he continued on hands and knees. Muddy water rushed down the path like a sluiceway of a dam, threatening to wash him off the face of the mountain. More than once, it almost succeeded. Chunks of dirt dissolved beneath his hands, and pieces of shattered limestone broke away above him, showering him with falling debris. Each movement dislodged pieces of mountain. He worried that a larger slab of limestone could crush him.

By the time he had gained two hundred feet in elevation, his arms and legs were burning from the effort. His jeans were ripped and knees were raw and bloody from scrubbing against the abrasive rock. His swollen fingers felt like sausages. Directly below him, the wash was a raging river draining into a small lake created as water piled up in front of the grated exit beneath the wall. He wouldn't have to worry about drowning if he slipped. The fall would kill him first.

The roar of Split Canyon Falls was deafening, a series of short ledges ending in a thirty foot cascade of water. It was difficult in the dark, but he finally spotted what he was looking for, an outcropping of rock jutting like a finger just beyond the falls. Beneath it, a narrow ledge, little more than a groove in the cliff, would provide a safe place to rest. Doubling the rope, he tossed the open loop over the finger of rock, praying that the rock could hold his weight, and then swung through the falls to the ledge.

The rush of icy cold water was a fist trying to hammer him against the rocks and break his grip on the rope. He had thought he was cold before, but the rain had been a sauna compared to the raging waterfall. He did a hard belly-flop onto the ledge, forcing the air from his lungs. He gasped for breath and fought to keep his hands from shaking, as he released one end of the rope.

With clumsy fingers he tied one end of the rope to a small knob of rock. The rope wasn't long enough to reach the ground, but he hoped it would get him to the point where the canyon wall sloped outward to meet the desert floor of the canyon. He could scramble down from there. It was too dark to see more than a few feet below him. He dredged his memory trying to recall exactly how far below the ledge the slope began, but it was still a guess. He had no choice. If the rain let up, he would be visible to anyone scanning the rocks.

He sighed and began climbing down the rope. He slipped several times on the wet rope, burning his hands each time he recovered. When he reached the end of the rope, he braced his back against the cold stone, and released the rope. He fell only a few feet before his feet hit the slope. The wet rock cushioned his descent, but tiny ridges and outcroppings played havoc with his body, slicing into his back and legs. He slid what seemed an eternity before his feet caught on an outcropping that sent him spinning head first into dark space. He expected to meet solid rock, ending his infiltration attempt. Instead, he landed in a pool of water ten feet below.

That wasn't so bad, he thought, as he shook himself off like a wet dog, massaging his sore muscles. *At least I'm alive.* He raced across the canyon floor, using the trees as cover. If he was going to take on a small army, he needed more than a pistol, a chef's knife, and a bad attitude. He hoped no one had found his buried weapons cache. He had to cross open ground to reach the chicken coop where he had stashed it. As he started across, he spotted a shadow detach from a tree, moving parallel to his path toward the chicken coop. He lost sight of the figure as it darted behind a row of lemon and orange tees. He hurried to reach the chicken coop first. He eyed with dismay the water-filled hole where his crate had been buried. Someone had beaten him to it. His plans were falling apart. At least he could eliminate whoever was following him.

He lay in wait beside the wall, as the shadowy figure approached. The figure made no attempt to move silently. He splashed through puddles and cursed aloud when he tripped over a fallen branch. His ragged breathing was loud enough to wake the dead. As the mysterious figure slammed into the side of the chicken coop, Jake lunged with his knife.

He stayed his hand just in time.

"Reed. What the hell are you doing here?"

Reed held up one hand for Jake to wait while he caught his breath. He pulled his inhaler from his pocket and took a puff. Finally, he spoke. "When I learned that you were still alive, I knew you'd come back here. When the storm hit, I figured it would be tonight." He pointed to the hole in the ground. "I knew you would come here first."

"Where is it? Does Levi have it?"

Reed grinned and shook his head. "No. I dug it up and moved it to the work shop. I've been making ammunition there for Levi.

They're afraid to come in because I've threatened to blow them up."

Jake shook his head in surprise at Reed's resourcefulness. "Where's Jessica?" Reed's hesitation caused a tight knot in Jake's stomach. "Is she all right?" he asked, fearing the answer.

"She's alive. Hawk came to get here a while ago. She's up there." He pointed toward the house on the ledge. "We're not leaving without her," Reed said, "are we?"

"We're not leaving," he growled. "They are. Come on. I need that crate."

The workshop was unguarded. Reed covered the window with a blanket before switching on the lights. Jake looked around. One table was covered with freshly reloaded cartridges. Gunpowder lay scattered in piles on the floor and table. He glanced at Reed.

Reed shrugged his shoulders and smiled. "I had to look incompetent to keep them away."

"I'm surprised you're still alive. How many of them are there?"

Reed immediately became serious. "Twenty-one; one on guard outside, two inside. I think a couple of them are guarding the river, but most are out of the rain in their tents eating. They change guard every four hours. We have another hour."

"There's eighteen now," Jake said.

He crossed the room to the dirty plastic crate, running his hands over its side. It was locked, and he didn't have his key. He picked up a hacksaw and began sawing away at the padlock while Reed watched the door. When the lock finally dropped away, he opened the crate and smiled. Reed came to peer over Jake's shoulder.

"What is that?" he asked.

Jake pulled out a tripod, set it up, and mounted the machine gun on top. "This is an M1919A4 Browning Light Machine Gun. It fires over 400 7.62 mm rounds per minute."

Reed snapped his fingers. "That's why you wanted the 7.62 mm ammunition from the armory."

"I have two full belts and two empty belts." He picked up one of the empty ammunition belts. "Now, start loading the two empty ones."

"Where did you get this monstrosity?" Reed asked, as he picked up one of the empty belts.

Jake grabbed a handful of cartridges from the 7.62 mm ammo box. "I bought it over the internet." He handed them to Reed.

Reed stared at him. "You're shitting me."

"No, I bought it as a museum piece, and then retro-fitted it to make it serviceable. We're going to need it."

Reed smiled as he took the ammo. "With this, we can take on an army."

"You can."

Reed's smile quickly faded. "What do you mean?"

"You're going to keep the troops busy while I pay Levi a visit."

"Me? I can't …"

Jake didn't give Reed the chance to consider refusing. This was a two-man job. He couldn't do it without Reed's help. "Yes, you can. You have to. I'm rescuing Jessica. Can you kill men?"

Reed's eyes narrowed. With a fierceness Jake had not expected from the gentle teacher, he answered, "I can kill these men."

Jake slapped him on the shoulder. "Good."

The plan was simple. Reed would mount the M1919A4 on the path leading up to the house. The added height would give him a clear field of fire over the entire canyon, while Jake confronted Levi. They spent fifteen minutes loading the two remaining belts. Jake knew time was of the essence, but a haphazard job could cause a misfire and jam the weapon. With a thousand rounds of ammunition, the machine gun could fire continuously for just over two minutes. They would need it operational for longer than that. Therefore, they would have to be judicious with their only assault weapon, firing it in short bursts to conserve ammunition.

Ideally, operating the machine gun was a two-man job. He reminded Reed of the dangers.

"You'll have to change belts on your own. You'll be vulnerable for that short period of time."

Reed nodded. "I understand. You save Jessica. I'll take care of Levi's men."

Finally, they were ready. He glanced at Reed, trying to judge his state of mind, but the pudgy teacher hid his emotions beneath a mask of determination. The rain fell in raging torrents, and thunder echoed down the canyon. Jake hoped the inclement weather would force most of the men inside their tents. Every minute of stealth increased their chances of success. One of the inside guards leaned against the side of the RV, using its bulk to deflect the wind-driven rain. He was so absorbed in his own misery that he failed to notice the two shadows sneaking up on him. Jake slammed the barrel of his pistol into the back of the man's head, producing a sickening crack so loud he prayed it would be indistinguishable from a peal of thunder. The guard slumped to the ground either dead or unconscious. Jake rolled his body beneath the RV.

The remaining guard stood in the open just inside the gate. He would be more difficult to eliminate. Jake placed the stunned guard's cap on his head and donned the man's trash bag parka. Cradling the man's rifle across his arms, he lowered his head and approached the guard. He was less than ten paces away when the second guard suddenly yelled out, "What's with you, Rafe? You're supposed to be walking the perimeter."

Jake swore silently. In a low grumble that he hoped mimicked Rafe's voice, he groaned, "Too damn rainy."

He held his breath as the guard stared at him for an uncomfortably long time before nodding and turning away to face the gate. Crossing the few feet separating them in three quick bounds, Jake swung the rifle butt just as the guard, alerted by the splashing, turned back to face him. The guard's eyes, illuminated by a flash of lightning, opened wide as the wood connected with his temple. Bone shattered and flesh tore asunder beneath the crushing blow. The guard fell backwards into the mud, his dead eyes still open and staring.

Together, he and Reed dragged the body and dumped it out of sight beside a row of motorcycles. As they were leaving, two figures left the path to the house, heading toward the kitchen tent. As soon as the pair had disappeared into the darkness, Jake grabbed the thirty-one pound machinegun, while Reed carried the tripod and ammo case. They reached the first ledge of the path undetected. There, partially hidden by a low rocky ridge thrusting like a castle's parapet along the edge of the ledge, Reed fed a belt of ammunition into the machinegun and settled down to wait. Jake threw his friend a quick grin and fled up the path.

The lights were on in the house. He didn't know how many people waited inside, but he was certain that Levi and his scared whore, Hawk, would be there. Of the two, Jake feared the woman the most. She was cold and vicious and in awe of Levi, if not in love with him. She was dangerous and deadly and would defend Levi with her last dying breath.

Jake stared at the house for several minutes, hoping to see movement beyond the windows to gauge how many people were inside. He used the time in a vain attempt to summon his courage, but a hard knot of fear remained in the pit of his stomach. He knew he could die in the next few moments. His biggest fear was putting Jessica in danger. Finally, he knew he could postpone it no longer. He crossed the plank bridge and pressed his body against the side of the house, listening. Entering through the front door would be a dangerous, bold move, but one Levi might not expect.

With his pistol in one hand and his knife in the other, Jake kicked open the front door and rushed inside. From his vantage point, he could see the entire house through the open door, including the bedroom. The house was empty. *No, not empty*, he thought, as a low moan reached his ear from the living room. A foot jutted from the edge of the sofa. His mind swirled with dread. Was it Jessica? Was he too late? He leaned over the sofa, gun aimed at whoever might be there. He was both surprised and relieved to see Hawk, her hand pressed against her belly. Blood spilled between her fingers to join a growing puddle on the floor. She glanced up at Jake, her eyes pleading, but they both knew the wound was fatal.

"He killed me," she whispered.

Jake knelt beside her. "Who killed you?" he asked though he knew the answer.

"Levi," she moaned, and then groaned as a spasm of pain hit her. When the pain subsided, she said, "He's got your woman. I tried to help her escape."

Jake found that difficult to believe. "Why?"

"He's mine," she said, as if that was reason enough.

He stared down at her.

"If I killed her, he would kill me. I thought ... I thought if she was gone ..."

Jake nodded in understanding. She wanted Levi for herself more than she wanted Jessica dead. She didn't comprehend just what a bastard he was.

"Where are they?"

Hawk reached out with her bloody hand and gripped Jake's wrist with a surprising amount of strength for a dying woman and pulled him closer. "He's gone to check on the guards," she whispered. "He's expecting you."

Jake swore. They were the two figures he had seen. He had missed them by two minutes. Hawk's grip tightened, and then relaxed as she fell back. Her eyes glazed in death, as her last breath left her body. Jake felt no sympathy for her. She would have killed Jessica if she had thought she could keep Levi by doing so. The machinegun began chattering outside. Now, they were trapped on the ledge, while Levi and his army were below them.

He had forgotten *Jake's Law #9 – Always have an exit strategy.*

21

There was no escape back down the path with Levi's men firing up from the canyon floor. His simple in-and-out mission had fallen apart around him. He had intended to free Jessica and quietly kill Levi, thus removing the gang's head, but she was gone and so was Levi.

Bullets began shattering the windows and smashing into the walls, as the men below began firing into the house. He dropped low and crawled back outside. Bullets ricocheted from the wall of the cliff, becoming doubly dangerous. He fired one volley from his pistol and raced for the plank bridge over the gorge. He was fully exposed to anyone with a gun. Bullets thudded into the wooden planks at his feet, showering his legs with splinters. One bullet tore through his loose shirttail, grazing his back. He quickened his pace.

Reed fired the machinegun in a blind panic in hopes of hitting someone, burning through the ammunition. Jake placed his hand on Reed's shoulder to calm him down. "Short bursts," he cautioned.

Reed looked up, grinned, and took a deep breath. The reminder helped him focus. He fired short bursts whenever someone moved or was revealed by lightning flashes. He yelped in triumph when one man spun and fell, as the man tried to move from the cover of the jeep to the foot of the path.

"Got him!"

"There are plenty more left," Jake reminded him.

He looked at Jake confused. "Where's Jessica?"

"Levi has her down there."

Reed swore silently, and then began firing the machinegun.

The return fire from the ground was intensifying as Levi rallied his men. Many of their weapons were fully automatic M16s and AK47s. He and Reed were outnumbered and out gunned. They had the machine gun, but it was a stationary defensive weapon. Jake estimated their chances as slim and getting worse as the night passed.

"We're sitting ducks here," he said. "I got us into this mess. I'll get us out."

"How?"

"I don't know. Can you keep their heads down for a while?"

He nodded. "Until I run out of ammunition."

"I've got a plan."

"What plan?"

"I'll make it up as I go. I have rope in the house. If I reach the canyon floor, I might have a surprise or two for Levi."

"I've got something that might help," Reed said.

"What?"

"Look beneath the gunpowder can in the workshop. There's a loose floor board. You might find a use for the package there."

He clasped Reed's hand. "Good luck."

"Save Jessica."

Before he could say something he might regret, he took off at a run across the bridge. Bullets stitched a line along the cliff, but the machinegun silenced them. He reached his house safely. Now, the fire targeted him. Bullets splattered against the stone walls and thudded into the thick pine logs. A few smashed the remaining windows and ricocheted around the room. He located his rope hanging on a peg in the closet. The AA-12 shotgun was still lying beneath the bed where he had left it. He checked to make sure the drum was loaded and slung the strap over his shoulder.

He lowered the end of the rope over the side of the cliff beside the house. A slight vertical depression hid him from sight of the shooters. He reached the ground safely. The rain was beginning to let up, but the wind still whipped down the canyon in gusts up to thirty miles per hour. As he crossed the canyon toward the creek, the roar of the falls drowned out the sound of firing.

His and Reed's only chance of surviving was to kill Levi. If he could circle around behind Levi's men, and then get among them, the AA-12 was an excellent weapon for close infighting. They would be firing blindly at each other. The panic would work in his favor. He would have his choice of targets. As he neared the work shop, Reed's words came back to him. What kind of surprise had he created? The firing was intensifying around the pathway to the house. Reed's machinegun stopped twice as he reloaded. Each time, Levi's men crept closer. He was running out of time.

Inside the workshop, Jake removed the almost empty gunpowder can and pried up the loose boards beneath it. He removed the plastic-covered object, loosened its wrapping, and smiled. He held in his hands a bundle of four pipe bombs wrapped in duct tape. A wristwatch timer was connected to a small plastic box. He removed the cover to see a nest of wires connected to an 18-volt power tool battery and a simple primer from a shotgun shell. He didn't have time to wonder how a high school science teacher knew how to manufacture an IED. The bomb nestled in its plastic sheathing gave him an idea.

The falls were cascading water into his small pond. It overflowed his stone dam and spilled into the creek bed, funneling down the narrow wash. If he could collapse the dam, a five-foot-high wall of water would rush down the canyon. Levi and his men would have no place to hide. But then, neither would Jessica.

Within minutes, Reed would run out of ammunition and all his options would be gone. He either had to abandon them both and run, or risk killing them all. He set the timer for fifteen minutes. It would take that long to locate and free Jessica. He sealed the entire package with layers of duct tape and taped it to an old plow shear. The weight would help the bomb sink to the bottom of the pond as close to the dam as he could place it. Just like the bouncing bombs used to destroy the Ruhr Valley dams of Germany during *Operation Chastise* in May of 1943, his 'dam buster' would let loose thousands of gallons of water on his small valley.

He threw the package as close as he could to the inside wall of the dam and watched it sink into his pond. He hoped Reed's expertise proved itself. If not, they would all soon die. He saw movement inside one of the tents. He threw back the tent flap with his finger on the trigger ready to fire. Instead of Levi's men, he saw three women, one pregnant. They were wet, frightened, and expecting death. They were also unarmed. He didn't know if they were willing residents, but judging by their bruises, they were as captive as Jessica. He might be a bastard, but he wasn't a woman-killing bastard.

"Get out of here. Get as close to the head of the canyon as you can. Climb as high as you can. If you don't, you'll die."

One of the women nodded. He watched them disappear into the darkness. He worked his way as near to the kitchen tent as he could before cutting loose with the shotgun, firing as quickly as he could pull the trigger. Keeping their heads down was more important than accuracy, but he watched one man fall holding his stomach. Just as he hoped, firing erupted all around him, as confused, frightened men fired in fear at anything that moved. He hoped Jessica didn't get killed in the crossfire. Twice, he had to shoot men who spotted him, but by crawling along the muddy ground and using whatever cover he could find, he reached the kitchen tent. It had taken longer than he had anticipated. Time was running out.

Levi stood just inside the tent silhouetted by the cook fire, yelling orders and gesticulating wildly with his pistol. Jessica lay on the ground at his feet, alive but afraid to move. For one brief moment, their eyes met. He saw the fear fade, replaced by hope. He motioned to her to remain on the ground out of harm's way. Then he raised the shotgun and aimed at Levi, a perfect target against the flickering flames. The rage inside him leaped from his heart to his trigger finger, as it slowly caressed the metal. One slight tug and it would all be over.

At that moment, two things happened. The bomb exploded behind the dam, sending a geyser of water soaring into the air, and one of Levi's men crossed in front of him, taking the full blast of the double-ought pellets. Levi, now alerted to Jake's presence, grabbed Jessica by the hair, lifted her from the ground, and used her as a shield. His eyes searched for Jake, and then, as the rumble from the collapsing dam increased, he pushed Jessica in front of him and raced toward the jeep. Jake tried to follow, but now several of the men spotted him. He hugged the ground and fired at them.

The final collapse of the dam shook the ground, as stones groaned under the pressure of the pent up pond of water. If he remained where he was, the water would wash him away with the rest of the filth. He jumped up, swept the AA-12 in a semi-circle as he ran, and raced after Levi and Jessica. They had already reached the jeep and were driving toward the open gate. He veered to intercept them, but then saw the five-foot high wall of water rushing down at him. He had to make a decision – run for the safety of the path, or risk death in pursuit of Jessica. He glanced one more time at the wall of water bearing down on him like a runaway freight train. He would never make it to the jeep. Jessica saw him, and for a moment, he thought he heard her call his name. Then the jeep was through the gate.

He reached the path just ahead of the rush of water. As he sprinted up the steps, he knocked down one of Levi's men seeking safety from the flood just as he was. The man tumbled into the water and was swallowed by the raging current. Men, trees, tents, his grandfather's house, the animal pens, vehicles, Reed's RV – all vanished in moments, swept away by the relentless flood and crushed against the stone wall. The wall bulged under the immense pressure as water cascaded over its top. It poured through the open gate seeking release, but there was too much water for the narrow opening. With a sound like a wooden board snapping in half, the wall collapsed at two points – the gate and the wash. The river erupted through the gaps and swept down the canyon, taking with it everything he had worked so hard to build.

He stood on the path and watched his past disappear like a bad dream. He doubted that the jeep could outrun the deluge, but for Jessica's sake, he prayed she made it. The full brunt of his failure struck him like a hammer blow. For a moment, he stood on the edge of the path and contemplated leaping in, joining his past and ending his bleak future. A hand gripped his shoulder – Reed.

"Is she …?" he asked, unable to complete the question whose answer he dreaded.

Jake shook his head. "She and Levi escaped in the jeep."

"Will they … will they make it."

"I don't know." His legs gave way and he collapsed on the ledge. "I don't know," he repeated.

Below them, the water was receding, flowing back into the banks of the wash, no longer impeded by the stone wall across the canyon. In its wake, it left total destruction. Of the seventy-year-old former ranch house, nothing remained to show it had ever existed. The canyon floor was swept clean. As if the hand of a blind avenging angel had come down to aid him at the cost of all he held dear. Of the dozen or so men, there was no sign. They, too, had vanished, victims of his revenge.

"Let's get out of this rain," Reed suggested and began trudging back up the path toward the house.

Jake remained where he was, staring at the aftermath of his binge of destruction. He had certainly lived up to *Jake's Law #10 – Serve revenge in big doses*, but he wasn't as certain that he agreed with *Jake's Law #11 – Be willing to lose it all*, not if all included Jessica.

* * * *

Jessica's head still reeled from the blow that had sent to her to ground at Levi's feet. She sat in passenger seat, too woozy to remove the seat belt and throw herself from the jeep to escape. The roar of the flood slowly receded behind them, only to increase in volume as the road threaded through the winding canyon. She could feel the ground trembling through the tires of the jeep as the wall of water rushed at them. She hoped it swallowed them.

Jake had come for her. She clung to that thought as the jeep bearing her and Levi plunged recklessly through the night. He might have only come for his ranch, but she preferred to think he had come for her, and for Reed. When she had seen him lying in the mud outside the tent, her heart had swelled with hope. Then, the dam broke. Jake had been willing to destroy everything he owned to free her. *Or to kill Levi*, another part of her acknowledged. She preferred the former.

Now, his ranch was gone, washed away by the flood. He might be dead as well. She had last seen him running from the flood. At least Reed was alive. He was the one on the ledge firing the machinegun, out of reach of the raging torrent.

Levi rounded one last corner and left the flood behind. He reached the river, a raging torrent, and drove through at full speed. The engine sputtered, as water poured into the cab, but didn't die. Then they were through and were safely on the other side. She found no comfort in her newfound safety. She had lived so that Jake could find her. Now, he was gone and she was still Levi's prisoner. She had no hope for her future. She would kill herself or force Levi to kill her. She only hoped she got one last opportunity to kill him.

"Your boyfriend's dead," Levi said, gloating.

"So's your girlfriend," she taunted. "I bet it hurts knowing she betrayed you."

"Not as much as the knife blade sliding into her belly hurt her."

"You're a monster."

"I'm alive. You're alive. That's a start."

"He destroyed everything he owned to kill you. He would have, too, if you hadn't run like a frightened rabbit."

Her insult struck home. "I ran from the flood, not Blakely."

"Yeah, keep telling yourself that. I bet you'll have a hard time sleeping at night, wondering if Jake is alive."

Levi slammed on the brakes. The jeep slewed sideways as it skidded in the mud, finally coming to rest facing the direction they had come. If the night had not been so dark, she knew she would be able to see veins popping out on his face and neck.

"If Blakely is alive, I'll make certain he knows where I am. After all, I have something he wants. You'll be my bait."

"That's big talk in the dark. Let's see what you look like in the daytime when Jake comes for you."

"Maybe you'll get your chance."

He slipped the jeep into gear and spun it in a circle on the road, pointing it toward San Manuel.

22

June 28, 2016   Galiuro Mountains, AZ –

Jake brushed broken glass from his favorite leather chair and sat down, a bottle of whiskey in his hand. He hadn't bothered with a glass. Sipping wouldn't wash away the pain. So far, half the bottle hadn't either. He still had his house, although it was a bit shot up and worse for wear. *And I've still got my health,* he whispered to himself, chuckling at his sarcastic wit.

As he took a long drag from the bottle, he noticed Reed's pained expression. He sat opposite Jake. Like Jake, he was thoroughly soaked and mud-streaked and uncharacteristically quiet. His glasses were gone, lost in the battle. At first, he thought Reed's sour expression was for his benefit, a reminder of his bitter failure. Then he noticed the blood on Reed's shirt.

"Are you hurt?"

"Just a scratch. I hardly felt it."

Jake pushed himself up from his chair. "I'd better take a look at it. You're bleeding like stuck pig. Take off your shirt."

Reed winced as he removed his shirt. Jake gasped when he saw the wound in Reed's stomach. "That's no scratch." He leaned Reed forward and searched his back. "The bullet's still in you." He stared at Reed. "It has to come out."

Reed's mouth dropped. "What do you mean?"

"I mean I have to operate."

"You! You're drunk."

"Do you see anyone else? And I'm not drunk, not yet. Look, the bullet has to come out. Otherwise, you'll bleed to death."

"Have you ever removed a bullet before?"

"No."

"Have you ever performed any surgery?"

"Still no."

"Well, that sucks."

Jake ignored him. "You're filthy. Go take a shower. I'll find my surgical kit."

Reed stood with Jake's help. He was unsteady on his feet. "If you kill me, I'll haunt you."

Jake winced at Reed's threat. He had enough ghosts haunting him now. He didn't need one more. "I'll be careful," he promised.

While Reed showered, Jake gathered the instruments and items he would need for the surgery. He had pieced together a small surgical kit from items looted from a veterinarian's clinic. He was sure Reed wouldn't mind that Fido may have been the previous patient on which the tools were used. Xylocaine was his only pain killer. He filled a syringe with the local anesthetic. He had nothing stronger with which to knock Reed out, nor the knowledge to use it if he had. Suture needle, thread, probe, forceps, hemostats, and scalpel – he had a limited kit, but it should suffice. If a large vein or artery had been nicked … He preferred to not to let his mind go there.

Reed entered wearing only a towel draped around his waist, his belly fat rolling over the edge. He was pale, forlorn, and frightened. He eyed the surgical tools warily. He held one hand over the wound, but blood still seeped between his fingers. "Where do you want to perform this miracle surgery?" A slight quavering in his voice betrayed the insouciance of his words.

Jake waved him toward the kitchen table, which he had cleared off. Reed shrugged and lay down on the table, which creaked and groaned in protest to his weight but held together.

"I can't knock you out," Jake warned, "but I can deaden the area with a local, xylocaine."

"Just make it quick," Reed replied.

"This may hurt a bit."

Jake drove the needle home and injected the xylocaine just under the skin near the wound, which was still bleeding. Reed winced and clenched his fists but said nothing as the needle went in. While he waited for the area to numb, he explained to Reed what he was going to do. Reed listened attentively until he reached the part about extracting the bullet.

"What if it's in too deep?"

Jake had worried about the possibility also. "If it was a small caliber slug. It shouldn't be a problem. If it was a high velocity bullet … well, I'll have to dig deeper." The longer it took him to extract the bullet, the more likely the sedative would wear off before he finished. The pain would be excruciating. "Can you take it?"

"I don't have much choice, do I?"

"No, not really. Are you ready?

Reed nodded. "Just try to make the scar small so it won't show when I wear my Speedo."

Jake understood that Reed's attempt at humor masked his fear. He was almost as afraid as Reed. He took a deep breath to try to quell his own apprehension. He had slapped bandages over wounds in Afghanistan and splinted broken limbs, but other than removing the cactus thorns from Jessica, his surgical experience was limited to stitching up a goat that had nicked its side on barbed wire. He prodded the area with his gloved finger to test the numbness. Reed didn't respond. He had to work quickly before the anesthetic wore off.

"Okay, here we go."

He hesitated on his first pass with the scalpel and realized he had cut too shallowly through Reed's excessive layer of fat, and made a second deeper pass. He wiped the blood spilling from the wound with a towel, wishing he had some suction to clear away the blood to see more clearly. The flow of blood didn't increase dramatically, a sign that no major veins had been severed by the bullet's passing or by his inexperience as a surgeon. Once the opening was large enough, he grasped the probe firmly with his blood-slick fingers, and gently pushed it into the wound and moved it around. Reed wriggled on the table. Jake hoped it was more from nervousness than from pain. The end of the probe encountered a hard object about three inches in. He hoped it was the bullet. He wished he had a retractor, as he held the wound open with one hand. He reminded himself of *Jake's Law #8 - Use the tools you've got.* He slipped the forceps inside the open wound. He was working blindly. It took three attempts to locate the bullet with the forceps. Glancing at the clock, he cursed at the time. Almost twenty minutes had passed. Finally, he grasped the bullet with the forceps and tugged. Nothing happened. The bullet was lodged deep in the abdominal muscle.

Reed's squirming became worse. "I can feel that," he said. He had an edge of panic in his voice.

The anesthetic was wearing off. Jake snapped at him. "Stay still. This is hard enough without you crawling all over the table."

"I, I can't breathe," Reed gasped.

At first, Jake dismissed Reed's complaint as panic, but Reed's breathing was becoming ragged. His body heaved as he fought for air. He had quickly read through the contraindications written on the xylocaine box and remembered that one allergic reaction was bronchial tightening. Since Reed already suffered from allergies his breathing could become worse. Jake couldn't break away from his surgery to find Reed's inhaler. He increased his pace.

There was no time for finesse or carefully cutting away the muscle to free the bullet. He resorted to brute force. He tugged and twisted the bullet, as Reed moaned and squirmed on the table. Jake worried that if he lost his grip on the bullet, he would never find it again or worse, push it deeper into the wound. Reed convulsed on the table, trying to sit up to ease his restricted breathing. Jake shoved him back down on the table, leaned his weight onto Reed's stomach, and yanked as if he were pulling a rotten tooth. The bullet popped free. He quickly pushed a wad of gauze into the open wound to temporarily staunch the bleeding, hoping the bullet hadn't splintered, and rushed to Reed's discarded clothing. He found the inhaler in Reed's pocket, and handed it to him. After three quick puffs, Reed settled down. His breathing was still ragged, but the inhaler acted as much as a placebo as a breathing aid, calming him.

Jake removed the gauze, pleased to see only a trickle of blood oozing out of the wound. He began suturing the wound, layer by layer, with dissolvable stitches. His handiwork with a needle would never earn him an embroidery prize, but he managed to stop the bleeding and close the wound. He set aside his instruments, removed and discarded his bloody gloves, and wiped the perspiration from his forehead. Only then did he allow himself to take a deep breath to calm his own nerves.

"I wrote my name with the stitches," he said. "I hope you don't mind."

"Did you get it?" Reed's voice was weak, but the panic in it was gone.

"Yeah." He held out the bullet for Reed to inspect. "It looks like a .38 round. Another two inches and you would have been singing with the angels."

"Thanks," he said, as he lay back on the table; then winced. "I think the xylocaine is beginning to wear off."

Jake suppressed a grin. "I've got some sedatives for the pain."

Reed shook his head. "No. I'll manage."

Jake washed the area with soap and water, and then alcohol to disinfect it. He placed a gauze pad over the wound and wrapped a bandage tightly around Reed's waist to hold it in place.

"If it doesn't become infected, you'll live."

He helped Reed down from the table and to the bedroom. After Reed was tucked away beneath the covers, Jake said, "I'll make some chicken soup."

"You don't have any chickens," Reed reminded him.

"I've got Campbell's. It'll do."

After placing the soup in a pot and setting it to simmer, he decided to take a shower to wash away Reed's blood. It would have to be a quick one. He doubted anyone had bothered refilling the water tank during his absence. With the well being washed away or buried beneath tons of mud, what water they had would have to last. The hot water revived him. He longed to linger beneath the hot needle jets, let them massage away his problems and the soreness of his muscles, but the need for water to drink or cook with overcame the urge to drown his sorrows in the shower.

After drying off and dressing in clean clothes, he carried a bowl of soup to Reed, but found him sleeping. He set the soup and a glass of water beside the bed and closed the door behind him as he left. He looked at his face in the bathroom mirror. He looked thinner and older than he remembered. He hadn't shaved in a week and several bruises glowed purple beneath the stubble. He made a fist with his hand. His fingers were swollen. He downed one of his Actos pills and a diuretic for the bloating. The window was still open from Jessica's escape. The floor and towels were wet from rain water. He closed the window gently to avoid waking Reed. Grabbing the bottle of whiskey from the living room, he strode out onto the balcony to bear witness to the destruction of his domain.

Darkness had hidden the true measure of destruction from him. By dawn's light, he could see that it was all gone. The flood had scoured the canyon clean like a bulldozer through a rain forest. Everything he had built, everything his grandfather had built, was gone as if it had never existed. Seventy-three years of history vanished, like the numerous native tribes who had inhabited the area centuries before, leaving only bits and pieces of their existence and numerous unanswered questions. Nature's fury had passed, but the echoes of the storm of gunfire still thundered in his ears. He took a swig from the bottle to silence them.

The single wash had become three separate channels, each bearing its load of silt-laden water down the canyon. As he watched, a fifteen-foot saguaro whose roots had been eaten away by the flood toppled into the stream and rushed away like a paper sailboat in a gutter. The wreckage of the RV was strewn about outside the tumbled wall, leaving a trail of breadcrumbs – a bumper here, a wheel there, a windshield glinting in the early morning sun. What appeared to be the front wheel and fork of a twisted Harley motorcycle projected from the mud, a mad artist's sculpture draped with limbs from the cottonwood tree and coils of razor wire. Shattered tree trunks, piles of rock, and heaps of metal rose from the mud and puddles of water like small islands. He saw no sign of the jeep that Jessica and Levi had been in and sighed a breath of relief. Levi still had her, but she was alive.

To his astonishment, three figures trudged through the mud and water, the three women he had freed. They had survived the flood. He felt a moment of joy. At least he had saved someone. He yelled down to them.

"Come up here and dry off. You're safe now."

He went back inside to check on Reed. He was awake and eating the soup.

"You're alive."

"So far," Reed replied.

"How's the pain?"

He hesitated before replying, "Manageable."

Jake was impressed at Reed's composure. He wasn't sure he could have put on such a brave face with such an injury. "Good. I have some questions for you."

He sat down in a chair beside the bed. Seeing the stern look on Jake's face, Reed set the bowl aside. "Shoot."

"How did you manage to build an IED with a timer, and before you say from books, you don't learn that kind of skill from books. I saw a few IEDs in Afghanistan, and that was an expert job."

Reed shook his head. "It's not important."

Jake pointed his index finger at Reed and cocked his head. "I think it is. You build bombs, you reload cartridges, you hotwire motorcycles – that seems strange for a high school science teacher. Just who the hell are you?"

"I'm Alton Reed, science teacher."

Jake shook his head. "No, you're more than that. No more secrets between us."

Reed sighed. "I taught science in San Manuel like I said. When things fell apart, I went to one of the FEMA camps in Phoenix. It was … less than I had hoped. Food was rationed, gangs ran wild, but the worst were the summary executions. If someone got sick, for any reason, the soldiers simply shot them and dragged away the body. Anyone caught stealing, hoarding, or trying to escape were shot as well. We were prisoners and they were the wardens. I heard about the military recruiting people for a special project and figured anything was better than languishing in the camp. I volunteered. The idea was to infiltrate uncontrolled areas, report on any activity, and if possible, recruit suitable people to help establish safe zones. They sent me back here because I knew the area."

Jake was floored. His anger coiled inside ready to explode. "A spy? You're a damned spy."

Reed shrugged. "Of sorts. An A-10 spotted your canyon on a flyover, and they asked me to investigate. I saw how well you had prepared and thought you might prove useful. I started the fire in the school hoping you would come."

"So you weren't just killing zombies."

"Oh, I wanted to kill zombies all right. That part was no lie, but I also needed to see how you would react."

"If I hadn't helped you?"

Reed shrugged again. "Then you probably weren't the man we wanted."

Jake released his anger, laughed, and took a swig of whiskey. "I'm still not."

"I think you are. You have the skills, and even if you pretend you don't, I know you care about people. You've proven that. You were willing to risk everything to rescue Jessica and me."

Had he? Had he come back for them or just for his ranch? Whatever his reasons, he wasn't going to give Reed the satisfaction of thinking he was right. "I was after Levi. He needed to die."

"If you insist. Still, you could have killed him without rescuing us. It would have been quicker and safer for you."

He decided to change the subject. "Did the military teach you to build bombs?"

"They taught me a lot of things. One of them was how to read people. I taught kids, so I was pretty good at reading people already. They taught me what to look for in the particular kind of person we needed to help rebuild."

Jake shook his head. "I'm not him."

"Jake, there are thousands of people in camp all over the country with no place to go. They're restless, half starving, and they're giving up hope. Suicides are up twenty percent. The cities are too dangerous for anyone to live in. Pacification, as the army calls their zombie killing expeditions, is going slow. They're too spread out. Splitting the survivors up into smaller groups, maybe fifty or sixty people each, is our only hope. They can become self sufficient until the military can complete its zombie operations."

Jake raised the bottle of whiskey and shook it at Reed. The liquor sloshed around. Some of it splashed out of the bottle onto his hand. "And you think I want to babysit a bunch of survivors." He licked the spilled whiskey from his hand.

"Yes, I do. For years, you showed people how to survive with your website. You're ex-law enforcement and ex-military. You've got a lot you can teach them – how to shoot, how to farm, how to survive. Why not put it into practice?"

The idea had a certain attraction to him, not babysitting a herd of people, but teaching them what he had learned over the years. Except for his house, everything was gone. He would have to start over. Could he do it alone? Could he trust the military to fulfill any promises Reed might make in their behalf?

"If I did, what help would I get?"

Reed smiled. "Food, weapons, equipment – anything, well, almost anything you need. Most of all, you would provide authority, enforce the law. You were a deputy."

He wondered how they would react to Jake's Laws, but decided they might find them a little harsh. "A bulldozer for the roads?" he asked.

"I'm sure they will help you locate one. They intend to clear the rails between here and Phoenix and Tucson to Yuma.

Eventually, they will run trains throughout the entire southwest linking new settlements. We can build new cities on the bones of the old."

"I like Tucson. I like my home."

"It's a strategic location. They won't abandon it."

"I'll think it over. If I decide, how do we contact them?"

Reed frowned. "That might present a problem. I had a satphone in the RV. I contacted them once a week. It's gone now. I guess we wait until they contact us. Now what?"

Now what? That was a good question. Did he want to sit around drinking whiskey and crying over lost possessions, or put the bit between his teeth and soldier on? If Jessica was alive, he would find her. He wouldn't rest until Levi was in the ground, or at least lying dead on it. Any chance at rebuilding would be useless if Levi was still around. He was chaos wearing a Stetson. Such men had no place in the new world. It was men like Jake's job to bring them to justice, justice according to Jake's Laws.

He set the whiskey bottle on the table and rose from his chair, a little shaky from the half bottle he had consumed and fatigue. "I need to locate a vehicle and find Jessica."

"Wait a day or two and I'll help you."

Could he afford to wait a few days to rescue Jessica? He didn't really have a choice. He didn't know where she was. He was certain Levi would find a way to let him know where they were once he was ready for another confrontation. Their business wasn't finished yet.

"There are three women on their way up, some of Levi's bunch. They survived the flood. I don't know if we can trust them, but they can nurse you back to health."

Reed smiled.

"What?" Jake asked.

"You saved them, didn't you?"

"I might have pointed out which way to run."

"Thanks. I saw how the women were treated. I think we can trust them."

"Well, you need to rest so your wound can heal. I left the ATV outside the canyon last night on high ground. Maybe it survived the flood."

"Jake?"

Jake looked down at Reed. His face was pale from the exertion of talking and fighting the pain. "Yeah?"

"I didn't like lying to you. I had to find out about you."

Jake smiled. "It's okay, Alton. I guess we both had our secrets."

"Thanks for coming back."

Jake left the room feeling ashamed at how he had treated Reed. If they had both trusted each other a little more, they could have avoided much of the problems they had faced. His pig-headed stubbornness to do things himself and follow only his self-written laws had almost cost him his life and the lives of the only two people he cared about. Maybe it was time to relinquish a little authority and follow Reed's advice.

He met the women at the foot of the steps. "There's a wounded man up there. Do what you can for him. Most of the food is gone, but you'll find a crate of MREs in the closet."

The pregnant woman spoke for the others. "Thank you for saving us. We …"

Jake waved her to silence. He had enough thanks for one day. "Take care of Alton."

He walked past the ruins of his ranch without looking at them. He had seen enough already. The loss was almost more than he could bear. It wasn't until he reached the first of the mud-encrusted bodies rising from the mud like zombies escaping their graves that he felt remorse for what he had done in unleashing the dam. Levi's men would have killed him, had in fact tried to do so, but breaking the dam now seemed somehow like cheating. Much like using his zombie army the first time he had encountered Levi. In the dark during the heat of battle, such thoughts had not arisen. He wanted them dead at any cost. Seeing their sun-bloated corpses littering the muddy canyon floor drove home the consequences of his actions.

Like a powerful one-two punch, the realization that rather than preparing for an apocalypse, he had been stumbling blindly through life since before E-Day, before he had the end of the world to blame everything on. The anger and self-banishment from the human race that had begun in Afghanistan had been reinforced as a deputy sheriff. Men did terrible things to one another for little reason. He had witnessed such horrors almost every day on the job. He, himself, had done terrible things in Afghanistan, things he had tried to bury deep in his subconscious, but like a black viscous pool of regrets, it had slowly bubbled to the surface and tainted his personal relationships with his fellow human beings, especially women. His distrust of Reed and of Jessica had placed them both in danger. He had almost lost Reed. He had lost Jessica. Only when a man loses everything can he truly be free.

Free to do what? He would find her, if at all possible. Somehow, he knew Levi would be in touch.

He found the ATV intact, high enough above the flood plain to survive the deluge. The seats were soaked and the water was three inches deep in the floorboards. He cranked it and drove it up an incline to spill out the water. Back at the ranch, vultures, drawn by the stench of death, circled overhead, a cloud of black undulating lazily on the thermals rising from the canyon floor. He knew he should bury the bodies, but hated to deprive the vultures of a meal.

To his astonishment, when he entered the house, Reed was sitting on the sofa. His face was flushed from the effort, but he had at least managed to make it from the bedroom. Two of the women fawned over him, trying to spoon feed him more soup. The third was preparing more MREs.

"You should be in bed."

Reed shook his head and tapped his chest. "I'm still having a little trouble breathing. I think it's the humidity. This monsoon weather feels like Florida. Sitting up is better. I'll be all right. I have these pretty nurses to help me."

One of the women, barely sixteen, tittered.

"You make a lousy patient."

"You make a lousy host. Where's the beer?"

"I'll see if our former guests left any."

The refrigerator had been ransacked, as had the pantry, but a few loose beers had managed to roll beneath a shelf and escape detection. He popped the top of one over the sink and allowed the hot beer to spew; then dropped a few cubes of ice in a glass and poured the beer over it.

"Drink it fast before the ice dilutes it," he said, as he handed the beer to Reed.

He took a sip and nodded. "I don't think he'll hurt her again."

Jake winced at the mention of Jessica. "Again?" He noticed the look of rage on Reed's face and guessed at how Levi had hurt her. "That's something else I owe him for."

"He'll keep her safe to use as bait. He'll make sure everything is just the way he wants it before he contacts you. He won't make the same mistake again."

"No, but he keeps making the biggest mistake. Why doesn't he just leave? We've beaten him twice. If he releases Jessica, I'll forget about him."

Reed shook his head. "No you won't."

Jake sighed and nodded. Reed was right. Some things can't be undone. "Yeah. He bothers me. Men like him don't deserve to live."

"I tend to agree with you."

Jake snorted in surprise. "You? I thought you were all for justice."

Reed took another longer swig of beer. "Sometimes justice comes from the barrel of a gun."

"There's hope for you yet."

Reed leaned forward in his seat and winced at the effort. One of the women pressed him back in his seat, took his glass from him, and set it down on the coffee table.

"Stay still," she said.

Reed ignored her. His eyes bore into Jake's as he said, "There's a time for revenge and a time for justice. In this instance, both can be meted out simultaneously, just as long as you remember that your primary responsibility is to free Jessica."

Thinking of Jessica in Levi's hands sent a cold shiver running through Jake's body. God only knew what Levi had already done to her. Would he take out his anger of him on her? Reed was right. He wanted Jessica back more than he wanted Levi dead, but the two outcomes were now inexorably intertwined. Levi would see to that. He doubted he could accomplish one without first achieving the other.

"I'll bring her back," he promised Reed. "I'll bring her back, or I won't be back at all."

23

June 30, 2016   Tucson Mall, Tucson, AZ –

She had endured their ceaseless torment for two days and nights. Sleep had become almost impossible, limited to short cat naps which were then interrupted by the zombies' wailing and their renewed attempts to get to her through the door. She had resorted to wads of paper towels shoved into her ears to dampen the sound. She was beginning to hope that Levi would return, hoping he hadn't left her to die alone and in the dark.

In the two days since their miraculous escape from Jake's ranch moments ahead of the wall of water rushing down the canyon, or rather Levi's escape with her as his prisoner, she had feared for her life. Levi's mood was such that she did nothing to antagonize him, certain that he would kill her in a homicidal rage. As long as she was still alive, Jake would find her. He had risked all and lost all to save her and Reed. Her heart had raced with joy when she had glimpsed him outside the tent. It had cried in pain, as she saw the wall of water rushing down on him. She chose to think he was still alive. He was a survivor. He would come for her.

She was in the Tucson Mall. She had recognized it by its silhouette against the pre-dawn sky. The roar of the nearby Rillito River drowned out Levi's curses, as he pushed her inside through the rear door of *Forever 21*, a clothing store. He hadn't given her time to explore her surroundings before shoving her into a cleaning closet and locking the door.

He had opened the door several hours later to glare silently at her. She had expected the worst, but he had tossed in a bottle of water, a bag of stale potato chips, and pull-open tab can of pork and beans. She couldn't believe that Levi still wanted to kill Jake. That such hatred could drive a man beyond reason confused her. He had spent so much effort in surviving, why would he risk his life for revenge?

"You must really hate him."

He closed his eyes and lifted his head. A look of ecstasy turned his face into a mask of evil. When he finally looked at her, he was smiling. "Oh, I hate him all right. He epitomizes all I detest in life.

He's a cop. The law. People like him have hounded me all my life. They beat me and tossed me away like so much garbage; left me to die with the other disposables. I owe somebody. He's as good a target as any. We make quite a pair, he and I. We understand each other. He knows what it is to be alone, and have everything ripped away. He hates me like I hate him. Our face off is as inevitable as dawn, as irrevocable as Judgment Day."

"He'll kill you," she said.

He took a step toward her. She backed away as far as she could, but he stopped a few steps away from her.

"He'll have to get to me first. This time I've raised an army of my own. We'll see just how good Jake Blakely really is."

Jessica's heart sank. She didn't think Levi cared if he died as long as he could take Jake with him. Then, he had opened the store's front door and let in the zombies before escaping out the rear door. No prison could have been more perfect or more deadly.

* * * *

Gunfire outside the door awakened her. At first, she had thought Jake had found her. That hope was dashed as the door opened to reveal Levi standing in the pool of moonlight. With his goatee and the brim of his hat turned up like horns, he presented the silhouette of a devil.

"Come with me," he said.

When she reached the door, he grabbed her, clamped her hands behind her back, and tied them with rope. The zombies inside the store lay dead on the floor, their blood staining the tile floor. He marched her through the mall, past *Macy's,* past a bath and beauty store, whose fragrances barely concealed the stench of rotting food and decaying corpses. She spotted several zombies in the distance, moving through the shadows, but they were moving toward the source of the gunfire in *Forever 21.* The sounds of glass crunching as the creatures trod through shattered glass revealed that more were inside the mall than she could see. When she glimpsed the stairs between the lower and upper levels, she at first thought he was taking her upstairs. Then he played his flashlight on a wooden barricade erected to block access from the top level, and then a second barricade pushed aside at the bottom of the staircase. Her heart tightened in her chest. She tried to stop, but Levi grabbed her by the neck and squeezed to keep her feet moving. He dragged her up the stairs to the first landing, and then secured her to the railing with a length of rope. She had just enough slack to stand and move a couple of paces. The scuffing feet of zombies grew louder.

"Don't leave me here," she pleaded.

"You'll be safe for a while. If Jake doesn't come for you, or if I don't come back, well, you're going to die a horrible death."

His maniacal laughter made her shiver, as it echoed through the cavernous space and continued for far too long. She suspected that he was becoming unhinged by his obsession for revenge. No sane man would go through so much trouble simply to kill another. Then she realized that Jake's death was not what he was after. First, he wanted Jake to suffer. Placing her in his path, with the threat of death hanging over her, would force Jake to decide which he wanted more – to free her or to kill Levi. To add insult to injury, he wadded up a rag that tasted of sweat and shoved it into her mouth, securing it in place with a second rag.

"Just so you're not tempted to warn him."

At the bottom of the stairs, Levi moved the second barricade into place. Zombies couldn't climb over or go around the barricades, but they could gather around her. Enough of them could smash or topple the barricade. It wouldn't keep them at bay for very long. She was trapped, silenced and trapped.

She watched Levi until he disappeared into the darkness, and then began frantically tugging on her bonds, trying to free her wrists, but the ropes were too tight. She only succeeded in burning her wrists. Next, she attempted to remove the gag, but the cloth securing it prevented her. Exhausted by her efforts, she sat down on a step to think. She noticed that she already had an audience. Two zombies on the upper level were clawing at the barricade. She cringed at each rattle and shudder of the makeshift obstacle Levi had cobbled together from wooden freight pallets and window shutters from a home accessory store. More zombies gathered on the lower level, drawn by the noise. They stared up at her with dead-set eyes, keening their hunger. Most of them were Shamblers, too weak to pose a serious threat if she hadn't been bound, but she feared Runners would be strong enough to wreck the flimsy obstruction.

After an hour, she was surrounded by zombies. She wondered why so many of the creatures would be in the mall since most of the stores had closed at the height of the infection. Then she remembered Levi's words. He was herding the creatures into the mall in preparation for Jake's arrival. He was setting his trap, a deadly gauntlet of flesh-eating creatures through which Jake must first pass to reach her, and then negotiate to escape. She suspected there would be more than just zombies in Jake's path. Somewhere in the vast labyrinth of darkened corridors and stores, Levi would be waiting, deadly eager for revenge.

24

June 30, 2016   Split Rock Canyon   Galiuro Mountains, AZ
—

Under the ministrations of his three nurses, Reed was mending, Jake's surgical skills notwithstanding. Some of the color had returned to the schoolteacher/spy's cheeks, and he was up and walking, if gingerly, about the house. It would be days longer before he would be fit to travel, but Jake was eager for his friend to heal. Reed could then contact his friends in Phoenix and begin the process of reintroducing civilization to Tucson. Jake had another destiny, one which might leave Reed alone to do the job. He had to find Jessica. Every day she was with Levi kept her in danger.

Jake had relented in his refusal to bury the dead and leaving them as vulture food, but it was to reduce the stench of death rather than any remorse on his part. He had dragged them to the same gulley he had disposed of the zombies. Their corpses were gone, of course, washed away by the rains, but he thought it a fitting final resting place. The smoke of their funeral pyre rose high into the air. He hoped Levi was watching and could guess at the smoke's source.

He methodically cleaned every weapon in the house. That included the machinegun for which he had no more ammunition. It helped to pass the time. By some quirk of the raging flood, or grace from God, the well wasn't damaged. The pump was missing, but the steel cap over the opening remained in place, protecting the well from filling with sand. With a new replacement pump, he would be back in business. Only the foundation of his grandfather's house remained to show where it had stood for seventy-three years. His smokehouse, his chicken coop, his fences, even his fruit trees were gone. All that remained was a lone ironwood tree standing at the edge of the wash, its roots so deeply imbedded in the earth that the flood couldn't uproot it.

Jake was beginning to worry that Levi might not contact him after all. His worst fear was that Jessica might already be dead and that Levi fled the area. Such maudlin thoughts nagged at him, played with his guilty conscience, as he watched the sunset over the mountains. Its passing left an icy cold stain in the center of his soul. *Mea culpa*, his mind whispered. *It's your fault she's gone.* He sat on the balcony all afternoon, ignoring the heat, humidity, and the biting insects. If any of them carried the Staggers' parasite, he no longer cared if he was immune. He was tired of waiting. His coffee had grown cold. He poured it over the balcony railing and, in a fit of rage, sent the cup sailing after it.

Three quick gunshots in the distance drew his attention. He knew without hesitation that it was Levi. He smiled. Reed had heard the shots too. He hobbled out onto the balcony.

"Did I hear gunshots?"

Jake nodded toward the foot of the canyon. "Levi." He turned to leave.

"You're not going out there?" Reed said. "He might be waiting with a rifle."

Jake's face was grim, as he said, "No, he wants to see me face-to-face before he kills me. He wants to make it up close and personal. I'll be safe."

He drove the ATV down the canyon, keeping his eyes on the rim of the canyon and the shadows around the base in spite of his assurances to Reed. He could be wrong about Levi. The newly erected waist-high cairn of rocks was visible enough without the glittering jeweled lawn ornament sitting on top reflecting the dying rays of the sun. As expected, Levi was nowhere to be seen. A piece of paper sat beneath the ornament. He picked it up and read it.

"Your lady friend is about to be become zombie food in the Tucson Mall. Come and get her. Come alone or she dies. Come tonight. If she's still alive in the morning, I'll kill her."

Jake wadded the note and squeezed, imagining Levi's neck in his grasp. He checked the sun. He had less than half an hour before nightfall. By the time he reached the mall, it would be full dark. It was the night of a waning crescent moon, but the sky was cloudy. He couldn't depend on moonlight and a flashlight would make him an easy target. He would have to trust his night vision. He lifted his head and cupped his hands around his mouth.

"I'm coming, Levi," he yelled to the surrounding desert. "I'm coming for you!"

He didn't know if Levi heard him, but announcing his attentions to the world made him feel better.

Back at the ranch, he explained his intentions to Reed as he prepared for his confrontation. Reed cautioned against a headlong assault. "Don't go after him like a bulldog. Sneak in like a mouse. That *mano a mano* shit will get both you and Jessica killed."

Jake stripped, donned black pants and shirt and smeared black paint across his forehead and cheeks with a camo stick. "Levi won't make it that easy," he said, as he slipped his Remington Model 1911 pistol into his belt beside his hunting knife. He loaded the AA-12 shotgun. It was large and clumsy and the noise would attract zombies, but its massive firepower might come in handy. He fitted four bolts into the quick-detach quiver of the Parker Concorde crossbow, and then added a second quiver beneath it. He would use the crossbow for silent work. The pistol and shotgun were for zombies or any other surprises Levi might have in store. The knife was for driving into Levi's heart.

"Let me go with you," Reed asked.

"You're in no shape to come," he answered, as he slung the crossbow over his shoulder by its strap. "Besides, if Levi is watching, he might kill her. He warned me to come alone." He glanced at the young girl who had claimed Reed as her patient. "You have to keep these ladies safe." She beamed at him.

"How do you know he won't simply shoot you down as soon as you walk in?"

He paused. "I don't, but there's no sport in that. Levi wants to gloat before he kills me. Call it professional bastard courtesy."

Reed grabbed a notebook and pen and began sketching on a page. He drew a rough diagram of the Tucson Mall and labeled the anchor stores. He hesitated, chewing on the tip of the pen as he thought, before filling in a few more names in a hurried scribble. "I don't know all the stores, but here's a few I do remember from visits there." He thrust the paper at Jake. "It might help you orient yourself."

Jake took the paper, glanced at it, and shoved it in his shirt pocket. "Thanks."

Reed grabbed Jake's shoulder. "For God's sake be careful, Jake. Get Jessica out safely before you start another war with Levi."

The pointed reminder of his last failed encounter with Levi wasn't lost on him. "I will." He glanced around the room, hoping he would see it again. "If I don't make it back ..." He left the rest of the sentence unfinished. If he didn't make it back, nothing he said would matter.

Reed's smile, as he said, "You will" was meant to comfort him. Instead, it looked more like a last goodbye.

As he started to leave, he saw his great grandfather's badge on the floor where Levi had discarded it. He picked it up, ran his fingers over it, allowing the history that had soaked into the tarnished metal through the years bleed into his soul. He had worn it as a reminder of his family's past. Now, as he pinned it to his chest, he wore it to remind him that there was no law but the law that came from the barrel of a gun – Jake's Law. In Levi's case, death was the only sentence that mattered, and he intended to carry it out *post haste*.

The road to San Manuel was now a series of washes still running deep from mountain runoff, though less raging than at the height of the storm. Parts of the road were washed away completely. Other sections were buried beneath feet of sand, mud, and gravel. He chose the most direct course, splashing through washes at full speed. In places, he left the road completely, dodging teddy bear cholla and saguaros with a blatant disregard for life and limb. Night fell as he passed through San Manuel, paying no attention to the zombies that came out to greet him. He had no time to linger.

The trip to Tucson, normally an hour's drive, took almost three. Traffic snarls of abandoned vehicles, trees blown over by the wind, and areas washed out by the rain plagued his journey. At the edge of the ridge sloping gently down into the Rillito River valley, he stopped. The twin beams of the headlights revealed a dead city. Abandoned and burned vehicles, piles of trash, smashed barricades, and skeletal corpses marked the scene of a past battle, some last stand along the banks of the river. Some of the dead wore military uniforms. It had been a last ditch attempt to save the city. It had failed.

After crossing the Rillito River, he parked the ATV beside the road and continued on foot along the river bank. He hoped the sound of rushing water had masked the noise of the ATV. He had no idea where inside the massive darkened mall Jessica might be, but he was certain Levi wouldn't make her rescue easy. Searching the mall from end to end would be the logical approach to finding her. He hoped Levi expected him to do exactly that, barging in through the main entrance, guns blazing. Part of him wanted to go in all gangbuster, but caution was safer. He chose to start in the middle and trust to luck.

A few lumbering shapes in the darkness betrayed the presence of zombies in the parking lot. Most he bypassed easily. One creature stood between him and the fire escape he wished to use to reach the upper level of Dillard's on the north side of the mall. The creature was just a dim shape in the faint moonlight. He aimed the crossbow carefully from the cover of an overgrown Palo Blanco tree, following the zombie's erratic movement. He braced his back against the tree's peeling white bark, held his breath, and fired. The bolt buried halfway into the creature's skull. Its hand reached upward for the offending feathered bolt, but dropped as the zombie collapsed on the pavement. None of the other creatures noticed its demise.

Jake sprinted across the parking lot and up the fire escape. He forced the lock at the top of the fire escape and entered Dillard's through the personnel only section. Navigating the near pitch black interior was difficult. Clothing, housewares, and handbags littered the floor from overturned shelves. Almost stepping into the decaying chest of a corpse, he lost his balance. He caught himself before falling on top of it, but brushed his right side against the corpse, releasing a nauseating stink. His leg and side of his shirt came away sticky from blood and rotting body fluids. The cloying stench of death and decay smell made him gag. He fought down the urge to vomit.

As he recovered, a figure loomed suddenly out of the gloom in his peripheral vision. He turned and had his finger pressed to the trigger of the shotgun ready to fire, and then chuckled silently when he realized that he had almost shot a Styrofoam store mannequin wearing a short summer skirt and long blonde wig. As he neared the store entrance onto the mall, the damage to the store became more severe and more recent. The glass sliding doors were smashed. Displays were overturned. Jewelry from a broken case carpeted the floor. He picked his way carefully through the rings, pendants, and broken glass to the edge of the door and peered out. He could barely make out the barrel vault ceiling overhead. The white columns supporting it stood like pale ghosts rising from the shadows. The tiled floor glistened with rainwater seeping through holes in the roof damaged by recent windstorms. The steady dripping became a background for the wails and high-pitched keening of the scores of zombies moving in the shadows on both levels of the mall. Levi had used his zombie army trick against him. Things had just gotten hairy.

He ducked back inside the doorway as a zombie stumbled down the walkway toward him. When it drew even with the doorway, it paused to sniff the air. Jake raised the crossbow and waited. If he cocked it, the hiss of CO_2 from the automatic cocking mechanism would alert the zombie. The zombie turned in a half circle, sniffing the air, and then continued down the walkway. Jake caught a whiff of the sickly odor rising from his clothing. The stench of decay on his pants and shirt had confused it.

The mall was a vast cavern of walkways, courtyards, stores, kiosks, and corridors. Searching the entire mall in the dark could take hours, and he knew he didn't have that long. He chose a direction at random, and moved southeast along the walkway past a telecommunications store, a looted jewelry store, and a restaurant reeking of rotten food. As he turned the corner at *Forever 21*, he heard the wailing and groaning of many zombies further down the mall and knew that his destination lay in that direction. The creatures were gathering there for a reason – Jessica. He stopped to consult Reed's crude map. The shot came unexpectedly, striking the glass behind him, shattering it, followed by a peal of raucous laughter. *Levi.* He ducked behind the railing. The shot had been close but not too close. Levi had intended his first shot to miss as the initial salvo of their game of nerves.

"Your lady friend is at the east end of the mall, Blakely," Levi yelled. "Better find her fast."

At least I chose the right direction. Jake searched the darkness across the mall for Levi but could see nothing. He was too well hidden in the shadows. For the bullet to strike where it had, the shot would have had to originate from the upper level. The gift card store or the coffee shop offered the best angle. Jake chose the coffee shop and fired two quick rounds from the shotgun, and then raced down the walkway toward Jessica. The discharge of the shotgun thundered in the cavernous space, rattling storefront windows and echoing back and forth down the twisting corridors until it finally rumbled silent. Glass exploded from the front of the coffee shop as Levi returned fire. Jake dove to the ground and slid on the rain-slicked tile floor headfirst through the open doorway of a tuxedo shop, sending a rack of ties and belts tumbling in all directions. He slammed into the corner of a wooden counter with his shoulder, dropping the shotgun. It skidded deeper into the store, disappearing into the yawning darkness within. Before he could recover it, a zombie rounded the corner and grabbed his right foot. He kicked the creature in the head with the other foot until it released him, but it lunged again. He pulled his knife from his belt and drove the blade into the top of the creature's head, twisting the handle until it went limp when the blade severed its hindbrain. It fell across his legs. He kicked it away with disgust.

As he got to his feet, another zombie, this time a more agile Runner, appeared from the store next door. Jake cocked the crossbow and fired. At 300 feet per second, the twenty-inch bolt passed straight through the creature's head and imbedded in the wall behind it. The Runner took one more step forward before crashing into and over the railing. It landed with a sickening thud on the tiled courtyard below, its blood mixing with the puddles of water. Jake leaned over the railing to see the crowd of zombies rushing to investigate the sound. A second shot from Levi struck the railing inches from his hand. Levi was through playing games. Now, he meant business.

The battle had become a game of hide-and-seek. Keeping low, he continued east along the walkway. Twice, he stopped to kill zombies that came at him, using his crossbow. He now had three bolts remaining. Simple math told him that three didn't go into dozens of zombies enough times to matter. It was time to change his tactics.

Knowing Levi could place a bullet in his back at any moment from the shadows, Jake stood to expose himself, reversed directions, and ran at full speed back the way he had come. Shots followed him, shattering windows and chipping brick behind him. He reached a crosswalk over the lower courtyard, raced across it, and hurdled down the stairs opposite three at a time. He didn't stop until he was safely ensconced behind a kiosk selling cell phones.

His bold move had taken Levi by surprise. Levi was now on the upper level where he would have to expose himself to shoot down at him, and he didn't think Levi was that stupid. He had bought a few more precious minutes in which to search for Jessica.

Using benches, planters, and other kiosks as cover, he crossed the courtyard until he was beneath the upper walkway. As he crossed in front of a perfume shop, the overpowering sickly-sweet miasma of comingled perfumes rose from broken bottles beneath his feet and brought tears to his eyes. In the silence, he could hear the faint ticking of numerous watches from a nearby watch repair kiosk, their batteries still functioning and beyond that, the soft scuffling of zombie feet. A sharper sound above him caused him to freeze. The sound was not repeated, ruling out a zombie crashing around. Levi was above him waiting for him to expose himself again. If he still had his shotgun, he would have been tempted to race out and empty it at the walkway in hopes of killing his adversary, but this was not simply about two men trying to kill one another. Another life was at stake, Jessica, and her life was more important than revenge.

The area of the courtyard in front of Macy's was a sea of zombies, illuminated by a thin sliver of moonlight entering through a broken skylight. They milled about on both levels in great numbers, raising a loud group moan. When he saw Jessica, her face pale in the moonlight, his heart thundered in rage. She was trussed up like an animal sacrifice on the stairs. The barricades at each end of the stairwell were flimsy and beginning to give under the combined weight of starving zombies. Her movements were frantic, as she tried to free herself. He knew any move he made toward her would reveal him to Levi. That was Levi's demented plan – toy with him before killing him. Even the automatic shotgun wouldn't have cleared a hole through the massed zombies. What could he do with a pistol, a knife, and three remaining crossbow bolts?

He needed some way to draw the zombies away from Jessica, create a distraction that might also fool Levi. Seeing the big ears of Mickey Mouse on a sign at the Disney Store gave him an idea. Inside the store, he searched for the items he needed for his diversion. After finding them, he crept back down to the mall courtyard and around a corner to prepare his surprise. He set his armload of foot-tall Buzz Lightyear action figures on the floor around him. Working quickly, he activated their lights and pressed their gauntlets to activate the toys' laser sound effects. Then he taped down the talk button with electrical tap and scattered them across the courtyard behind him, as he raced back toward Jessica. Multiple Buzz Lightyear voices filled the mall, and the laser lights and sound effects drew the zombies' attention. He waited behind a wall as a phalanx of the creatures filed past him to investigate.

To his horror, he saw that the upper barricade protecting Jessica was beginning to topple. He used his remaining three crossbow bolts to kill the creatures nearest it. Jessica saw them fall dead and increased her attempt to free herself.

"Nice try, Blakely," Levi called out from above him. "But you'll never make it."

Levi was probably right, but he had to try. He pulled out his .45, took a deep breath, and fired three quick rounds into the walkway directly above him. He tossed the useless crossbow in one direction and made a mad dash for the stairs.

* * * *

Jessica watched in horror, as the zombies tore at the flimsy barricade with the vigor of the starving. Dozens of the creatures surrounded her, close enough to smell their stench. She knew it would not be long before the barrier fell, and she would die in a most gruesome manner. She didn't see Levi again after he left her, but she knew he was somewhere within the darkened mall lying in wait for Jake. In spite of her certain grisly death, she hoped Jake wouldn't come for her.

The first report of gunfire echoed down the mall courtyard, followed by Levi's insane laughter, attracting the attention of some of the zombies. *Jake!* He had come for her. In spite of her earlier wish to the contrary, she was relieved and grateful that he had come. A handful of the creatures shuffled toward the sound, but most remained gathered around her. She feared Jake was dead until she heard twin shots from his shotgun. She smiled. A few more rifle shots a short while later proved Jake was still alive and getting closer. Then, ten minutes passed in silence. She began to worry that something had happened to him. To her surprise, and then amusement, the familiar sound of a dozen Buzz Lightyear's voices brought a smile to her face. He was drawing the creatures away from her. Now, most of the creatures abandoned their vigil and moved toward the flashing lights and sound. Her smile faded as a window shutter toppled from the upper barricade and skidded down the stairs. Not all of the creatures were fooled. Some preferred the food closest at hand. *Not long now*, she thought.

She tugged on the ropes but they wouldn't yield. Her wrists were bloody from her earlier attempts, but not slick enough to force them through Levi's tight knots. A few minutes later, the rest of the barricade came crashing down the stairs. She tried to scream through the gag. One zombie took two steps down the stairs, and then fell with an arrow protruding from its head. *Jake*. The two remaining creatures suffered similar fates. She heard Levi's voice taunting Jake from across the courtyard. Jake replied by firing three shots and running toward her. She tried to warn him back, but couldn't. He raced by the foot of the stairs, tossing his knife onto the landing as he passed. She pounced on the knife to keep it from falling off the edge of the landing. He fired three more rapid shots in Levi's direction and disappeared behind the staircase.

"Come out now or I'll kill her," Levi shouted.

He stood in the shadows, but she could see the brim of his Stetson and the barrel of his rifle pointed at her glinting in the moonlight. Shifting as little as possible, she positioned her body until she could reach the knife with her hands. Her bonds were so tight that she could barely grasp it.

"If I come out, you'll just kill us both," Jake replied.

"Drop your gun, step out where I can see you, and we'll finish this man to man with knives."

She pushed until the hilt of the knife wedged against her stomach, and then moved the rope over the sharp blade. The knife kept flipping over, but she wriggled it back into position each time and continued to saw at her bonds.

"Throw out your rifle first," Jake called out.

She started at the clatter of a rifle skidding across the tiled floor. She hadn't believed Levi's offer, but he had thrown out his weapon. He still might have another weapon.

"I'm coming down," Levi yelled.

Fool, she wanted to yell at Jake. *Don't trust him. You don't have your knife and I can't give it back to you.*

Jake's pistol followed Levi's rifle onto the floor. He was going to take Levi at his word and meet him weaponless.

"What about the shotgun?" Levi asked.

"I lost it in the tuxedo shop upstairs. I think it's in the cummerbund section if you want it. Let's do this."

Jake stepped out from behind the staircase, his empty hands held out in front of him. He looked up at her and smiled encouragingly. Levi walked around the walkway until he was standing above her at the head of the stairs, and then took the steps one at a time. When he reached her, he paused, glared down at her, and continued. He didn't see the knife beneath her. When he had passed, she continued to work on the rope. Slowly, the knife was parting the tough nylon of the rope. As the rope loosened, she forced her hands apart to break it, biting back on a scream as the circulation returned to her wrists. Then she removed the gag.

"Don't do it, Jake," she yelled. He didn't reply. His gaze was fixed on Levi. "Here," she said and tossed him the knife. He caught it with one hand. Levi stopped moving until he saw that it was only a knife.

"Run," Jake called out to her. "Go to the upper level. Exit through Dillard's. Head west along the river until you reach the ATV. Go home. Reed's hurt. He needs you. I'll join you later."

She couldn't believe what he was saying. He was sending her away. "No. I can help."

"No. This is between me and him."

Rage rose in her. The image of his body on top of her clouded her vision. "After what he did to me," she screamed. "I want to kill him."

Levi looked up at her with a sneer. "You can wait and watch your man die, and then I'll take real good care of you."

"Like you did Hawk," she shot at him.

His face clouded for a moment. "She forgot where her loyalties lay."

"Go," Jake repeated.

He walked to the middle of the courtyard and crouched with his knife pointed towards Levi. Levi moved to meet him, stopping a few yards away. The two circled one another warily, each feeling the other out. She retreated to the upper level, staring back at the two adversaries the entire time. She wasn't leaving. She couldn't leave Jake alone. Most of all, she couldn't leave without knowing that Levi was dead. She wanted to see his dead body on the ground. She hugged the shadows inside a doorway and watched.

25

June 30, 2016   Tucson Mall, Tucson, AZ –

Jessica was free. That was all that mattered to Jake. Between his diversion with the Buzz Lightyear toys and the noise he and Levi were making, she shouldn't encounter any zombies. They would be coming to him. Instead of the heat of battle he had experienced in Afghanistan or a rage of anger at what Levi had done, a sense of calm washed over and through him, as if his entire life had been a prelude to this moment. He could see nothing beyond the instant he was now in. He felt relief.

Levi was grinning, enjoying the rush of adrenalin that his eagerness to kill pumped through his veins. Jake hoped his eagerness pushed him to take risks. Jake moved slowly and deliberately, knowing the longer he could prolong the fight, the further Jessica could escape in case he lost. With his eyes on Levi, his foot slipped in a puddle of water. As he regained his balance, Levi rushed in and slashed at his chest. Jake ducked to avoid the blow, but the blade sliced into his shirt. He swung his knife upwards at Levi's arm but missed. Levi retreated three paces backwards and stared at him, breathing heavily. The foul stench of decay drifted from Levi's clothing. *So that's how he managed to avoid zombies. He rolled in a corpse like a dog in road kill.*

"When I kill you I'm going to rip that Ranger's badge off your chest and wear it to remind me to kill my enemies quickly," Levi boasted.

"Soon, you won't have to worry about enemies. I'm going to rip out your guts and feed them to the zombies, one loop at a time."

As they circled, Jake had been keeping one eye on the zombies. The zombies were ignoring Levi. However, the smell on Jake's pants leg wasn't enough to fool them, especially after sliding through the water and washing most of it away. They were beginning to understand that the lights and voices from the toys were not food and were moving back toward the sounds of fighting.

Levi began tossing his knife from hand to hand. "I've had plenty of practice with shivs in prison. You don't scare me, copper."

Jake ignored the 'copper' comment. "I don't want to scare you. I want to kill you."

He crooked his finger at Levi and motioned him to come on. Levi growled and lunged at him. This time, he was ready. He waited until the last second, and then turned and sidestepped Levi's knife thrust. As he turned, he made a backhanded swipe at Levi's exposed back, slashing his shirt and drawing blood. Levi reached back with his free hand and felt the shallow gash. He looked at the blood glistening on his fingers.

"Barely a scratch," he said

"I wasn't trying to kill you," Jake said. "I just wanted to draw blood." He motioned toward the zombies surrounding them. A few heads were turning toward Levi. "Now they smell fresh blood. I don't think your corpse stink will fool them for very long."

Levi cast a worried look at the zombies. Jake waited until the closest one zeroed in on him, and then kicked it in the stomach, knocking it to the floor face down. Casually, to send a message to Levi, he stomped on the back of its neck with the heel of his boot. With the sound of its spine shattering, the creature ceased to move. He then turned his attention back to Levi. He saw a glimmer of worry cross Levi's face and smiled.

"What say we get this little soiree over with," he said.

Holding his knife low, he moved toward Levi. When he was within three feet, Levi suddenly whipped off his Stetson and sent it spinning Frisbee fashion at Jake's head. As Jake ducked the hat, Levi faked a move high to the right before moving low to the left. The unexpected feint left Jake's right side open. He saw the knife coming too late. He reached out his free arm to block it, but he felt the blade sink into his flesh like a red-hot branding iron. Only his grip on Levi's forearm prevented the blade from going in deep enough to reach a vital organ. Still, the pain was excruciating. He pushed Levi's arm back and stumbled away, pressing his hand over the wound. Waves of pain lanced through his side, radiating from the wound like aftershocks of a tremor. Blood seeped between his fingers and ran down his side. He gritted his teeth, released the wound, and faced Levi.

"Now we're even," Levi said, grinning.

The zombies, smelling the fresh blood, were becoming agitated. Their focus shifted from him to Levi, confusing them as the two moved in a circle. Their shuffling feet beat a staccato counterpoint to their hungry wails and moans. More and more of them spilled onto the courtyard around the stairs. Both men were forced to dodge their outstretched arms while watching out for their opponent. Levi used them like blocking dummies, keeping one of the creatures between him and Jake, as Jake tried to reach him. Jake grew tired of the game and shoved one creature away from him. It collided with another, creating a domino effect of falling zombies. If not for the severity of the situation, it would have been comical. Levi, having lost his zombie barricade, closed in quickly, forcing Jake backwards toward the zombies. He couldn't turn to look without letting down his guard. One of the creatures, a Runner, fell on him from behind the stairs, wrapping its arms around his neck. The Runner was strong. Jake couldn't break its grip. As its head closed on his neck, Jake jammed his knife twice into its throat. It released him and staggered backwards, wrenching the knife from Jake's hand. Seeing that he was now defenseless, Levi rushed in for the kill.

Jake's gaze fell on the staircase off to his right. He loped up the stairs, stopping on the first landing to face Levi. He was unarmed, but now Levi would have to come at him straight on from below. As Levi mounted the steps, Jake grabbed the piece of rope from that had bound Jessica's hands from the floor. Using it as a whip, he flailed it at Levi's face, keeping him at bay. He knew he couldn't fend off Levi for long with a length of rope. His foot brushed against one of the zombies he had killed with the crossbow. He reached down and plucked the bolt from its head, just as Levi danced beneath the rope. In one swift movement, he fell to the floor, reached up, and jabbed the bloody bolt into Levi's leg just above the knee. Levi yelled in pain and fell backwards, tumbling down the stairs.

As much as Jake wanted to finish off his opponent, Levi was still armed and he wasn't. He believed wholeheartedly in *Jake's Law #3 – A fool and his life are soon parted.* He searched the courtyard for his pistol and saw it being trampled beneath the feet of zombies merging on the prostate Levi. Then he noticed the rifle

Levi had thrown out, an M16, at the base of a planter. Following the direction of his gaze, Levi saw the weapon a moment later, and he was closer. Jake vaulted over the stair rail to the courtyard below. The impact on the hard tile produced a bone jolting pain that shot through his wounded side, taking away his breath. His vision clouded for a moment as he fought to breath. Even wounded and dragging his injured leg behind him, Levi reached the rifle first.

Before he could train the barrel on Jake, he was inundated by a mob of zombies. He pushed them away with the butt of the rifle, and then fired two short bursts into their midst, but those not hit by the stream of bullets continued to press him backwards into the entrance of *Macy's*, firing the M16. Jake ignored the pain and leaped over a planter, headed for his pistol. Before he could reach the pistol, a bullet shattered the tile beside it.

"Next one goes through your head," Levi called.

Jake stopped and turned slowly, arms raised in the air. He preferred dying facing his killer than to receive a shot in the back. Half a dozen zombies lay dead around Levi, but they had done some damage to him. His arm bled from three wounds, and his shirt was ripped and covered in blood from deep scratches to his chest.

"You're tougher than I expected, Blakely, but I don't have time for a slow death for you. Thanks to you, now I have to escape through the zombies."

"I hope they chew your liver," Jake spat at him.

Levi took two steps toward Jake and raised the M16 level with his chest. Levi's hand trembled, but from so close a distance, he could hardly miss. Jake prepared to die. Then, Levi's body folded at the waist and he lurched backwards, as if struck by some invisible hand. His chest turned crimson. Jake realized whose hand it was when the sound of the shotgun reached his ears. *Jessica.* The look of utter surprise on Levi's face was worth all the pain he had endured. Levi's eyes lifted skyward just as a second blast ripped open his side. The M16 clattered the floor.

"Come on, Jake," Jessica yelled at him.

He watched Levi crawling across the floor toward the rifle until the zombies fell over him. His screams filled the mall and seemed to continue far beyond his death, as the creatures ripped into his body with hands and mouths. Jake watched for a few moments more, and then went upstairs to Jessica. As she stared down at Levi's mutilated body, her chest heaved. Her grim expression frightened him.

"I said I would kill that bastard," she said.

"You did." Jake took the shotgun from her trembling hands. She fell into his arms and began sobbing, not from any weakness on her part, but as a catharsis. Now, she too had murdered. It didn't matter that it was a man who needed killing or that she had done it to save his life. Once that thin line was crossed, one could never retreat. He had crossed it in Afghanistan, and it had changed his life forever. Her future would be forever marred by this one moment of revenge. He knew how she felt, but this time, he knew how to save her, as she had saved him.

"Come on," he said. "Let's go home."

26

July 1, 2016   Tucson Mall, Tucson, AZ –

Jake sat with Jessica on the bank of the Rillito River and watched the sun come up over the Catalina Mountains. The wound in his side ached but had scabbed over and stopped bleeding. It would need stitches, but he would live.   Jessica was slowly recovering from the shock of her first killing. He had tried to reassure her that she had done nothing wrong, but getting through the thick veneer of her civilized moral code would take time. He didn't want to destroy her beliefs, just amend them to the new world. It would take her a while to recover from her trauma, but he would see to it that it didn't take as long as it had him. He would see that she didn't descend into the dark places from which he had barely escaped.

The dawn broke clear and bright. An omen, he hoped, of things to come. The morning was cool after the monsoon rains. A mist hovered over the river and hung to the tops of brush and trees. Over the rush of the river, the soft cooing of a mourning dove and the rustle of a pack rat stirring from its burrow lent a pastoral air to the morning. Another sound broke the stillness of the morning – vehicles. He glanced toward Oracle Road and saw a line of military trucks approaching. They stopped at the bridge beside his ATV. He shook Jessica to get her attention. Her eyes were red-rimmed from crying, but she smiled until he pointed at the army trucks.

"Looks like we have company."

Her hand went to the AA-12 shotgun beside her. He stopped her.

"No, we can't fight them."

An officer stepped down from the lead truck. His eyes searched the riverbank until he spotted them. Behind him, another figure appeared – Reed. He saw the pair and waved. Men spread out and headed toward the mall. Reed and the officer walked toward them.

"I guess Reed managed to get through to his friends."

Jessica looked at him in confusion.

"I'll let Reed explain." When Reed reached them, Jake said, "You're a little late, but I appreciate the gesture. How did you get through to the army?"

Reed smiled. "An A-10 flew over when I didn't call. I signaled with a flashlight. Morse code," he explained.

Jake shook his head. "You are a true boy scout." To Jessica, he said, "Jessica, meet Alton Reed, high school science teacher and part-time spy for the military."

She stared at Reed in a new light. "All this time …"

"Jake can explain. Later. Right now, let's get you back home."

"Is anything left?" she asked.

"Enough to build on," Jake said. "If you still want to hang around a while?"

He removed the Arizona Ranger's badge from his shirt and stared at it. It had gotten him through some dark times, but it was time for him to step into the light. He flung the badge into the river and heard it splash.

"Reed offered me a new job, Sheriff of San Manuel. We're going to start rebuilding for the future. Are you up for it?"

She kissed him. He thought he felt in her kiss more than gratitude for saving her life or an exchange for services rendered. He felt enthusiasm. He hugged her and kissed her back with a passion he had not expressed in many years. He turned to see both Reed and the officer smiling.

"Levi's dead." He didn't mention who had killed him. That would remain his and Jessica's secret. "Let's go home."

"Home," Jessica repeated. "That sounds lovely."

To Jake's surprise, it sounded lovely to him too.

The End

James (J.E.) Gurley haunts the deserts of Arizona with his Prepper and Survivalist friends, waiting on the zombie apocalypse. When not writing, he pays guitar and keyboards in local bands, hoping someday to become a traveling bard after the apocalypse chronicling the fall of mankind. he live with his wonderful wife, Kim, and his two cats, Shoes and Coco.